How the Murder Crumbles

How the Murder Crumbles

A COOKIE SHOP MYSTERY

Debra Sennefelder

CROOKED
LANE

NEW YORK

Published in the United States by Crooked Lane Books, an imprint of The Quick Brown Fox & Company LLC.

Crooked Lane Books and its logo are trademarks of The Quick Brown Fox & Company LLC.

Library of Congress Catalog-in-Publication data available upon request.

ISBN (hardcover): 978-1-63910-280-8
ISBN (ebook): 978-1-63910-281-5

Cover design by Jesse Reisch

Printed in the United States.

www.crookedlanebooks.com

Crooked Lane Books
34 West 27th St., 10th Floor
New York, NY 10001

First Edition: June 2023

10 9 8 7 6 5 4 3 2 1

For my husband, George.

Chapter One

"Why was the cookie so angry with the baker?" Kip Winslow asked the group of five women as they tied their aprons. He waited a beat.

Mallory Monroe paused as she walked out of the bakery's kitchen. She tried not to roll her eyes at her friend and employee's joke, knowing the punch line was going to be just terrible—and that she'd laugh all the same.

"He had a chip on his shoulder," Kip finished with a chuckle.

The women, who had signed up for the beginner cookie decorating class, laughed at the silly joke. Though Mallory noticed one of them, who had introduced herself as Elana Peterson, barely cracked a smile. Even Kip's worst jokes usually got a small smile. Or a groan. *Something.*

Once the women were settled, Kip returned to the kitchen to make sure the sugar cookies would be ready to swap out when it came time to start decorating. Mallory took her spot at the farmhouse table she'd found while antiquing. Because of her tight budget, which had no wiggle room, she had to be creative regarding the bakery's décor. But, thanks to flea market trips, learning how to sand and paint, and a lot of elbow grease—hers and Kip's—she had unique furnishings that added the extra oomph she wanted for the bakery.

"Are you ready to decorate?" Mallory looked at each woman, and four out of five nodded enthusiastically. The fifth, Elana, gave only a slight nod, and even that seemed half-hearted. Her friends noticed, and their excitement seemed to temper. Mallory didn't need the group's energy dipping. To keep the upbeat mood—after all, cookies were supposed to make people happy—Mallory quickly launched into the story of how she had become the owner of The Cookie Shop.

"I'm so happy you're here today because I get to share with you my passion for cookies and cookie decorating. When I was a little girl, I visited Wingate and I spent most of my time right here with my Aunt Glenna." Her voice choked, and she wondered when she would be able to talk about her aunt without getting emotional. It seemed like only yesterday Aunt Glenna had given her blessing at the re-grand opening of the bakery.

"She was a wonderful woman," the woman to the right of Elana said. "Excellent baker."

"Thank you. It was here, with her, that I discovered my love for baking and decorating cookies." Mallory blinked, hoping to keep back the tears. She missed her aunt so much. She missed how her aunt smelled of cinnamon, nutmeg, and ginger—her own spicy fragrance from hours of baking. She missed how her aunt whispered, "When it's made with love, the recipe is never wrong," when Mallory messed up a batch of cookies. She smiled at the memories and then continued.

"Back then, I dreamed of being a baker like my aunt. But then life happened. I grew up, got a degree, and found success in advertising."

"You've had quite a change in your life," the gray-haired woman seated across from Mallory said.

"I have. The one thing that never changed, though, was baking and decorating cookies every chance I got. Then one day, I discovered cookie bouquets, and I was hooked. I made them whenever there was a birthday or new baby or promotion." The last word stuck in her throat, and she swallowed hard. She hated to admit it, but she still harbored some bitterness after not getting the promotion she'd worked so hard for. Looking back, perhaps it had been for the best. It was one of the reasons she had taken the biggest leap of faith in her life—buying the bakery. And then changing pretty much everything about it.

"You've certainly made this place your own," said the woman seated next to Elana.

Mallory nodded as her gaze traveled around the bakery. She'd loved the bakery just the way it was, but her vision for the space was more colorful and whimsical than her aunt's had been.

Once the keys were handed over, Mallory had gotten to work. She'd revamped the front of the bakery. The white walls were given a fresh coat of light green paint, and then she added framed wallpaper panels. She chose a floral wallpaper with giant rhodo-dendrons in pastel colors. Over the antique wood floor stood a long console table she'd found at a tag sale. After stripping and painting it lime green, she used it to display a variety of cookie baskets she offered. An oversized, chunky pedestal table in the center of the bakery had also been stripped and then painted a deep coral. She topped it with two smaller pedestal stands. There she displayed smaller cookie baskets and the hand-dipped gour-met apples she also sold.

She continued speaking for another minute, wrapping up her story, and then got to work. For the class, they were making sim-ple cookie pops. Gathered together, they'd make a sweet bouquet. She demonstrated how to roll out the sugar dough, cut out the daisy-shaped cookies, and insert the bamboo stick.

She made her way around the table to check everyone's prog-ress. This wasn't exactly a difficult task. Mallory expected these women to have had some experience with this basic skill of baking.

Once they were all done shaping their cookies for baking, Mallory collected them on baking sheets and excused herself to the kitchen.

She walked across the bakery and behind the counter, which had also had a remodel. Gone was the long bakery case. In its place was a smaller one to hold individual cookie pops and assorted cookies, including the cookie of the month. As a tribute to her aunt, Mallory had decided to feature one cookie each month from her aunt's recipe book. This month, the cookie was Almond Meltaway. Next to the case was a counter to ring up sales and a desk area to take special orders. She pushed the swinging door and entered the kitchen.

Along with well-used baking equipment, there were three workstations in the cramped kitchen. Each was set up with a mixer and supplies, which allowed the spaces to be used simultaneously or independently.

"I'll take those." Claudia Allen stepped away from the dough mixer and moved toward Mallory. Her footsteps were heavy despite the lightweight clogs she wore. Glum-faced, she carried the baking sheets to her station and set them aside. Her tidy work-space was the result of twenty years' experience working as a baker. "Those are ready for your students." She gestured to the sheet pan rack. Mallory's aunt had hired Claudia to work the counter, but within weeks discovered that Claudia had a talent for baking and moved her into the kitchen. It wasn't long before Claudia became Glenna's right hand and most trusted employee. "You saw those burgundy mugs came in, right?"

"I did. I already made up a prototype for Gil," Mallory said.

Frame & Brewster, a business supply company, was about to celebrate its twentieth anniversary. Gil had ordered two dozen cookie mugs. She'd designed three cookies for the mug—one rectangle with the company's logo and two star-shaped with the words Thank You and Celebrate written on them.

"I hope he likes the bouquets." Exhilaration buzzed in Mallory. Not only was it the bakery's most significant order so far, but it was also their first corporate order. First of many, she hoped.

Claudia dusted her table with flour and then plopped down a ball of dough before reaching for a rolling pin. She worked efficiently and competently, which made her an asset to Mallory, as she had been to Glenna. She'd also been Glenna's friend. Mallory wondered if they'd ever be friends, not just employer and employee.

"If he doesn't like them, I doubt he'll complain. It's not like he's an actual customer," Claudia said without looking up.

Mallory hated to admit it, but Claudia had a point. Gil wouldn't complain if he was unhappy with the cookies or their presentation. However, regardless of what Claudia thought, Gil was an actual customer . . . who was also her boyfriend. She knew her designs would knock the socks off everyone at Frame & Brewster. Gil would get a slap on the back for his unique gift idea. And she'd be one small step closer to paying back the mega loan she had taken out to buy the bakery.

Claudia looked up from her perfect rectangular sheet of cookie dough. "I've said it before, and I'll say it again—"

"Must you?" Kip said as he passed through the kitchen and then disappeared into the storeroom.

Claudia harrumphed. "As I was saying, it's never a good idea to mix business with pleasure. Of course, Glenna never did . . . except when she made the mistake of doing a favor for that horrid Beatrice Wright."

"I appreciate your advice." Mallory pulled the baking sheet from the rack and headed toward the door. Before pushing the door open, she looked over her shoulder. "Don't forget, I'm leaving after the class is over. Claudia, you'll cover the counter."

Out of the kitchen, Mallory carried the baking sheet out to the table, inhaling the sweet fragrance of vanilla and sugar and butter all baked into perfect little cookies. Her nose wriggled. They smelled heavenly.

"Here we go. These cookies have cooled and are ready for the next step." Mallory set the tray in the middle of the table. "Please take three each, and then I'll demonstrate how to decorate them."

As her students reached for their cookies, Mallory noticed that Elana checked her cell phone and frowned before taking her cookies.

"Okay, let's make these pretty." Mallory set three cookies in front of her and picked up her first piping bag. "What you want to keep in mind is not to go too fast or too slow. You want to get into a steady rhythm of flow."

"Sounds kind of woo-woo," one of the students quipped.

"Perhaps. But trust me, this method works. The icing bag is an extension of your hand." Mallory leaned forward and positioned her piping bag over a cookie and squeezed with just the right amount of pressure. "Be sure to grab the bag with your dominant hand so that your thumb wraps around the top of the icing bag." She started piping from the center of the cookie, moving out to the edge of each petal and coming back into the center. She repeated until the whole cookie was covered in white icing.

"Wow, that's amazing," Elana said in awe. Her comment surprised and delighted Mallory. Maybe there was hope for the woman enjoying the class. "I'm not sure I can do that."

"Give it a try." Mallory set down her piping bag and then walked around the table, stopping at each student. She adjusted hand positions, grips on piping bags, and fixed mistakes. Next, she showed them how to fill the center of their cookies with yellow icing. Conversation between the girlfriends waned as each concentrated on what they were doing.

The next thirty minutes flew by, and Mallory was soon waving goodbye to her students. In addition to their own decorated cookies, they'd purchased a few chocolate-covered apples and Almond Meltaways to take home. They also received a coupon for twenty percent off a cookie bouquet or basket.

Mallory was catching up on her emails at the desk when Elana emerged from the restroom. On her way to the counter, she peered out the door. Mallory expected she was looking for her friends.

"They said to meet them at Heavenly Roast." The coffee shop was a few stores down from the bakery. "I hope you enjoyed yourself today."

Elana gave a half-smile as she walked to the counter to pick up her cookie pops. Up close, her face looked drawn, her eyes tired and puffy—like she'd been crying. Is that why she'd dashed to the restroom? To cry?

"I really did. You're very talented and an excellent teacher." Elana sounded sincere. "It's just been . . . rough lately. And I'm not sleeping well."

"I'm sorry to hear that. A cup of chamomile tea usually helps me when I can't sleep." Mallory knew all too well about sleepless nights. For months before taking the buyout package from her agency, she'd felt the weight of the world crushing her shoulders.

Elana shrugged. "I've tried that. It just all feels too overwhelming." Her chin trembled, and she teared up.

"Oh, my." Mallory quickly reached for a tissue and handed it to Elana. "There are things that sometimes feel more overwhelming than they actually are."

"Trust me, this isn't one of those times. I wish it were." Elana dabbed her eyes and she sniffled. "Look at me . . . who am I these days? Dumping my problems on you."

Mallory shook her head. Elana hadn't really dumped her problems on her. She had no idea what was bothering the woman. But if she could help, she'd welcome Elana unloading on her.

"Sometimes it's easier to talk to a stranger than someone close to you."

"Well, if you have any marital advice to offer, I'm all ears." Elana's half-smile returned.

Mallory's lips pressed together. She knew about a lot of things, but marriage wasn't one of them. Nope. Walking away from an advertising career to chase a dream? That she knew about.

"I'm sorry, I'm not married, but I'm dating someone. Though I'm sure whatever the problem is, you'll be able to work it out."

"Thank you. You're very kind." With her cookies in hand, Elana spun around and left the bakery.

Mallory watched through the front window until Elana was out of sight. She couldn't help it, her curiosity about Elana and her husband had been piqued. She exhaled a breath. She wouldn't stick her nose into the woman's business even if she had practically laid it out for Mallory. Getting entwined in people's private stuff was a recipe for disaster. Especially in a small town.

With her resolution set, Mallory turned and walked into the kitchen to say her goodbyes, prompting Claudia to march out to the front of the bakery. And Kip let out a relieved sigh.

"It's going to take some time," she said, patting him on the shoulder as she made her way to her office. Having two very different personalities in the small kitchen was challenging. But she was confident they'd work things out.

With her apron off, she grabbed her cookie mug prototype for Gil's company. On her way to the back door, she picked up her backpack. When she reached her bike, she set the cellophane-wrapped mug in the basket and then unlocked the bike. So many things had changed when she made the move from Manhattan to Wingate. She had traded her one-bedroom with a Hudson River view for a cottage. She had swapped her beloved high heels for supportive shoes. And her commute had gone from subway to bicycle.

A lot of changes in a short period for someone who craved stability and had an aversion to making spontaneous decisions. But it had seemed that the stars had aligned a few months ago. A lost promotion, a merger that made her position at her company vulnerable, and a backstabbing colleague had Mallory craving career independence. Then her aunt had called with the news that she wanted to sell her bakery, the place where there were so many memories of her childhood. By the end of the call, Mallory had said she would buy the bakery. Over the following weeks, she had pulled together a business plan and shared her vision of what she wanted her bakery to be. Then, with her aunt's approval, she went for it. She'd never felt so exhilarated and scared to death at the same time.

She hopped on her bike and cycled down the driveway along the two-story building that housed The Cookie Shop. On the second floor was a studio apartment that was currently between tenants.

Then she turned onto Main Street. The winding street was Wingate's central hub of activity and was postcard-perfect from one end to the other. Century-old lampposts dotted the long stretch of sidewalk where historic brick-façade shops mingled with Victorian painted ladies and stately Federal period buildings. Once a manufacturing town, Wingate was now known for its shops, restaurants, and galleries. Being named one of the Top Ten Shopping Destinations in the state for eight years running by *CT Life and Style* magazine, the town had become the place that had something for everyone—from thrifty shopper to antique connoisseur to weekend explorer.

Her next turn took her down Lilac Lane, a residential street where front yards bloomed with bright spring colors, and birdsong filled the air as she pedaled along the road. At the stop sign, she made a right onto Old Lantern Road, and within a minute, her rental cottage came into view.

Her for-now home was a hodgepodge of architectural styles—part cottage, part Craftsman, part Victorian. The sage green dwelling with a picket fence was utterly delightful. When she found it, she hadn't hesitated to write the check for the deposit and one month's rent. She also wasted no time in purchasing an Adirondack chair to sit by the pond where she could ponder her life-changing decisions. Unfortunately, though, she'd yet to have time for the reflective exercise.

Mallory pedaled her bike around the side of the cottage and got off, leaning it against the flowering arched arbor. She plucked the cookie mug out of the basket and unlocked the back door. She entered the kitchen through a small utility room, and Agatha, her gray and white cat, greeted her. The feline meowed loudly and slinked her body along Mallory's legs.

"Hey there, little girl." Mallory bent over to scratch Agatha's head. The cat purred, lapping up the attention. She'd been named after Mallory's favorite mystery author. "How was your day?"

Mallory set her things on the counter and then prepared Agatha's meal. While the cat feasted, Mallory dashed upstairs for a quick shower and then dressed in something sexier than her daily uniform of jeans and a T-shirt.

Back downstairs, dressed in a green wrap dress, strappy heels, with her strawberry blonde hair swept up into a bun with wisps framing her heart-shaped face, she quickly swapped out the backpack for a sleek clutch. On the way out of the kitchen, she patted Agatha and then picked up the cookie mug. She walked along the stone path to the detached garage where her Jetta was parked. The car was used, but good enough for the limited travel she would be doing.

She and Gil hadn't had a proper date in weeks. When they first met at an acquaintance's dinner party, they both lived in the city and enjoyed date night practically every night. Then a year ago, Gil relocated to Connecticut for a better job. Neither wanted to break up, so they did what they had to do to keep their relationship intact. When she bought the bakery and moved to Wingate, she thought it would be easier for them. After all, they were finally in the same state. No more slogging through traffic or racing to get to Grand Central Station for a train out of the city after work. It turned out she'd been wrong. Both were working long hours and Gil had started traveling more for work. So tonight, she was going to surprise him with a romantic dinner.

Her takeout order was waiting for her when she arrived at the restaurant, and then it was a ten-minute drive to his condo. When she arrived at Gil's unit, she spotted his sedan parked in the driveway. As she slowed the Jetta to park at the curb, she saw Gil walking along the path to the front door.

He wasn't alone.

She shifted the car into park and then turned off the ignition.

A woman was walking beside Gil.

Her eyes widened when she noticed they were walking closely together. *Too closely.*

She pushed open her door, stepped out, and headed toward them, juggling the bag of food and the cookie mug.

She stopped in her tracks when she noticed Gil's arm wrapped around the redhead's slender waist. Her heart slammed into her chest when she saw Gil kiss her. On. The. Lips.

"Gil!"

He pulled back from the redhead, and then flashed Mallory a deer-in-the-headlights look.

"Mallory! I . . . I wasn't expecting you."

"Well, that's obvious. Do you want to tell me what's going on?"

"Go . . . go . . . going on?" Gil removed his arm from the redhead's waist. "What are you doing here?"

"Who is she, Gillie?" the redhead asked, putting space between them.

"I have the same question about you, *Red*. I'm his girlfriend," Mallory said.

"Girlfriend?" Red swung her head around and glared at Gil. "You said you recently broke up with someone?"

Gil's gaze darted between the two women. "It's not serious," he finally said to Mallory.

"Not serious?" Red propped her hands on her hips. "What about last weekend? Our romantic getaway."

"You told me you had a business trip." Mallory's head spun, and she felt queasy. Was this really happening? "Lying and cheating. I don't even know you anymore."

"Look . . . I . . . didn't expect . . ." Gil looked at Mallory and then at Red, and then his gaze narrowed on the bag of Chinese takeout in Mallory's hands. "You bought dinner? For us?"

"Hey!" Red whacked him on the shoulder with her hand, and he grimaced. "Forget about the food. You have some explaining to do, remember?"

Gil nodded and then shrugged. "I guess things change," he finally said to Mallory.

"They most certainly do." Mallory shoved the bag and mug into Gil's hands. "Here's dinner and your cookie mug. Enjoy!"

She whirled around and stomped back to her car. *Don't cry. Don't cry.* The last thing she wanted to do was to break down in front of Gil and Red. Instead, she picked up her pace. She didn't know how long she could keep it together.

When she reached the car, she yanked open the door and slid in behind the steering wheel. She started the ignition after closing the door harder than she needed to.

Before Mallory pulled away from the curb, she gave one final look at the cheating couple. Her stomach clenched as her gaze zoomed in on the cookie mug in Gil's hand, and she remembered she had to deliver a bunch of them to his office.

She dropped her head against the headrest as Claudia's words echoed in her mind.

It's never a good idea to mix business with pleasure.

Not only had she just broken up with her boyfriend, but she also had to admit Claudia had been right. Could things get any worse?

Chapter Two

The following morning Mallory hit the snooze button three times before she crawled out of bed to face the world with a brand-new status—single. The thought sent a stabbing pain through her heart. On her feet, she grabbed her kimono and slipped it on while Agatha stretched out on the bed. The cat's not-so-lean body elongated, and a twinge of envy flicked in Mallory. She'd love a good yoga session. With no time in her schedule for a Warrior or Pigeon pose, she padded into the bathroom. She flicked on the overhead light and stared at her reflection in the mirror over the sink. She cringed. Her eyes and nose were red and swollen thanks to last night's cry fest. Her shoulder-length hair looked like a rat's nest from a night of tossing and turning.

"It's going to take a miracle," she muttered, shaking her head. As much as she wanted to slink back to her bed, she couldn't. There was no time to wallow and definitely no time to waste another thought on Gil the Cheater and his gal pal, Red. She had a business to run and an interview to give. Of all the days for Dugan Porter, a reporter with the *Connecticut Chronicle*, to show up at the bakery, it had to be the day after her heart got broken. He'd reached out to her two weeks ago with the offer to write a profile on her. He wanted to explore her path from an advertising account manager who decorated cookies as a hobby to becoming a cookiepreneur.

Cookiepreneur. It was a funny word, but it summed up the direction her life was going. So, with no time to dawdle, she began the process of trying to make herself look presentable. Oh, what she'd give for a glam squad.

An hour later, she gave Agatha a pat on the head, slipped out the back door, and got on her bike. The ride to the bakery lifted her mood slightly as she passed flowering shrubs and the early morning air filled her lungs.

When she arrived at the bakery, she dropped her backpack on her desk and tied on an apron. In the kitchen, she found Kip and Claudia preparing for the day's baking.

"Come on, bring it in." Kip held his arms out. He'd been her one phone call last night. He had listened to her rant, sob, and promise never to fall in love again. *Never ever.*

Mallory walked into Kip's embrace, welcoming his comfort. But not for too long. The weight of Claudia's stare from across the kitchen had her lifting her gaze. *Oh, boy.* Claudia had a deep frown on her face and an annoyed look in her dark eyes. Unfortunately, it seemed it was her default expression every day.

"What are we going to do now about the order from Frame & Brewster?" Claudia reached for the carton of eggs on her worktable. She cracked six open with precision, separating them into two stainless steel bowls.

Mallory pulled herself from Kip and cleared her throat. She needed to make sure she spoke with authority and confidence, even though on the inside she was a hot mess.

"We'll deliver them. We have a contract." And unfortunately, there wasn't a breakup clause in it.

Claudia arched a thin brow. "I expect that should be an interesting delivery for you to make."

"I'm happy to make it." Kip walked to the refrigerator and pulled out a slab of unsalted butter. "I wouldn't mind giving Gil a piece of my mind."

Mallory's heart swelled at the protective tone in her friend's voice. He always had her back, just like her sister. Unfortunately, though, she couldn't allow him to rip Gil a new one while representing the bakery.

Claudia tsk-tsked as she poured the egg whites into her mixer.

"Is there something you want to say, Claudia?" Kip asked, unwrapping the butter. He cut a chunk off and set it on the food scale.

Claudia looked up from the mixing bowl. "Well, since you asked. It's my considered opinion that personal business should be left at the door before coming into the bakery."

Mallory swallowed her first reply—wouldn't it be nice if she could tuck her life into neat little compartmentalized boxes like Claudia did? But Mallory's life was sometimes messy. Like now.

"Thank you for sharing your opinion." Mallory then turned back to Kip. "Thanks for the offer, but I'll make the delivery." She was a big girl and could handle the undoubtedly awkward situation. At least she hoped so.

She dashed back into the office and opened the safe for the money bag. Out at the counter, she filled the cash register and then flipped the closed sign around and unlocked the door.

Because today was a special day for her and the bakery, she set up a complimentary coffee station for customers. She also displayed mini-chalkboards on the farmhouse table. She'd used her best fancy script to write the details of upcoming cookie decorating classes. Her goal was to fill them all.

It didn't take long for customers to come in, and Mallory was thankful for the busy morning for two reasons. First, it kept her mind off her breakup. Second, it kept her from overthinking the interview with Dugan Porter. She sold a half-dozen premade baskets, took orders for three custom baskets for delivery, and bagged several of her gourmet apples. She'd added them to the bakery's offerings because, like cookie bouquets, they were great for gift giving. And there was a nice margin on them. The most popular so far were the white chocolate–dipped green apples covered in pastel-colored sprinkles. Wrapped in cellophane and tied with a yellow bow, they were perfect for spring. Finally, just past eleven, she took a breath and a sip of coffee while a mom with two little girls sat at one of the three café tables in the nook by the bay window. As the mom paid for her cookies and apples, she expressed how grateful she was that Mallory continued to sell the bakery's traditional cookies. She loved the Almond Meltaways and had been disappointed when Glenna had stopped selling them.

Twenty minutes later, there was a line of customers at the counter while others browsed and helped themselves to coffee. The shop was filled to bursting. Exactly what Mallory had hoped for during the interview. She checked her watch. Dugan Porter would be arriving at any moment.

Kip, who came out to help at the register, nudged her and then whispered, "That's him."

Mallory made eye contact with Dugan and nodded at the young reporter. Dressed in a plaid button-down and khakis, he had a shock of ash brown hair and wide eyes that matched his eagerness to get a story. He crossed the antique flooring, passing a huddle of customers at the pedestal table who were trying to decide which decorative cookies to purchase.

"Dugan!" Ginger Dupont waved from a café table where she was seated with two other women. Wingate's resident romance author smiled, her perfect white teeth framed by bright red lipstick. "Loved my profile. Thank you!"

Dugan tipped his head to Ginger as he continued toward the end of the display case while Ginger leaned forward at the table and said something that had her companions nodding. Mallory remembered the profile on the romance author. It had been very flattering and quite comprehensive. Hopefully that boded well for Mallory's piece. She hurried to greet Dugan and led him to the end of the counter. There she answered his basic background questions while customers glanced over at them. Her body buzzed with pride that she was being seen giving the interview. Getting press coverage was vital for small businesses. When the interview was published, everyone would talk about it. She refocused on Dugan and answered his questions. He ate up her answers and continued with his questions until the front door opened again and in walked Beatrice Wright, aka Queen Bea.

Of course, no one called her that to her face.

Mallory cut a glance at Kip, who returned it with a shrug before pasting on a big smile and welcoming Beatrice to the bakery.

Instantly, she thought he was wasting his time smiling. And she chided herself for the unkind thought. But everything about Beatrice seemed severe—her thin lips, her chin-length bob, her tailored dress. Mallory couldn't fathom someone so serious being a food blogger. The few people Mallory knew who blogged were creative souls who had a passion for food. Beatrice appeared to lack creativity and passion.

"Good to see you, Beatrice. What brings you by today?" Kip stood ready to take an order or ring up a sale.

"I came to settle something once and for all. With *her*." Beatrice's expression was determined as her gaze fell heavily on Mallory.

Mallory's stomach knotted. Now wasn't the time for a visit from Beatrice. Unfortunately, though, there probably wasn't ever a good time.

"Excuse me a moment," Mallory said to Dugan and hurried to join Kip. "How can I help you?"

Beatrice set the cookie tin on the counter and, with her bony hand, removed its lid. "I baked these this morning. Please try one."

Mallory looked in the tin and found a layer of what looked like her Almond Meltaways. Then, in a low voice, she said, "Right now isn't a good time for me."

Beatrice looked toward Dugan and grinned. "You're being interviewed, aren't you? I guess this is serendipity."

"Serendipity, my sugar cookies," Mallory muttered as her nerves frayed and her heart pumped faster.

"Don't say something you'll regret," Kip whispered in her ear and then backed away.

"Perhaps we could talk later?" Mallory offered before looking back at Dugan, who was watching her and Beatrice with interest. *Darn it.*

"I'm here to give you notice." Beatrice's voice ratcheted up, and all the heads in the bakery turned toward her.

"I . . . I don't understand what you're talking about. Notice for what?" Mallory pushed Kip aside and hurried around the counter. In her haste, she collided with a man, sloshing his coffee.

"Oh. My. Goodness," she gasped. "I'm so, so, so sorry."

Mallory shuffled to a nearby napkin dispenser and grabbed a handful. She returned to the man, and began blotting his crisp white shirt and couldn't help but notice his firm, broad chest.

He obviously worked out. She glanced up to his caramel-colored eyes and saw a glint of amusement flickering.

"It's not a big deal. It was an accident, right?" he asked, his voice as smooth as the color of his eyes.

She was tempted to ask him to repeat himself. But instead, she gave herself a mental shake. She'd just broken up with Gil and wasn't looking for a rebound. She had enough to deal with at the moment.

"Yes . . . it was an accident. I'm really sorry." She continued patting his shirt, aka his chest. "Oh, no. It looks like I'm making it worse."

His hand raised up and covered hers, stopping the wiping action. "It's only a shirt. Accidents happen."

Mallory bit her lower lip. His touch was warm and gentle. *Focus, Mal, focus.* "It *was* an accident. I should have looked where I was going. I'll pay for dry cleaning."

"I appreciate the offer, but it's not necessary." A small smile tugged on his lips, making Mallory wonder why he wasn't more upset with her. "You have a lot going on. Don't worry about me."

"I'm giving you notice to stop selling my recipe," Beatrice said, bringing Mallory back to the bigger problem at hand. "Or I'll contact my lawyer."

"I'm good. Everything is fine. Don't let me keep you," the stranger assured Mallory before walking toward the nook by the bay window where the café tables were set up. He claimed one. Everything about him seemed confident, cool, and something else, but she couldn't pinpoint what it was. After sitting, he took a sip of what was left of his coffee.

Mallory's attention returned to Beatrice, who clomped toward her with her finger jabbing in the air.

"I'm waiting," Beatrice said.

And so was Mallory. She was waiting for the grace and kindness to deal with Beatrice, but it was darn hard to muster. The woman was so insufferable, so rude, and so unlikable. How had her aunt ever been friends with her?

"Cat got your tongue?" Beatrice prodded.

Mallory's whole body tensed as she felt the eyes of curious onlookers boring into her.

Kip hurried to Mallory's side. "Oh, come on, Beatrice. It's not like there's only one recipe for Almond Meltaways."

"There's clearly a misunderstanding," Mallory said. "The recipe was my aunt's. I have every right to bake and sell them."

"Your aunt stole the recipe from me," Beatrice said.

Mallory gasped at the accusation. "Wait a minute, Beatrice. My aunt never stole a thing in her life."

"Then tell me why she stopped selling them?" Beatrice asked.

Mallory didn't have an answer. She guessed it was because they hadn't been a big seller. It wasn't uncommon for Glenna to experiment with new recipes, and if they weren't a hit with her customers, she took them off the menu.

"Your aunt at least had the decency to stop selling my cookies when I confronted her about it. I expect you'll do the same thing," Beatrice said.

"Do you have proof that your recipe was stolen?" Dugan asked.

Mallory's mouth dropped open. What was happening? Her profile as an up-and-coming cookiepreneur was being turned into a piece about a stolen recipe? She had to get her interview back on track.

"How about I give it a taste test?" Dugan asked.

"Marvelous idea." Beatrice extended the tin, and he helped himself to a cookie.

Dugan took a bite and then swallowed. "Very delicious. Tender. Not too almondy." After finishing the cookie, he looked to Mallory.

Oh, for goodness sakes.

Mallory marched to the display case, plucked a piece of tissue paper from its container, and slid open the door behind the tray of Almond Meltaways. She lifted a cookie from the display and handed it to the reporter.

At first glance, the little cookie was unassuming. A simple shortbread cookie with almond icing, nothing fancy. But when bit into, it was a lightweight cookie that melted in your mouth. The sugary flavor of the icing and the buttery shortbread mellowed the strong taste of the almond extract, creating a burst of cookie goodness that had you reaching for another one.

He took a bite and then swallowed. "Also very delicious. And not too almondy. Tender and light." Dugan finished the cookie.

"The verdict?" Kip asked, earning him a glare from Mallory.

"They taste the same." Dugan said.

"That's because she's using my recipe," Beatrice said.

"Or you stole Glenna's recipe," Kip countered.

Beatrice's mouth formed an O. "How dare you accuse me of stealing recipes. You think I would risk my reputation by doing that?"

"You think Mallory would?" Kip asked.

Mallory had had enough. Customers were gawking, and her interview had been derailed. Finally, she raised her palms to put an end to the ridiculous conversation.

"The Almond Meltaway cookie recipe came from Aunt Glenna, and I have no intention of pulling it from the menu. In fact, I've decided that it will stay on the menu for the foreseeable future. So there. Put that in your icing bag and pipe it."

Oh, no, no, no. Did I just say that out loud?

Mallory heard what sounded like a snicker and glanced in its direction. There she saw the cool, calm, and collected coffee guy lower his gaze as he sipped his coffee. So he thought this was funny? Her lips pressed together in frustration. There was nothing funny about having your reputation at risk of being ruined. Especially when you had a huge loan to pay back.

Beatrice stepped closer to Mallory. "How dare you speak to me like that. Even your jealous recipe stealing aunt never stooped so low."

Mallory's attention returned to Beatrice, and since she was already in for a penny, as her aunt used to say, why stop now?

"You can't go around accusing people of stealing recipes and threatening legal action. Words have consequences. You'll see. One day you'll regret saying those things about my aunt."

Beatrice pulled back as if Mallory had struck her. "I believe you just threatened me."

Mallory shook her head. "Don't be—"

Beatrice raised her hand. "No . . . we have nothing more to say to each other." She spun around and marched out of the bakery, leaving a room full of gaping stares and frenzied whispers.

"Good grief," Mallory muttered. She looked to Kip and then at the perplexed faces of her customers and then at Dugan, who was doing his best to hide a grin. She knew he was pleased as punch because his story about her had just gotten a whole lot more interesting. Then it hit her—she'd asked for this last night when she had thrown the question out to the universe whether things could get any worse.

The answer was yes, and now she had to find some way to fix this mess.

*   *   *

After Beatrice's dramatic exit, it hadn't taken long for the bakery to clear out, including the hot coffee guy. Right behind him was Dugan. He quickly wrapped up the interview. Before he left, Mallory gifted him with a sport-themed basket. She'd found out he was a die-hard sports fan. He marveled at the football-shaped cookies and chuckled at the personalized football jersey cookie. He thanked her and was off.

Mallory closed the front door and turned to face her employees. Claudia had a sour look on her oval face, while Kip had a worried look in his green eyes. He must have had the same feeling she had—that the profile wasn't going to be as flattering as they'd hoped. She wasn't two steps away from the door when it opened. Her cousin, Darlene Hughes, breezed in with a stack of flyers in her hand.

Darlene looked relaxed in a midi floral dress and white sneakers. Her shoulder-length dark-blonde hair was styled in loose, bouncy curls. She removed her oversized shades, and her eyes narrowed in on her cousin.

"Heard there was quite a ruckus with Queen Bea," Darlene said.

"Already? That was fast." Mallory continued to the counter and busied herself with tidying up the area.

"Wouldn't surprise me if somebody took a video of the whole scene and you end up going virus," Claudia said right before she disappeared into the kitchen.

Kip shook his head. "Viral. The word is viral," he called out to her. "Not everyone should try to be hip."

"Do you think someone did that?" Mallory asked him.

He pressed his lips together and gave a half-hearted shrug before darting into the kitchen.

"Not helpful." Mallory's body sagged at the thought of her encounter with Beatrice being viewed by the masses. "Why did she have to come in here today of all days?"

"She obviously heard about the interview. Do you think she'd pass up a chance to be a part of it? A few years ago, she crashed Mom's television segment," Darlene said.

"That's right. I remember . . . Aunt Glenna was on the five o'clock news at Christmas. I was here that day," Mallory said.

Darlene nodded. "They were friends. Mom wanted to share the big moment with her. But Beatrice wasn't content to sit on the sidelines. She practically took over the segment to promote her blog. When Mom told her how upset she was, Beatrice accused her of being unsupportive. Let me tell you, the woman has a lot of nerve." Darlene set the flyers on the counter. "Anyway, I'm not here to gossip."

Mallory lifted a brow. Her cousin was in the thick of Wingate's gossip mill. Born and raised in town, she was a social butterfly, volunteering at the drop of a hat, and she was also a member of the PTO. Which meant Darlene was privy to all that was being talked about in town.

"As you know, I'm on the Spring Garden Tour committee, and we're asking all the local merchants to put these flyers up. I know there isn't steady foot traffic here since you've taken over."

"There's *enough*." Mallory took a flyer. Her cousin had been unhappy with the changes at the bakery and never passed up the chance to express her displeasure. The fact that her mother had given Mallory her blessings to make those changes didn't seem to matter to Darlene. Mallory suspected it had more to do with Aunt Glenna's death than with her. So she tried her best not to take what Darlene said too personally. Yet sometimes her words stung.

"I suppose so." Darlene's cool gaze swept across the empty bakery and made its way back to Mallory. "Anyway, the bakery has always donated cookies to the tour. So I expect you'd like to keep the tradition? Or would you like to change it?"

There it was, another jab at Mallory's changes to the bakery. And she let it slide. *Again.* Someone had to take the high road.

"I'm happy to donate a tray of cookies along with two cookie bouquets for the raffle." The proceeds from the Garden Tour and its associated events went to fund programs at the senior center, which she was happy to support.

Darlene's expression faltered. "Very generous. Thank you."

Mallory wondered how much that hurt her cousin to say. She wanted to ask, but there was something more important she needed to know.

"Do you know where your mom got the recipe for the Almond Meltaways?"

Darlene shrugged. "Not really. She got a lot from my grandmothers, and the rest came from her experimenting."

That answer wasn't helpful to Mallory. Time to move on to another question.

"You know Beatrice better than I do. How should I handle her?"

"Are you actually going to listen to my advice?"

"What's that supposed to mean?"

Darlene sighed. "Never mind. I really have to go." She spun around and headed for the door. But before she pulled it opened, she looked back at Mallory and clearly decided to offer a piece of advice after all.

"You handle Queen Bea very carefully."

Chapter Three

The rest of the day flew by, and before Mallory knew it, it was time to flip the open sign over and close the bakery. Thankfully, she had had little time to think about Gil because the afternoon was jam-packed with work, from social media scheduling to baking dozens of sugar cookies to working the counter after Claudia clocked out. At the bakery's back door, she double-checked the lock with Kip by her side. In her hand, she held her aunt's recipe book. When she had first pulled the Almond Melt-away recipe, she'd skimmed the notations on the card and then transferred the recipe to an electronic file. As much as she hated to admit it, maybe she had missed a note about the recipe coming from Beatrice. She and Kip parted ways with a promise of getting together later for a movie night, complete with pizza and wine. Now at home, she barely had time to unwind because of Agatha's demands to be fed.

After setting her backpack down, Mallory quickly opened a can of salmon paté and dished it out. Agatha trotted to her place-mat and waited impatiently. Her meows went from a she-devil tone to lyrical once Mallory set the bowl on the mat.

With her cat fed, Mallory grabbed the recipe book and headed for the staircase. She wanted to change before Kip arrived. Passing through the living room, she made a quick stop at the old chest she used as a coffee table. There she set the book on top of a stack of mystery novels. Those books, including her favorite Miss Marple title, *4:50 To Paddington*, were waiting to be organized on the bookshelves in the living room. At some point she'd have the time to get her house in order.

Yawning on her way to her bedroom, she wished she hadn't agreed to movie night. What she really wanted was a hot bath and her bed. When she reached the room and saw her queen-sized bed, she considered calling and canceling. But she couldn't do that to Kip. He was looking forward to their movie night. She hoped at some point she'd get a second wind.

From her dresser she pulled out a pair of stretchy pants and a T-shirt. She quickly changed and then slipped on her fuzzy slippers. Standing in front of the mirror over her dresser, she unpinned her messy bun and combed her fingers through her hair. She stared at her reflection one more time and inhaled a deep breath. She reminded herself she'd get through the five stages of the breakup. They were listed on a blog she had read months ago.

Mallory turned and headed toward the door. The first phase was denial. It was that period when you believed he'd come back. Well, she had definitely bypassed that phase. She didn't want the cheater back. Stepping out into the hall, she walked toward the staircase. The second phase was sadness. Yep, she was there. She trod down the stairs and headed into the kitchen. Next up would be anger. In the kitchen, she pulled out a bottle of wine and two stem glasses along with plates and napkins and set them on a tray. Mallory paused a moment. It felt like sadness and anger were mixed. So maybe she'd get them both over at once. She grinned. There was nothing like multitasking.

She lifted the tray and headed back to the living room. The next phase was rebound. The face of the good-looking guy she spilled coffee on flashed in her mind.

"No, no, no," she murmured as she set the tray on the old chest, shifting the unruly stacks of books to make room. "Not going to happen. I'll skip right over that and go onto the last stage, which was . . . newfound confidence. Yep, that's where I'll go."

The knock at the front door alerted her to Kip's arrival with dinner. And just in time. Her stomach had rumbled more than once. Quickly, she crossed the scuffed wood floor that creaked in too many places to count and let him in.

"Why did the cookie go to the doctor?" Kip asked as he stepped over the threshold.

"Ugh." Mallory closed the door. "I don't know. Why?"

"Because he felt crummy." He laughed as he carried the pizza box into the living room.

Mallory also laughed, but it was more at the fact that Kip loved to crack himself up with those silly jokes. She followed him into the living room and noticed Agatha had appeared from the kitchen. She'd perched on the arm of the tufted wing-back chair and was washing her face.

"Does she have to do that here? We're about to eat." Kip placed the box on the old chest and then he dropped onto the slip-covered sofa.

"This is her home." Mallory joined Kip on the sofa after opening the box. "Pour the wine. I've been thinking about this pizza all afternoon."

"Yeah, you needed something to look forward to after the day you had." Kip poured the wine and then swirled his before taking a sip.

"Tell me about it." Mallory lifted a hot, cheesy slice of pizza from the box and took a bite. After she swallowed, she said, "I'm trying not to dwell on what happened with Beatrice. I'm going to pick a new novel to start reading tonight." She gestured to the stacks of books.

"You won't be reading tonight because you'll be fretting over the incident. Face it, Mal, you want people to like you."

"Do not!"

Kip gave her an appraising look. "So why haven't you told Claudia to hit the road yet?"

"She's . . . Claudia is . . . experienced, and it's in the best interest of the bakery's success to keep her on." And because her aunt would have wanted her to make every effort to keep Claudia at the bakery, despite her being a cantankerous individual Mallory would have canned in a heartbeat at the advertising agency. Even though Claudia hadn't come out and said it, Mallory believed she was still grieving Glenna's death. Plus, all the change at the bakery couldn't be easy for someone so set in her ways.

"If you say so." Kip took a bite of his slice and chewed.

Mallory studied her friend as she tried to form a rebuttal to his statement about her personality. But she couldn't. And he knew it. Darn it.

"You can't please everyone." Kip set his slice down and then took another sip of wine.

"You're speaking from experience."

He nodded thoughtfully. "I am. Look, when I went against the family tradition of public service to bake cookies for a living, I certainly didn't please the Winslow clan. But I couldn't worry about what everyone thought. I had to do what was right for me."

What had been right for Kip was a two-year pastry program at culinary school. He graduated at the top of his class and landed a good job at Corrigan's, a chain of grocery stores in New England, in the bakery department. Now he was working at The Cookie Shop. Was he saving the world? No. But he was making people very happy with his baked goods.

"I know that was hard. But you know your family is proud of you." She and Kip had been friends since they were ten years old. It was the summer when Mallory's parents decided to rent a house by the lake. Before then, she and her family had always stayed at Aunt Glenna's house. Her parents had said it was getting too crowded in Glenna's antique colonial. Looking back, Mallory believed that the home's one and a half bathrooms weren't enough for three girls, two of whom were preteens. One afternoon Mallory was sitting by the lake with her nose in a Nancy Drew book when Kip showed up with his sister, Lauren. They started talking and never stopped. She and Kip bonded over their love for baking. Even when Mallory returned to the city, they called, emailed, and texted. And whenever Mallory returned to Wingate, during the summers or holidays, they got together. She had watched him struggle with his decision not to apply for the police academy, like his sister, father, and uncles had done. Instead, he had enrolled at North Haven Tech College.

Kip shrugged off Mallory's comment and then reached for the remote control. "Let's choose a movie." He had a talent for telling the worst jokes *and* for avoiding talking about himself.

While Kip searched the guide for movies, Mallory's thoughts drifted back to Beatrice.

She knew Beatrice would probably never like her, but she had to deal with the recipe stealing accusation.

"Oh no," Kip said, pausing the scroll of the television guide.

"Oh no, what?"

"You have that look. You're going to try and fix this thing between you and Queen Bea."

"What choice do I have? Either I nip this in the bud now or it's going to snowball."

Mallory set what was left of her pizza on her plate and reached for the thick recipe book. She opened the book and flipped through the pages that had been marked up with notes from her aunt. She found the Almond Meltaway recipe. It was neatly written on an

31

index card and taped to the lined sheet of paper. She took time to reread the recipe and scanned the handwritten notes that documented the baking times Aunt Glenna had experimented with. There were no notes about Beatrice.

"Ah-ha! I was right. I didn't miss any mention of Beatrice." Mallory closed the book.

"What are you going to do?"

Mallory glanced at her watch. "She lives on Spruce Lane, doesn't she?"

"Number sixteen. Right next door to Evelyn Brinkley." Kip stared at Mallory. "Oh no, you're not thinking of going over there?"

Mallory popped up from the sofa with the recipe book in hand. "Why wait? She'll probably be more agreeable if we talk in private. She won't have an audience to play to. I'll show her that it's indeed Aunt Glenna's recipe." She patted the book.

Kip snorted. "Or she could call the cops on you for trespassing."

Mallory waved away the notion. "I don't think there will be any need for the police."

Kip shrugged. "You're forgetting who you'll be dealing with."

"Then come with me."

"Oh, no way, sister. I'll wait right here for you to get back or take your call if you need bail money." Kip picked up his slice again and took a bite.

"Fine. I don't expect to be long." As she passed by the wing-back chair, she patted Agatha on the head. "Don't let him eat all the pizza." The cat blinked, and Mallory smiled. She could always count on Agatha.

She walked through the kitchen, picked up her backpack on her way to the back door, and dropped the recipe book inside. There she kicked off her slippers and slid into a pair of sneakers.

She pulled the door open and exited the house, heading for the garage.

Behind the wheel of her Jetta, Mallory turned left out of her driveway. Her GPS navigation system had mapped out the seven-minute drive to Spruce Lane. She traveled slowly along narrow roads while watching for deer leaping from wooded areas with no advance warning. The turn-off for Spruce Lane was at a two-way stop and, with her blinker flicked on, she turned right.

She eased her foot off the accelerator and coasted along the gravel road looking for number sixteen. Up ahead on her left was the house, according to the mailbox. She pulled into the driveway and shut off the Jetta's engine. Subtle lighting of the driveway and garden beds created a warm welcome to the rambling ranch set back from the road. With her backpack in hand, Mallory exited the vehicle and walked along the brick path to the front door. Interior lights were on, which meant Beatrice was home. And that's probably the reason why Mallory's stomach knotted.

When she reached the door, she sucked in a fortifying breath and then pressed the doorbell and waited. How long would Beatrice leave her standing on the welcome mat? Growing impatient and worried she'd have to leave before having a chance to talk to Beatrice, Mallory peered into the sidelight window, looking for any sign of the homeowner.

There was none.

She pressed the button again and waited.

Beatrice had to be home. Practically all the lights were on.

Her phone buzzed. She reached into her backpack for it and saw Kip was calling.

"How's it going?" he asked. "Did she let you in?"

"There's no answer." Mallory stepped back from the door. "But all the lights are on."

"Guess she's sending you a message. Come back home. I got *27 Dresses* queued up and ready to start. And your cat is staring at me. I think she wants to kill me."

Mallory rolled her eyes. "She's a house cat, not a lion. Maybe Beatrice is in the back of the house and didn't hear the doorbell." She spun on her heels and walked back to the driveway.

"Mal, don't go looking for trouble. She clearly doesn't want to talk to you."

"She confronted me today at my place of business. So now it's my turn, and she's going to listen to what I have to say." Too bad Mallory wasn't sure exactly what that would be.

"I don't like this," Kip said.

Mallory ignored his naysaying and followed the brick path around the two-car garage to the patio off the rear of the house. When she reached the back of the house, the slider door was partially open, and she approached it.

"She's home. The slider is open." Mallory reached for the door and slid it open wider and then called out for Beatrice. There was no answer. She tried again, this time louder. When there was no reply, she continued into the kitchen.

The lit-up space was impressive. Beatrice's kitchen was decked out with high-end appliances and even had a built-in espresso machine. The stainless steel appliances sparkled from regular polishing, and the massive island was topped with a thick slab of granite. However, the cream-colored tile floor appeared dusty.

Mallory looked closer at the floor, and she realized it wasn't dust.

"Flour?" She hadn't taken Beatrice for a messy cook.

"What are you talking about?" Kip asked.

"There's flour on the floor."

"Wait. You're inside her house?"

"The door was open. Hold on." Mallory took another few steps and saw a ripped bag of flour on the floor. "Huh. Looks like Beatrice dropped a bag of flour." It had happened to her a couple of times. Moving too fast, not paying attention. But then she saw a sensibly shod foot peeking out from behind the island. "Uh-oh."

"What's wrong?"

"I'm not sure." Cautiously, she moved forward and stopped when she found Beatrice sprawled out on the floor in an outline of flour. She gasped.

"What . . . what's happening?"

Mallory's eyes widened when she saw the bloodied marble rolling pin beside Beatrice's body.

"I have . . . have . . . to call the police."

"Why?"

Mallory gulped. "I found Beatrice. I think she's dead."

Chapter Four

Mallory leaned against her car with her arms crossed to ward off the night chill. She should have grabbed her fleece jacket when she left her house. Since she was thinking about should-haves, she should never have come to Beatrice's home in the first place. Kip had been right; it was a mistake that ended with the police being called.

She stared at the scene in front of her. Flashing strobe lights, radio squawks, crime scene tape stretched along the patio, and neighbors gathered on the road watching with morbid curiosity. Too far to hear what they were saying, she had a pretty good idea of what was being whispered.

"Something terrible has happened, hasn't it?"

"Is Beatrice okay?"

"Isn't that the cookie bouquet lady who threatened Queen Bea earlier?"

Mallory shook her head to dislodge the voices just in time.

"Miss Monroe, we meet again."

Her gaze flicked toward the deep voice that was all too famil-iar. The hot coffee guy from the bakery! What was he doing there? Then she saw it. His unbuttoned blazer revealed a badge fastened to his belt as he approached.

She swallowed.

Hot coffee guy was a police detective.

She groaned.

The night couldn't get any worse.

Wait. She needed to take that thought back, and fast. Things *could* get worse if she was taken away in handcuffs.

"You're a cop?" Mallory straightened, uncrossing her arms. She resisted the urge to run her fingers through her hair and give it a little fluff. They were at a murder scene, not in a meet-cute moment from one of her beloved romantic comedies. A woman was dead. A woman she'd had harsh words with. Some of those words the detective had heard.

Put that in your icing bag and pipe it.

Why on earth did I say that to Beatrice?

He nodded. "Detective Will Hannigan."

"And this is your case now?" There was a sliver of hope in Mallory that he was just passing by and another detective would be there shortly.

He nodded again, flipping open his notepad. "I'd appreciate it if you tell me what happened."

Mallory exhaled a deep breath. She wasn't going to catch a break.

"Honestly, I'm not sure. I found Beatrice . . . dead . . . she's dead, right?"

"Very much so."

Mallory rested her palm over her heart. It squeezed tightly at the thought of Beatrice taking her last breath in her kitchen. Had she suffered? Or had she succumbed quickly to the deadly blow?

"Why don't you walk me through what happened this evening? Starting with before you found her."

"I can do that." Mallory nodded. "When I arrived, I rang her doorbell. When there was no answer, I thought she might be in the back of her house and hadn't heard the bell. So I walked around the side of the house, saw the back door open, and went inside. Then, of course, I called out to her because I didn't want to startle her."

"Do you often enter other people's homes uninvited?"

Mallory opened her mouth to speak but then closed it, her lips pressing firmly together. The way he framed the question and the tone of his voice set alarm bells off in her head. She needed to proceed with caution.

"As I said, I didn't think she had heard the bell, and when I saw the back door open, I made sure to announce my entry. I just stepped inside. I didn't go through the house. It's not like I was stalking about." Mallory searched the detective's eyes, looking for some sign he agreed with her statement and came up with nothing.

"You and the deceased had a disagreement earlier." He stated the cold, hard fact without emotion, not even an inkling of one. She guessed it came with years of experience as a police detective.

"That's why I came here tonight. I came here to settle . . . I mean to straighten out the misunderstanding." Mallory whipped her backpack off the hood of her car and unzipped it. She pulled out her recipe book. "See, this is my aunt's recipe book, and here is her recipe for Almond Meltaways. I wanted to compare it to Beatrice's recipe."

Detective Hannigan cast his cool gaze on the well-used book. "Why at this hour?"

"I didn't have a chance to go through the book until I closed my bakery. Then I had to go home and feed my cat."

"Cat, huh?"

"Her name is Agatha, after my favorite author."

"You like mystery fiction?"

"Obsessed with it. Until I moved to Wingate, I ran a mystery book club. Once a month, a little food, a little wine, and a whole lot of murder." Mallory realized she might have gone too far with her explanation. She quickly reined herself in and got back on track. "Anyway, after feeding Agatha, my friend and employee, Kip Winslow, came over for dinner. He's Chief Winslow's son." Mentioning her connection to the chief ten months ago had gotten her out of a speeding ticket. The officer had let her drive away, at the speed limit, with only a verbal warning. Perhaps her longtime relationship with the chief would help her not be a murder suspect.

"He's the *baker*." Hannigan's emphasis on the word baker told Mallory what he thought of Kip's career choice. "I'm finding there are a lot of connections between people in Wingate. None of which impacts how I do my job."

Uh-oh. If Hannigan had been the cop who had pulled her over, she would have gotten a ticket. Maybe two. Time to move past her friendship with the detective's boss.

"While we were talking, the idea suddenly popped into my head, and here I am." She'd have to remember to take a long pause next time before acting on her ideas. "Who would have done such a thing to Beatrice?"

"Someone who disliked her immensely. Perhaps someone who had a public row with the victim."

Mallory started nodding in agreement, and then her head froze. "Wait . . . you think I killed her? Because we argued over a cookie recipe? That's ridiculous."

The detective jotted something on his notepad before looking back at Mallory. That wasn't good, was it? She gulped.

"If I remember correctly, Miss Monroe, you told Mrs. Wright, quote, 'One day you'll regret saying those things.'"

He'd quoted her exactly. Great. Apparently, he had the memory of an elephant.

"That doesn't mean I killed her. This is crazy. We're talking about a cookie recipe." Gosh, she couldn't believe when she first met the detective, she'd thought he was hot. What had she been thinking?

"Things have a way of getting out of control . . . fast."

"So much out of control, I'd hit her on the head with a marble rolling pin?" Realizing what she just said, Mallory clamped her mouth shut.

Detective Hannigan arched his brows and held his gaze on her for a long moment. Even though she was innocent, she suddenly felt flushed and guilty. She needed to say something, to proclaim her innocence.

"I didn't! I came here tonight in hopes of settling the question about whose recipe I'm using and putting this incident behind us." Her chin trembled as tears pricked the back of her lids. She willed herself not to cry. "Instead, I found her on the floor. Her head was bloody, and she looked dead. I . . . I didn't know if her attacker was still in there. That's why I ran out of the house and locked myself in my car until officers arrived."

Detective Hannigan's sharp brown eyes softened, and he took a step forward and rested his hand on her shoulder. He gave a small, reassuring squeeze.

"I understand discovering the body was a traumatic event. You did the right thing. What I need from you now is your full cooperation so I can investigate and apprehend the person responsible. Can you do that?"

Mallory nodded as she composed herself. Breaking down in public wasn't a good look, and she needed a clear head to help the police.

"Detective! The *Chronicle* is here!" an officer called out before he disappeared into a police vehicle.

The *Chronicle*? Mallory inwardly groaned and looked toward the crowd that had gathered, and there was Dugan Porter with a camera in hand. Shoot. Panic clawed at her insides. He'd been at the bakery when Beatrice came in and made her scene. Now he'd have an even juicier story for his readers. How large was the *Chronicle*'s circulation?

"Detective Hannigan, can I go home? I've given my statement to Officer Winslow, and I've answered your questions." She said a silent prayer he'd agree to let her leave.

He shifted his attention back to Mallory. He looked hesitant for a moment and then nodded. "Yes. I think we have all we need now. I'll be in contact."

Mallory didn't waste any time. She shoved her recipe book into her bag and then tossed it into the car as she opened the driver's side door. By the time she slipped in behind the steering wheel, the detective had turned and headed toward the crime scene. Thinking of Beatrice's kitchen as a crime scene sent a shudder through Mallory. A tap on the driver's side window startled her. She started the ignition and then lowered the window.

"You okay to drive home?" Officer Lauren Winslow asked. She was the first officer to arrive after Mallory called 9-1-1. She was also Kip's older sister and her friend.

"Yeah, I think so." Her hands had finally stopped shaking, and the shock of finding Beatrice's body seemed to be wearing off.

"I can have someone drive you home." Lauren rested her hands on her utility belt.

Mallory had no idea how the petite brunette managed to carry so much weight around her waist.

Mallory considered the offer for all of two seconds. Getting a lift home meant she'd have to come back to this house to pick up her car later. Even in daylight, she really didn't want to come back.

"It's not necessary. I'm okay. But I do have a question."

Lauren gave a sly smile. Mallory remembered the same one from when they were teenagers, talking about boys. "He's single."

"No! My question isn't about Detective Hannigan."

"Oh, my bad." Lauren gave a contrite look. Too bad it didn't look sincere. "Lots of ladies have that question about him."

Mallory raised her palm and said, "Well, I'm not one of them." Detective Hannigan's marital status was none of her business. So why had her heart skipped a little beat at hearing the information? Her thoughts zipped back to the five stages of breakup article she'd read. No way was the detective going to be her step number four—rebound. Nope. No matter how hot she thought he was when she first saw him.

"What do you want to know?"

Lauren's question jogged Mallory out of her thoughts about the detective.

"Any idea when Beatrice was killed?"

"Not yet. But she was still warm when I arrived, so it appears she wasn't dead for long by the time you arrived."

"Maybe if I didn't wait so long at the front door—"

"Don't do this to yourself." Lauren leaned forward. Her voice softened. "You're not responsible for her death."

"Tell that to the detective. He all but said he suspected me of killing her."

Lauren glanced over her shoulder and then returned her gaze to Mallory. "He's only doing his job. He has to ask hard questions. No one is going to believe that you murdered Queen Bea."

Mallory appreciated the vote of confidence. "She sure did ruffle a lot of feathers, so the detective is going to have his hands full investigating."

"That's why he gets paid the big bucks." Lauren stepped back from the car. "You get home safe."

"I will." Mallory shifted the car into gear and slowly drove out of the driveway, past the group of onlookers and Dugan Porter. She forced herself to concentrate on the road, not what the reporter would write about Beatrice's murder. And her connection to it.

*   *   *

Mallory carefully eased beneath her covers so as not to disturb a sleepy Agatha. At least one of them was ready for bedtime. She dropped her head on her pillow, resting her phone on her chest. She'd just finished a group text with her sister, Liz, and their mom. As a rule, she hated group texts, but at times like these—finding a murdered woman and being questioned by the police—they seemed to have a place. Looking back, this text was one of the most awkward to start.

Hey, just want you to know I found a dead body tonight. I'm okay.

Her sister's reply was classic Liz—**You didn't. Miss Marple did. We've talked about this before.**

Her mom's reply was expected—**This better be a joke. If it is, it's not funny.**

No, it wasn't funny. Mallory had spent the next fifteen minutes sharing as much information as she thought she could without jeopardizing the police investigation and assuring her family she didn't need them rushing over. Liz was minutes away, while their mom was a good hour from Wingate. After her parents retired from teaching, they purchased a bed and breakfast in the shoreline village of Craggy Neck. Mallory's move to Wingate not only allowed her to follow her dream but also to be closer to her family. Though sometimes the closeness felt a little too much. Finally, her mom and Liz calmed down and both agreed to stay home when they learned that Kip was staying over.

She stretched her glance across the bed to Agatha. The feline's eyes were closed, and her body was curled into a fluffy ball.

Somebody was drifting into a deep sleep, just like someone else in the living room.

She'd left Kip downstairs snoring on the sofa since the bed for the guest room hadn't been delivered yet. He'd insisted on staying until she returned home and then put the kettle on so they could have a cup of tea. He said it would help settle their nerves. He'd been a bundle of nervous energy from the time she left for Beatrice's home, and it had increased tenfold after the body was discovered. To be honest, she wasn't sure who was comforting whom as they sipped their tea.

She now stared at her ceiling and wondered if the vision of Beatrice's body would haunt her dreams. That was, if she could get to sleep at all.

Tapping her fingers on her phone, her mind raced with what-ifs. Those what-ifs were just as bad as should-haves. Once her mind started, it was hard to stop.

What if she hadn't gone to Beatrice's house? Then she wouldn't have been questioned by Detective Hannigan and have her words tossed back into her face.

What if she had never made those Almond Meltaway cookies? Then Beatrice wouldn't have stormed into her bakery and made a scene.

What if she had arrived a few minutes earlier? Would she have come face to face with the killer?

That last thought had her heart pounding. Would she have been killed too? She squeezed her eyes closed, hoping to shut down her racing mind. She inhaled deeply and exhaled slowly. Mallory reminded herself she was safe and was in no danger. Her eyes opened.

What had Lauren said?

Beatrice's body was still warm, so it appeared she hadn't been dead for too long when Mallory found her. Did that mean there was a chance that the killer could think she saw him . . . or her?

The cell phone buzzed, startling Mallory. Her body jerked, and the phone slid off to the side. Fumbling for it, she disturbed Agatha, who gave her an irritated look before tucking her head back down.

"Sorry." Mallory stroked the cat and then checked the caller ID—Unknown.

A shudder rippled through her body at the simple word. Now, it was reasonable to assume it was a robo-caller on the other end. Still, a little niggle in her mind sent her on high alert.

She dropped the phone like a hot potato, disturbing Agatha yet again, and she tossed her covers off and slipped into her slippers. She double-checked her locked windows and then headed downstairs to check the doors, just in case.

Chapter Five

Mallory attempted to stifle a yawn, but she wasn't successful. It appeared there wasn't enough coffee in all of Wingate to energize her. Exhaustion had consumed her despite the fact she'd drunk ample amounts of caffeine before arriving at the bakery and after tying on her apron.

"Hey, why don't you take a break?" Kip nudged her shoulder with his. He looked well-rested despite having slept on a sofa. Meanwhile, Mallory had settled on her mattress—cloud-soft with cooling technology that cost way more than her original budget—and barely gotten a wink of sleep. Between a never-ending movie reel of the crime scene playing in her mind and hearing every little noise throughout the night, slumber had been elusive.

"Thanks. But you need to work the counter today." Mallory pointed to the swinging door as she carried a half baking sheet to the oven. "I can't possibly show my face out there."

As soon as the bakery opened, a steady stream of customers had paraded in. It would have been a godsend to have such brisk business on any other day. But it wasn't. It was the day after she had discovered Queen Bea's body. And the customers weren't exactly spending big money. Instead, they were buying one or two cookies as cover for their info-seeking mission. Not one of them ordered a cookie bouquet. In fact, by noon, three orders had been canceled.

Mallory tried not to read too much into those lost orders, but she had a suspicion those customers suspected her of being involved in Beatrice's death. She inhaled deeply to calm the racing thoughts of doom swirling through her mind.

"Are you sure?" Kip closed the oven door for Mallory.

Mallory nodded. She hadn't the energy or bandwidth to engage with customers. There was also the fact that her presence would encourage questions about last night. She felt Detective Hannigan wouldn't be pleased if she shared details of the crime scene. Then again, what would it hurt to get her side of the story out since she was innocent?

"What's going on up there?" Kip pointed to Mallory's head. "Care to share?"

"Maybe I should call Dugan Porter."

"Why on earth would you do something like that?"

"To tell my side of the story." Mallory walked away from the oven. "That I went there to smooth things over with Beatrice. I'm sure he'd like an exclusive interview."

"Of course, he would love an exclusive that he could twist to his advantage."

"You think he would?"

"Mallory, Mallory, you're so naïve it'd be almost adorable if you weren't a suspect in a murder," Kip said.

She opened her mouth to protest but was cut off by Claudia. "He has a point."

Kip's head swung around so fast Mallory was sure he got whiplash. "I do?"

"Even a broken clock is right twice a day." Claudia dropped a mound of cookie dough on her worktable and used a cutter to divide the dough in half.

Kip looked back at Mallory and gave her a *what-the-heck-does-that-mean* look. "As I was saying, the last thing you want to do is talk to the press. So don't call him." He pivoted and walked out of the kitchen. He wasn't gone a minute before he popped his head back in. "There's somebody here to see you."

Mallory wiped her hands on her apron. "Who?"

"Go on out and see." Claudia dusted her work surface and then grabbed her rolling pin.

Mallory's stomach flip-flopped as the bloodied rolling pin she saw near Beatrice's body flashed in her mind. She gave herself a mental shake to dislodge the vision.

"She says her name is Aspen Leigh and she met you the other night." He must have seen the less than enthusiastic look on her face. "It's safe to come out. It's only her."

"You can't stay hidden in here forever." Claudia glided her rolling pin over the rugelach dough.

Oh, how Mallory hated when Claudia was right. Her shoulders slumped, and she walked toward Kip. Stepping out of the kitchen, she was shocked to see Gil's gal pal Red standing on the other side of the bakery case.

Mallory stopped short, and Kip crashed into her. She glanced over her shoulder and glared at him, prompting her friend to scoot back quickly.

"There you are, Mallory!"

"What are you doing here?" She wasn't in the mood to hear Red gloat about how Gil was all hers now. Before she could turn and head back to the kitchen, the front door opened and in marched her cousin Darlene, holding a document in her hand.

"You're all set, Aspen." Darlene approached the redhead and handed her the paper. She then unfolded her right hand, revealing a set of keys.

No. No. No.

While Mallory's aunt sold her the bakery business, she had left the building to her daughter. Darlene had been actively looking for a tenant for the studio upstairs. It appeared she had found one.

Aspen plucked the keys from Darlene's hand and smiled widely. "You've been such a dear. I promise I'm going to be the best tenant ever. And I even have a friend in town already."

"You know her?" Kip whispered to Mallory.

"Sort of." Mallory inched closer to the counter. "Red . . . I mean Aspen, what's going on? Why are you renting the studio apartment?"

"It looks like you two have some catching up to do." Darlene gave a half snort. It appeared Aspen had filled her landlady in on all the details of how she knew Mallory. Darlene quickly recovered from her amusement at her cousin's situation. "Before I go, are you okay, Mal? Last night must have been very upsetting."

"It was. And I'm okay," she lied. Mallory was far from fine, but she knew her cousin wasn't looking for a heart-to-heart conversation.

"Good to hear. I hope that what happened last night won't have a negative impact on your business. My mother managed to run her bakery for decades without a whiff of scandal," Darlene said.

"Are you talking about the murdered woman? I heard about it this morning. You knew her, Mallory?" The cheeriness in Aspen's voice had disappeared as her cornflower blue eyes went wide with curiosity.

"Oh, she knew her, and she also found the body. After they had a very public dustup right here yesterday, didn't you, Mal?" The corner of Darlene's lip turned upward.

The front door opened and Detective Hannigan sauntered in, giving Mallory a nod as he scoped out the shop. Her pulse rate kicked into overdrive. What did he want? She doubted he was there to buy a dozen cookies or order a cookie bouquet. Though she could easily make a law enforcement–themed bouquet like the one she had made for a former coworker's sister. The bouquet included a personalized gold-colored badge, a police squad car, and, of course, a couple of donut-shaped cookies. It was absolutely adorable and was received with much praise.

"Do the police think you killed that woman?" Aspen asked.

Aspen's question dragged Mallory from her thoughts. "What?"

"That would be crazy of them," Aspen continued. "You couldn't kill anyone."

"How can you be so sure?" Detective Hannigan joined the conversation with ease. Clearly, he had experience barging into conversations.

Aspen swiveled her head and gave the detective an appraising look before answering. "Because she didn't kill Gil when she found us together the other night."

Mallory's gaze zeroed in on the detective, and she didn't miss his spark of interest in what Aspen had just said.

"Though if she had, I wouldn't have blamed her," Aspen continued.

Mallory needed to take control of what was quickly turning into a three-ring circus, with the act in the center ring being her put into handcuffs and read her rights.

"Kip, why don't you give Aspen a cookie on the house and set her up at a table while I talk to the detective."

"Detective?" Aspen cooed, but Kip intervened as requested and lured the redhead along the bakery case and showed her an assortment of cookies.

"Thanks for stopping by, Darlene. See you later." Mallory gave a small wave and, in return, got a perturbed look from Darlene before she spun around and left the bakery in a huff.

Meanwhile, Kip grabbed a giant chocolate chip cookie from the bakery case and hustled out from behind the counter. He guided Aspen, who teetered in four-inch heels, to one of the café tables.

"Looks like I interrupted something." Though there wasn't any remorse on the detective's face as he walked closer to the counter. "Who's your character witness?"

"Aspen Leigh. Turns out we were seeing the same guy."

"You found them together?"

"I wanted to surprise Gil with dinner. But I was the one who was surprised." She rested her palms on the counter. "What brings you by, Detective?"

"Just a few more questions if you have the time?"

Mallory sensed his question really wasn't a question.

"Of course I do. Actually, I'm glad you came by because I'm worried about something. Do you think that the killer saw me last night? I mean, Beatrice was still warm, according to one of your police officers." Mallory didn't want to get Lauren into trouble, so she decided to keep her as an unnamed source. Though she'd probably have to reveal Lauren's name if the detective pressed her, because cookie bakers didn't have sources. "Late last night, I got a call from an unknown caller."

"You thought the killer called you last night?" Kip's voice deepened with concern as he stopped in his tracks halfway back to the counter. "Why didn't you wake me?"

"Oh, no need to worry. It was me!" Aspen swung around in her chair. "I wanted to tell you my news."

"You two were together last night?" The detective's gaze darted back and forth between Mallory and Kip.

"You moved on fast, didn't you?" Aspen winked.

"No, I haven't moved on. I mean . . . I plan to one day . . . when I meet the right person . . . Kip slept on my sofa. You know, my overnight guest isn't important." Mallory stopped talking and propped her hands on her hips. Then she realized something. "How did you get my phone number, Aspen?"

"I got it from Gil's phone. After you left the other night, we went inside, and he started groveling. So when he went into the kitchen, I checked his phone to see if there was anyone else. That's when I got your number."

Mallory was tempted to ask if there had been other women, but she didn't think she could handle the answer. At least, not today. Nor could she take the answer to another question that loomed over her now—why hadn't Gil groveled to her?

Her eyes narrowed in on Red, and heat worked its way through her body, from her toes stuffed into her clogs to her fingers, itching to wring Gil's neck and everywhere in between. The anger she was feeling toward Red was irrational and displaced. It belonged to Gil, but he wasn't there at the moment.

"It appears now may not be a good time for you." Hannigan's statement got a *no-kidding-Sherlock* look from Mallory, and he flashed that same slightly amused look she'd seen the day before. "Why don't you come to the station for an interview?"

Mallory gulped. The police station for an interview? It sounded so official. And word would spread quickly that she was summoned to the police station for questioning.

"Are you arresting her, Detective?" Aspen stood, grabbing her purse.

"I just have a few questions I'd like to ask Miss Monroe," the detective said.

"Does she need a lawyer?" Kip raced behind the counter to Mallory. There he stood solid by her side.

"As I said, it's just an interview," Hannigan assured, but it didn't calm Mallory's worries.

"It's never that simple." Aspen's tone changed, and suddenly she sounded cool and professional, which confused Mallory. What was Aspen up to?

The only lawyer Mallory knew was the one who had assisted her with purchasing the bakery and setting up her new business. Maybe he knew someone who could help her.

"I don't have a lawyer," Mallory said.

"You do now." Aspen marched toward the counter. "I'll represent you."

"You're a lawyer?" both Mallory and Kip asked in unison.

Mallory needed a moment to digest what was happening. She was asked to come to the police station for an interview, her ex's girlfriend had just rented the apartment upstairs, and she was now her lawyer.

"Whoa. A real-life Elle Woods, though yours is a redhead," Kip whispered to Mallory.

Mallory swatted her hand at him and then stepped out from behind the counter. "Thank you for your offer, Aspen, but I think I can handle answering Detective Hannigan's questions. I want to help find the person who murdered Beatrice."

"That's what all my clients think. They say, *I can handle this* or *I got this*. Well, let me tell you, you don't." Aspen pivoted and then pulled out a sleek case from her purse. She whipped out a card. "Detective Hannigan, I'll call to set up a time for us to come to the station."

The detective took the card and smirked before he slipped it into his blazer's breast pocket. "I look forward to our conversation. See you both later." He turned and left the bakery.

Aspen looked at Mallory. "Don't worry. You're in good hands."

Somehow those words from Gil the Cheater's gal pal weren't reassuring to Mallory.

* * *

Delivering a cookie bouquet was the perfect opportunity to brainstorm ways to fix the mess that was now her life. Alone on her bicycle, Mallory's mind churned over ideas with no outside interference. Before she left the bakery, Kip and Claudia had shared their thoughts on how to handle the police interview, how to deal with Red, and how not to let rumor and innuendo ruin the bakery. For once, the two of them agreed on things, and she had to admit they offered some excellent advice. Now she needed to make some decisions.

She slowed her pedaling as she approached the delivery address. When she reached the quaint robin's egg blue home, she admired the view of the lake from the front yard. She leaned her bike against the split-rail fence and then lifted the Field of Cookie Flowers Supreme from the bike's rear basket.

It was one of the most expensive bouquets she offered, and clearly, Natalie Kellogg's son wanted her to know how much he loved her. Or, if he was anything like Gil's younger brother, he was priming his mother to ask for a loan. She groaned. She wouldn't think about her ex or his family. When she broke up with him, she'd officially cut all ties with them.

Yet somehow she had ended up with Aspen.

She made her way along the grassy stone path to the front porch. The home sat on a small lot that needed mowing. The past two weeks had been rainy most days, which meant two things in New England—mud and lush lawns with early spring flowers. Before Mallory reached the door, it swung open, and Natalie appeared with a delighted look on her face. She swooped out on the porch with her arms extended, beaming like a child on Christmas morning. Hands down, this was the best part of the job for Mallory.

"Your son really wanted to make sure your day is special. Happy birthday!"

"It's stunning," Natalie said, taking the basket. She inspected the bouquet made up of seven floral-shaped cookies—four daisies, two butterflies, and one flower with the message *Happy Birthday* written on it. Surrounding the container was a tray filled with two dozen soft-baked cookies—chocolate chip, macadamia nut, walnut chocolate, and peanut butter.

"You are truly an artist. Look at the intricate detail on the cookies."

Mallory felt her cheeks flush with color. "Thank you."

"Is it true you worked in advertising before taking over the bakery?" Natalie asked. "You're far too creative to have been stuck in a cubicle."

"I was an account executive." She loved advertising and for a while thought that was where she'd spend her entire career. But then the ad agency merged with a powerhouse in the industry, and it was as if all the stars aligned. They offered her a package, her aunt was selling the bakery, and because she had been a fiscally responsible adult with a good credit rating, she had been approved for a loan.

"When you called earlier to let me know you were coming, I didn't know what to expect. I've never received a cookie bouquet before. This is truly magnificent. They're too pretty to eat." Natalie laughed as her gaze drifted over the bouquet again.

"I hope you do eat them. The flower cookies are sugar cookies, and they are delicious if I do say so myself." Mallory had spent years perfecting her secret recipe.

"I'm sure they are. Your aunt was an amazing baker. May she rest in peace." Natalie's gaze flicked upward for a moment. "Though I hear it wasn't peaceful in the bakery yesterday. Beatrice always made things lively by stirring up trouble. Of course, she won't be doing that anymore. Let me tell you, when she got something in her mind, she was like a dog with a bone. Just ask Ernie Hollis."

"I don't know who he is."

Natalie lifted her chin and angled her head slightly. "He lives just down the road. Like you, he's an excellent baker and was on a winning streak in the Pie Baking Contest."

"The one that's held during the Spring Garden Tour?" Ten years ago, the senior center had added an Afternoon Tea along with the Pie Baking Contest to draw more attendees to the tour. In addition, this year, a container garden workshop was scheduled. "You said he was on a winning streak. What happened?"

"I guess Beatrice got tired of losing to him, so she pitched a fit. She claimed he cheated, and she deserved the first place ribbon. Can you believe that? Anyway, the contest was eliminated because they didn't want a repeat of last year."

"Just because she complained?" Mallory asked.

Natalie arched her brow. "She's the chairperson of the general committee and has been running the garden tour for years."

Mallory's jaw slacked. She knew she shouldn't have been surprised by that; after all, they were talking about Queen Bea. And they were talking about fundraising. While Wingate wasn't a big city, the medium-sized town did have its own form of cutthroat behavior. Community members jockeyed for committee positions to advance their own agendas, garner attention, or obtain a little power.

"Poor Ernie. What a shame."

"It devastated him. He started baking after his wife passed away. But he was more furious with Beatrice. Tarnishing his reputation by saying he cheated. After all, he's a respected administrator at Abernathy College. They got into a heated argument more than once about it." She shrugged. "It looks like he won't have to worry about Beatrice anymore. Guess every cloud has a silver lining for someone."

Mallory felt a chill at her words. How could anyone's death be a silver lining for someone?

"Did that sound terrible? I apologize. Though you should be grateful Beatrice had many enemies in town. It means you won't be the only suspect. Thank you again for this wonderful gift. I know what I'll be sending my friends on their birthdays." Natalie turned and entered her house, closing the door behind her.

Mallory, uncertain of what to say, chewed on her lower lip as she descended the porch steps. It should have elated her to hear Natalie intended to send cookie bouquets to her friends. But instead, she fretted over what would be in store for her next if she didn't nip the outrageous allegations of her being a suspect in the bud.

Chapter Six

Mallory checked her watch. She had a few minutes to spare before she needed to be back at the bakery. Usually, she would have raced back because there was so much to do, and she felt the need to oversee everything. With her business only a few months old, now wasn't the time to let go of the reins. But with the rough start to her day, she needed a little pick-me-up, and that was an iced matcha tea.

She secured her bike, grabbed her backpack, and then pulled open the door of Heavenly Roast Coffee Café. The name did not lie. It smelled divine inside, with the aroma of freshly roasted beans luring you in deeper. The clank of cups, the hiss of the professional coffee machines, and soft music played through speakers above brought a smile to her lips. Her gaze traveled over the café tables that dotted the front of the shop by the large picture window. However, instead of looking out onto the town's charming Main Street, most customers were busy tapping on their computer keyboards while others scrolled on their phones. And she would chug down her iced matcha tea, worrying about things that were out of her control. Oh, boy. A pity party was forming in her head, which was the last thing she wanted. Her gaze stopped, landing on a corner table.

Elana Peterson sat alone, circling the rim of her coffee cup with her forefinger, her gaze fixated out the window. She looked as distracted as she had during the cookie decorating class the other day.

Mallory detoured from the line at the counter to make her way toward Elana. As she wove through the tables, she caught some of the glances from the other patrons. She knew in her bones that they had all heard about Beatrice's murder and how she had found the body. She gulped. Maybe venturing out in public the day after the murder wasn't such a good idea.

"Good to see you." Elana's greeting lacked genuine joy. She pulled her finger from her cup and set her hand on the table. A floral headband kept her dark brunette hair with subtle gold highlights off her face, and she wore demure hoop earrings and a simple wedding band. Everything about the woman emanated class and sadness.

"Same here. I just popped in to get an iced tea to go." Mallory hitched a thumb over her shoulder toward the counter. She wasn't sure why she had made an effort to come over and speak to Elana. Maybe it was because of how unhappy she seemed after the cookie decorating class, and she wanted to check on her.

"Well," Elana leaned forward. "I was hoping to hear all about last night. You know, everybody's talking about Beatrice's murder. And you were there!"

Mallory couldn't help but notice that the distant, contemplative look on Elana's face had morphed into morbid curiosity.

"I'm not surprised someone killed Queen Bea. The woman was awful." Elana sipped her coffee. "Forgive me, but I have to ask. Was it you?" she asked in a hushed tone that was followed by a sly smile.

"No! Of course not."

Elana gave a half shrug. "My bad. But I had to ask. I mean, everyone is probably thinking the same thing. Well, in my opinion, whoever did it should get a medal for ridding our town of Queen Bea."

The iciness in Elana's words chilled Mallory and changed how she viewed the woman. She'd gone from distraught wife to possible murder suspect in the blink of the eye. Now it was Mallory's turn to ask a question. She pulled out the chair across from Elana and sat without an invitation. Her mother would have been mortified by her action, but a tiny breach in etiquette was acceptable considering the circumstances.

"I'm curious. Why did you dislike Beatrice so much?" Mallory set her backpack on her lap.

Elana took another sip of her coffee before answering. "She had a way of hurting people and was never held accountable. Now that she's gone, maybe my husband and I can move forward with our lives." Her cell phone chimed, and she glanced at the device next to the saucer. "Sorry, I have an appointment I can't be late for. Nice chatting with you."

Before Mallory could inquire further about how Beatrice had impacted Elana and her husband's lives, she was out the door. How had she moved so quickly?

Mallory's phone buzzed, and she opened her backpack's front pocket to retrieve the device. The incoming text confirmed the photo shoot with food photographer Luke Collins. She groaned. She'd hired him to take photos for her social media and website. Given the turn of events in the past twenty-four hours, her gut instinct was to cancel. With a cloud of suspicion hanging over her, she wasn't sure if her new business would survive the storm that had hit. But she'd already paid a nonrefundable deposit. So she sent a quick reply, confirming the session.

She tucked her phone back into her bag and stood. She made her way to the counter, feeling the weight of stares.

Was it you?

The urge to jump up on the counter and proclaim her innocence was strong, but Mallory resisted. Doing something like that would make her look either guilty or insane. Or both. Well, then at least she'd have a defense.

*   *   *

Mallory returned to the bakery with her drink and a renewed desire to hide out in the kitchen for the rest of her life. Unfortunately, Kip thwarted her plan by leaving early for a dental appointment. And Claudia needed to bake more Almond Meltaways. Since Beatrice's fuss over the cookies, they'd been the bakery's bestseller.

Even Michaela "Mac" O'Toole, a Wingate mail carrier, asked for a half-dozen when she entered with the day's mail.

A lifelong civil servant, she carried on the family tradition of delivering the mail. Her father and grandfather had both been mail carriers and had each served as the town's postmaster. Mallory wondered if Mac had the same aspiration. About a decade older than Mallory, Mac kept her tall, solid frame lean by walking her route five days a week. She also added a little flair to her standard uniform by wearing a silk scarf around her neck and a pearlescent decorative comb in her honey-colored hair.

"Here you go." Mallory exchanged the bag of Almond Meltaways for a small stack of envelopes. It seemed Mac always had a pile of mail and a hot sheet of the newest chatter in town.

"Doozy of a night, wasn't it?" Mac joked as she pulled out a cookie from the bag.

"I guess it's what everyone is talking about today," Mallory said as she sorted through the mail. Mostly junk since she did most of her bill paying online.

"You got that right. It seems everyone has a theory about who did it. I was just in Curls N' Waves, and I think they have a pool going on. If you ask me, that's just gruesome."

Mallory nodded in agreement as she discarded the junk mail.

"Do you know Ernie Hollis?" Mallory asked as she carried the remaining envelopes to the desk.

"I know him, but he's not on my route. Jimmy Delaney delivers his mail. Nice enough fella. Quiet. And he was a devoted husband. I knew his late wife. She worked at Curls N' Waves, so I saw her pretty much every day. He's the admissions director at Abernathy College," Mac said before eating her cookie. "Liz must know him."

Mallory nodded. Her sister was a literature professor at the college. And she believed in networking and attending all faculty and staff events. She knew everybody at the college.

"It was a shame what Beatrice said about him. He was only trying to keep his wife's legacy alive. Before she got sick, she was a regular competitor in baking contests all summer long. I think there was an article about her in the *Chronicle*."

"Who had an article in the *Chronicle*?" Claudia asked as she appeared from the kitchen with a tray of cookies.

"Patty Hollis," Mac said. "Mallory was just asking about Ernie."

"Why are you asking about him?" Claudia slid open the bakery case door and added the freshly baked cookies to the tray.

"Natalie Kellogg told me that Beatrice accused him of cheating," Mallory said.

"Ha! Natalie is as slippery as they come, and you shouldn't listen to anything she says." Claudia grabbed the empty tray and headed back to the kitchen door. "Mac, do you want to get dinner before book club?"

Mallory shifted just a bit to get a better look at her employee. "You're in a book club?"

"We've been in the romance book club for years," Claudia said.

"Let's meet around six. I better get back to my route." Mac turned and departed the bakery.

"Romance book club?" Mallory asked. She never would have guessed. Claudia seemed more of the nonfiction type.

"We're discussing Ginger Dupont's new book tonight. So I need to leave on time." With that, Claudia disappeared back into the kitchen, and Mallory was left dumbfounded.

*   *   *

Lunchtime rolled around, and Mallory ducked out to meet her sister for lunch. She arrived at the café on the Abernathy College campus a few minutes late. There she spotted her sister at a table for two by the bank of windows overlooking the quad.

When Liz noticed Mallory, she set her phone down and waved. She'd gotten their father's brown hair, which she enhanced with strategically placed bronze highlights. Her toned body was thanks to rigorous boot camp sessions, which Mallory saw as torture. Instead, she preferred to ride her bike for exercise. While most of the professors at Abernathy dressed casually, Liz favored the more polished style of structured blazers and crisp trousers. On her way to join her sister, Mallory glanced at her jeans and T-shirt. She shrugged. Her profession was messier than teaching literary classics. When Mallory reached the table, she dropped onto the chair and then set her backpack down.

"You don't look good." Elizabeth Monroe Lewis wasn't one to mince words. *Ever.* It was a trait her students rarely appreciated, and at the moment, neither did her younger sister.

"Geez, thanks." Mallory pushed the menu aside. She already knew what she wanted—chicken Caesar salad. Oh, and a redo of the past forty-eight hours would be great. "You won't believe my day so far."

"It can't possibly be worse than last night? Or the night before? I can't believe you found Beatrice's body, but I'm still so angry with Gil. How could he cheat on you? I have a mind to pay him a visit."

Mallory had the best big sister. The morning after her breakup, she had called Liz on her ride to the bakery and filled her in about the unexpected ending of the relationship. Liz suggested they both ditch work and have a spa day. While Mallory would have liked a day of pampering, she couldn't play hooky. After all, she was the boss. And she didn't want to think about what would happen if she wasn't there to referee Kip and Claudia for an entire day.

"Thanks, but maybe we weren't meant to be together forever." Saying it out loud hurt her heart. She figured it would take time to get over the betrayal and over Gil. After all, he hadn't come groveling like he had with Aspen. Oh, Aspen. She exhaled a scant breath and then shared the latest twist in her real-life saga with Liz.

"You have to be kidding me! The nerve of that woman. And what was Darlene thinking renting the apartment to her?"

"I wish I was joking." Mallory lifted her water glass and took a sip. "It gets better. Aspen is now my lawyer."

Liz had been taking a drink of her water, and she choked. She set her glass down and, when she stopped coughing, she asked, "Your what?"

Their server appeared to take their order. Once she was out of earshot, Mallory filled her sister in on what had happened with Aspen and Detective Hannigan at the bakery.

"I hear he's good-looking. Hot, even." A sly grin crossed Liz's face as her eyes flickered with a hint of mischief. Even though she'd been the studious one throughout school, she had gone through a boy-crazy phase in her teens. And now she lived vicariously through her younger sister since she was a self-described old married woman at the ripe age of thirty-four. While Liz was outraged at Gil for cheating, Mallory bet her sister was secretly happy because that meant Mal would get out and start dating again at some point.

"He's not horrible looking." Mallory was loath to toss the detective a compliment because it was as clear as day he considered her a suspect. And if he didn't but was questioning her in order to check an item off his investigative to-do list, then he needed to broadcast to everyone in town that she was not a suspect. Besides Mac's purchase of cookies and Mrs. Carmichael buying three Triple Chocolate Dipped Apples, there had been no other sales before Mallory left for lunch. She couldn't sustain a business with those low sales numbers.

"Ah-ha!" Liz leaned back and clapped her hands. "You think he's hot. But because he's doing his job, you're being a little witchy."

"Am not."

"Are so."

Mallory rolled her eyes. "Can we talk about something else?"

Liz shrugged. "Okay. What do you want to talk about?"

"I had to make a delivery to Natalie Kellogg. It's her birthday, and her son ordered such an amazing basket of cookies," Mallory said. "Anyway, she told me that Beatrice managed to have the Pie Baking Contest canceled because she didn't like losing to Ernie Hollis. Who does that?"

"I'd heard she accused him of cheating. How? How would he have cheated? He's an excellent baker. His pies are delicious."

Their server arrived at their table with their meals. Mallory's nose twitched at the aroma of her lunch special, signaling her empty belly to grumble. Just as she was about to lift her fork, Liz raised a hand and waved. Mallory looked over her shoulder and saw a middle-aged man approaching their table. He wore dark khakis and a knit vest over a white button-down shirt. His salt-and-pepper hair was neatly trimmed, and his dark eyes were sandwiched between bushy brows and heavy bags.

"Good afternoon, Ernie," Liz said as the man came up to the side of their table. "I'd like you to meet my sister, Mallory. Mal, this is Ernie Hollis."

"Nice to meet you." Ernie extended his hand. "Liz tells me you bake and decorate amazing cookies. I'm a pie baker myself, but I've thought about dabbling in cookie artistry."

"I hear you make delicious pies. I'd love to try one someday." Mallory took back her hand. "I can never make a good crust. Maybe you can give me some tips."

Ernie beamed. "It would be my pleasure."

"Hey, ya." A student dressed in an Abernathy hoodie sweatshirt and distressed jeans came up behind Ernie, slapping him on the back. He towered over the admissions director. "Mr. Pie-Pie, what's baking?" He let out a loud, obnoxious laugh.

Ernie flinched, and Mallory wasn't sure whether it was the slap on the back or the nickname. Either way, whoever the kid was, he was a class A jerk.

"Chad, I hope you're prepared for tomorrow's exam," Liz said, channeling her serious professor voice.

"Hey, Professor," he said, tipping his head with a grin. "I'm not sweating it."

"Maybe you should. Your grades are important." Liz reached for her glass.

Chad waved off the comment. "I do just fine without worrying about grades. Right, Mr. Pie-Pie?" When Ernie didn't reply, Chad laughed again and pulled his hand from the admissions director's back.

"Chad! Come on! We're going to be late," called another student from the entry of the café.

"Got to go." Chad flashed a toothy smile before he turned and swaggered toward his friend.

"Who was that?" Mallory asked.

"Chad Bellamy, one of my students. His ego is as big as this room." Liz tucked a lock of hair behind her ear. "He never studies,

barely passes his exams. Honestly, I have no idea how he graduated high school, much less ended up here."

Mallory wanted to remind her sister that the person responsible for every student's admission was standing right there. But it
would have been a wasted effort. Liz said what was on her mind.
No holding back.

Ernie shifted his attention back to Liz and offered a tenuous
smile. "The reason why I crashed your lunch date with your sister
is to remind you that the budget meeting is at two sharp. We've
moved it around so much this week, I almost forgot." He chuckled.

"Having a busy day?" Mallory asked.

Ernie did a double-take. "Actually, I didn't sleep well last
night."

"It's in my calendar. I promise I won't be late." Liz lived her
life by the calendar app on her phone. She time blocked everything, from her morning coffee to her classes to her reading for
pleasure. Mallory kept a schedule, but it wasn't as rigid as Liz's.
She didn't need a reminder from Ernie because one had been set
on her phone. Mallory was certain of it.

"I think a lot of people had a rough night. Beatrice Wright
was murdered," Mallory said, keeping her gaze trained on Ernie
for his reaction.

His amiable expression faltered, and then he turned his head
away from Mallory with a snap. "See you later, Liz." With that, he
dashed off in a hurry without so much as a look back.

"Why did you have to bring up Queen Bea?" Liz pierced a
grape tomato in her salad with her fork.

Before Mallory could answer, her cell phone rang. She dug it
out of her backpack. The caller ID told her it was Aspen. After
finding out it was she who had called last night, Mallory had
added her number into her contacts. She hesitated at first. After

all, adding Aspen into her contacts cemented some type of relationship between them. And she wasn't sure she wanted one.

"Mallory, I talked to Detective Hannigan. He wants to speak with you at the station in one hour," Aspen said.

A creeping feeling of dread worked its way through Mallory's body. She was innocent, couldn't he see that?

"Not much notice, is it? Do we really have to go?" Mallory asked as her sister stopped eating and looked up from her baked ziti. Liz must have heard her voice tighten.

"Technically, no. Though it's in your best interest to be seen as helpful. Besides, you have nothing to hide. But if you do, you can tell me."

"There's nothing to tell. I'll see you in an hour." Mallory ended the call and did her best not to overthink the upcoming appointment.

"What's wrong? Who was that?" Liz asked, setting her fork down.

"Aspen. The police want to talk to me. *Again.*" Mallory slumped into her chair. A headache stretched along her forehead as her mind raced with too many thoughts. What if the detective didn't believe her? What if he'd been successful in building a case against her with only circumstantial evidence? She knew it happened all the time thanks to true crime podcasts. Where would she get the money to mount a legal defense? Then one final thought settled on her brain. "I think I'm really a murder suspect."

Chapter Seven

"Not too shabby." Aspen dropped her designer handbag on the table in the interview room that an officer had led her and Mallory into. "It's important to take your cues from me and don't allow the detective to bait you."

Mallory hung her backpack on the back of her chair. She tried her best to quell the flutter of nerves in her belly. She'd never been in a police interrogation room. Sure, the officer had called the square space with a bland table and chairs and a camera an interview room, but she knew better.

"I'll do my best." Mallory set her hands on the table and clasped them together. "How many criminal cases have you taken to trial?"

"Oh, I've never been inside a courtroom to try a case. Well . . . during law school, I did. One of my courses had me doing traffic court."

Mallory's head jerked back as a heavy feeling plopped in her stomach. "What do you mean you haven't been inside a courtroom? Aren't you a criminal defense lawyer?"

"I'm a corporate attorney. I take care of all the legalities and contracts. That's how I met Gil. His company hired the law firm I worked for, and then he asked me out to lunch. Then next was dinner . . ."

Mallory raised a palm. "I get the picture." She also got the fact that she was in more trouble than she thought. When she had agreed to do the official interview with Detective Hannigan, she'd thought she had a qualified attorney to look after her interests. Now all she had was a paper-pushing lawyer whose experience consisted of "sign on the dotted line." No. This wasn't good.

Aspen rested a hand on Mallory's shoulder. "Don't worry. I assure you I can get you through this interview. While I haven't been in a courtroom defending a serial killer, I have been in depositions. Breach of contract or murder, the same legal parameters apply. Don't give the plaintiff's attorney or the prosecution, or in our case today the detective, anything they can use against you. And I took criminal law in law school."

"Just so there are no more surprises, I have to ask, did you pass the bar exam?" Mallory asked.

"Of course! Or else I wouldn't be here with you today."

Mallory let out a small breath of relief.

"I promise you that if we reach a point in the interview where I believe I cannot represent you because you need an experienced criminal lawyer, I will tell you. Cross my heart." And she did just that with her manicured finger.

The door opened, and Detective Hannigan entered, carrying a file folder. He pulled out the chair on the opposite side of the table and sat, setting down the folder.

"Thank you for coming. This won't take too long." He opened the folder and scanned the papers.

Smooth. Real smooth. Like he wanted to make her sweat. Make her nervous. Maybe nervous enough to confess to something she hadn't done. Because there was no way he hadn't reviewed those documents before coming to the interview. Mallory doubted Hannigan would ask questions he didn't already know the answer to. At least she hadn't when she dealt with clients and their advertising campaigns. She went into meetings prepared. And she could count on one hand the number of times a meeting had gone sideways, and those had happened early in her career. The detective didn't appear to be the type who let interviews go sideways too often.

"Last night, you arrived at Mrs. Wright's house uninvited. Is that a correct statement?" Hannigan lifted his gaze from his paperwork, and it landed on Mallory.

Mallory looked to Aspen, and she nodded.

"It is a correct statement," Mallory said.

"You knocked on the door, but there was no answer, correct?" he asked.

"Not exactly. I rang the doorbell." Ha! Just as she suspected. He was trying to get her to slip up and then catch her in an inconsistency that he could exploit. Mallory wouldn't let him trip her up. She remembered every grim detail of last night.

Hannigan gave a slight nod and continued with more questions. They were variations of what he'd asked last night, and Mallory kept her answers consistent. They also covered her relationship with Beatrice, which wasn't really a relationship. Until yesterday morning, she had had little interaction with the food blogger.

"Do you know her husband, Daniel Wright?" the detective asked.

"No, I don't. Though he might have come into the bakery. I don't know all my customers personally, and I don't always work the counter," she said.

"Of course you don't. You're the cookie artist. You decorate all those pretty cookies," he said, making her smile.

Darn it. She hadn't wanted to smile.

"Just one more thing to cover before we can wrap this up." He shuffled the papers in front of him.

That was music to Mallory's ears. She'd wanted the interview wrapped up as soon as Hannigan entered the room.

"Here is a photo of the crime scene." Hannigan pulled an 8×10 photograph of Beatrice's body in her kitchen from his folder and slid it toward Mallory and Aspen.

Mallory bit back the comment on the tip of her tongue—thanks for the reminder. The image of Beatrice's body lying on her tiled kitchen floor with a bloodied rolling pin nearby had been burned into her brain. There was no need for photographs.

Aspen gasped and diverted her gaze for a moment.

"Someone used that rolling pin"—Hannigan tapped on the photo—"to hit Mrs. Wright on the back of the head, killing her. Not only did we find her blood on the rolling pin but also some brain matter."

"I can't believe someone would do that to her," Mallory said.

Aspen composed herself and returned to the conversation. "Is that flour around her body?"

"Yes. Our theory is that she was baking when the attack occurred." Hannigan leaned forward and tapped on another spot on the photograph. "You see here? By her hand? It appears she wrote something. Perhaps a name."

Mallory and Aspen leaned forward, taking a closer look.

"Like the name of her killer?" Mallory asked.

"They look like letters," Aspen said.

"Yeah. M and A. Ma?" Mallory asked.

Hannigan shrugged. "Maybe. Or maybe she was writing Mallory." He pulled back the photo and placed it in the folder, which he closed with authority.

A breath hitched in Mallory's throat, and then her mind raced over everything she'd seen last night. She hadn't noticed the initials in the flour. But then again, she was busy freaking out over the dead woman on the floor.

How the Murder Crumbles

Aspen leaned in close to Mallory and whispered, "I think you need to get that criminal defense attorney now."

*   *   *

Mallory emerged from the police station and put as much space between her and the brick building as possible. She teetered on the edge of the curb, ready to jaywalk and head back to her bakery. But she paused a moment to soak up the warmth of the afternoon sun. Being in the interview room with Hannigan and his crime scene photos had felt stifling, and now outside, she just wanted to breathe.

The early spring air swelled her lungs as her gaze returned to the police station. It was sandwiched between two shops. Bit of Britain was the go-to stop for everything British, from food to gifts to clothing. Its bright, red-painted door had welcomed shoppers for fifty years. On the other side of police headquarters was the Yarn Nook. The knitting shop's window displayed baskets of yarns and sweaters cozy enough to tempt non-knitters like Mallory into the shop.

"I'd hoped the interview would have gone better." The lines between Aspen's eyes furrowed. "Though you did a great job in there."

Mallory shot Red an *are-you-kidding-me* look.

"I'm serious. You didn't give him a reason to continue looking at you as a suspect."

"What about those initials Beatrice scrawled as she was dying? The first two letters of my name," Mallory said.

"Those letters could spell out a thousand words. Besides, you didn't have a powerful motive to murder her. Also, the time of death will play a part in this," Aspen said.

"How so?"

"Once it's determined, they will be able to piece together your movements."

"Lauren, she's Kip's sister and a police officer, said that Beatrice hadn't been dead for long before I arrived. That doesn't look good for me."

"No. It doesn't. However . . . if that is true about the time of death, the police will be able to piece together your alibi. When you arrived at Beatrice's house, you were on the phone with Kip. Prior to that, the police can use your phone's location data to pinpoint where you were, and before leaving your house, Kip was there. So don't get too discouraged. The detective is just doing his job, and I'm sure you'll be ruled out soon."

"Then why did you suggest I should get a criminal defense lawyer?" Mallory asked.

"It seems the prudent thing to do. I know someone. At least have him ready just in case," Aspen said.

"Hi, Mallory!" Jake Lewis waved from a few feet away. Tall with pale skin and reddish-brown hair, he had a boyish charm about him. That's probably why he was such a successful real estate agent. Plus, he was a natural-born seller. Mallory had known him since childhood and he'd always sold the most wrapping paper for school fundraisers. His long, purposeful stride had him reaching Mallory and Aspen in the blink of an eye. "I heard what happened. It must have been awful finding Beatrice's body."

"Oh, it was—" Mallory started but was cut short.

"Awful. Yes, yes." He stepped past Mallory and Aspen. "Almost late for a meeting. But don't worry. I'll have news about the bakery building's sale in a few days." He tapped his earbud, rejoined a conversation, and continued walking.

"Wait." Mallory reached out and snagged his arm, keeping him from walking away.

"What are you talking about? Darlene is selling the building? What about my bakery?"

Jake's eyes tightened at the corners, and he offered a "be right back" to whoever he was on the call with before tapping his ear-bud again. "You should probably talk to Darlene. I don't want to get into the middle of a family thing. You understand, right?" He tapped his earbud and then continued walking along Main Street.

"I didn't know the building was for sale. I just signed a one-year lease," Aspen said.

"Neither did I." Mallory's lips pressed together, and she glanced back at the police station. She might end up back in there soon, because she was going to kill her cousin.

Chapter Eight

M allory had done some rapid-fire, if not psychotic, texting on the way back to the bakery. She fired off not one, not two, but five text messages to her cousin asking if what Jake said was true—was she selling the building?

Mallory wasn't sure what it meant for her if it was true. She did have a lease, so that should offer her some protection against a rent increase, right? If not, she'd find a way to pay more rent or find a new location. Right now, all she could do was wait to hear what Darlene had to say about the matter.

The rest of the afternoon was slow. She wasn't sure if it was still because of the murder or just the day of the week. Foot traffic was fickle. Whatever the cause, Mallory opted not to dwell on the negative and put her "free" time to good use by catching up on paperwork.

Tops on her to-do list was to register for upcoming bridal shows in early fall. She'd missed out on the shows at the start of the year because she was busy launching her cookie business. But she wouldn't miss out on the next opportunity to reach the bridal market.

Looking at the preliminary numbers for attending the shows gave her a moment of hesitation. Those bridal shows were high-cost, high-risk venues, like all trade shows. She'd make no actual sales at the events, but she'd get leads. At least she hoped so.

Not only were there transportation costs to consider, but she'd have to create cookies for sampling, eye-catching printed promo cards with a discount offer, and branding for her table.

Though she was confident once she lured the brides-to-be to her table, she'd be able to entice them to place orders. After a decade in advertising, she knew just how to tap into the hopes and dreams all those brides held for their wedding days. Ordering decorated cookies from The Cookie Shop would mean they'd have unique favors, welcome gifts for VIP guests from out of town, or thank-you gifts for the wedding party.

While it would take a lot of work, it would be worth it. Not only would she be in the midst of her target market, but also she'd have the opportunity to network with other vendors for cross-promotion.

In between filling out registration forms and spending money she really didn't have, she sent off three more texts to Darlene and left two voice mails. They all went unanswered. Clearly, she was avoiding Mallory.

Mallory leaned back and stretched, her arms rising toward the ceiling, and slightly arching her back. The stretch felt good after nearly an hour of concentrated work at the computer. Then, needing a break, she pushed her chair away from the desk and stood. She swiped up her reusable water bottle and walked out of the small office. Not much had changed in the tiny room since her aunt had handed over the keys to the bakery. Mallory had thrown all her money and effort into revamping the front of the bakery. The office could use a fresh coat of paint and maybe a new desk chair. The one there now wreaked havoc on her back after a long session of bill paying.

In the modest-sized entry by the back door, where the staff kept their outerwear and bags, Claudia stood, slipping on her navy trench coat over her daily uniform of black chef's pants, white polo top, and black clogs.

"Is it that late already?" Mallory glanced at her watch.

Claudia reached for her tan bucket hat and stepped in front of the oval mirror. She adjusted the hat over her gray pixie cut, sweeping her bangs from her brow. A month ago, she'd celebrated her sixtieth birthday and murmured something about retiring. While Kip had struggled not to smile, Mallory didn't want to lose Claudia. Not yet. She needed her. And she was determined to forge a friendship with the woman.

"Guess time gets away from you when you're distracted."

Mallory couldn't argue with Claudia about her being distracted. She hadn't exactly been present in the bakery that day.

"I heard the Garden Tour has reinstated the Pie Baking Contest." Claudia took her sensible black purse off the coatrack and dug inside for her car key.

Well, that was fast. Beatrice hadn't been dead for a full twenty-four hours yet.

"And Darlene has stepped in as the new chairperson for the Garden Tour. Your cousin is a very busy bee, isn't she?"

She most certainly is. Busy selling this building and keeping it a secret.

Mallory shook off those bitter thoughts. Besides, for all she knew, Darlene could have had an emergency with her daughter. But then again, if there had been one, Darlene had managed to find time to volunteer to take over Beatrice's role.

"Perhaps things will simmer down with Darlene in charge. Beatrice always seemed to ruffle feathers." Claudia gave a pointed look at Mallory. "I guess I'm not telling you something you don't already know."

"Have a nice evening. Enjoy your book club." Mallory pivoted and headed into the kitchen. By the time she reached the doorway, she heard the back door open and close. Claudia had left the building, and she felt her whole body breathe a big sigh. She had to find a way to stop feeling relief every time Claudia left work. Then again, it did take two people to make a relationship work.

Mallory entered the kitchen and found Kip checking his phone. He had a deep frown on his face.

"Everything okay?" Instantly, she regretted asking the question. Then as Kip lifted his gaze to meet hers, her breath caught in her chest. What had happened now?

Kip's shoulders slumped, and he murmured "sorry" as he held up the phone for Mallory to see. She tramped forward, bracing herself for bad news. Good thing she was prepared.

"You've got to be kidding me!" Though she wasn't laughing when she snatched the phone from Kip's hand and read Dugan's article on the *Chronicle*'s website. She scrolled, reading to the very end of the story.

"No one is going to believe you killed Beatrice. Even if they read that article," Kip said.

"Just because he threw in the word 'alleged' and the phrase 'person of interest' when talking about me instead of using 'prime suspect,' it isn't exactly a ringing endorsement of my innocence. Look, he even included my interview with Hannigan." To think, yesterday she couldn't wait for everyone to read the article she'd been interviewed for. Her aunt always said, be careful what you wish for. She shoved the phone back into Kip's hand.

"You'll get through this, Mal. I know you will." Kip slipped the phone into his back pocket.

"But will The Cookie Shop survive too?" Mallory glanced around the kitchen. The space was small, the equipment decades old, but it was all hers. "I can't just sit around and wait for my name to be cleared."

"What can you do?" Kip walked back to his workstation and gave it a final wipe down for the day.

"I'm not sure. But I know there's no shortage of people in town who had reason to not only dislike Beatrice but hate her. Maybe she pushed someone too far." Mallory moved toward the swinging door. She had to close the register and tidy up the front of the bakery before calling it a day.

"Wouldn't be surprised." Kip discarded the wipes and then leaned against the table and crossed his arms. "Are you thinking what I'm thinking?"

"I don't know. What are you thinking?"

"That you should pull a Nancy Drew on Wingate and find the person who Beatrice pushed too far." Kip pushed off the side of the table and scooted closer to Mallory.

"Nancy Drew?"

"You'd rather be a meddling spinster?"

Mallory pursed her lips as she considered her options. "Nancy Drew is more modern. Okay. Okay. That's what I'm going to do. Before it's too late."

"Before you're arrested?"

"No! I didn't kill Beatrice, and Hannigan will eventually figure that out. But I can't wait that long. Each passing day means I'm more at risk of losing my business, and my reputation will be ruined beyond repair."

"Right. Sorry," he said with a sheepish grin. "You know you can count on me. Whatever you need."

"Looks like we're doing this." Even though doubts raced in her mind, Mallory knew her decision was the right one. She'd only be asking a few questions, and whatever she learned, she'd immediately turn over to Hannigan.

"Yeah, we are!" Kip high-fived Mallory to seal the deal. "Come on, I'll help you close up."

Mallory nodded and then opened her hand to push the swinging door. When they stepped out of the kitchen, they stopped short.

There was a customer. She hadn't tapped on the bell on the counter. Maybe Mallory needed to put up a sign to let customers know why it was there.

"I hope you're not closed yet." A tall, lithe woman dressed in a denim jumpsuit stood at the counter with two white chocolate–dipped apples covered in nuts set in front of her. "I've been meaning to stop in since you opened. These apples look decadent. And I'd love some of those Almond Meltaways." She pointed toward the bakery case.

"Yes. We're still open. I apologize you had to wait." Mallory shuffled toward the counter, grabbing a sheet of tissue on her way to the tray of Almond Meltaways. "How many would you like?"

"A dozen, please. I've heard they're yummy. And after all the work I did in my garden today, I deserve a treat." She smiled and tiny lines feathered out from her close-set eyes.

"Gardening is a lot of work. You absolutely deserve a treat." All the worries and tension Mallory had felt for most of the day vanished. Having a one-on-one conversation with a customer while packaging cookies was precisely what she needed. "I'm Mallory Monroe." She closed the pastry box. Then she pulled out a small bag from beneath the counter and set the two apples inside.

"Hi, Evelyn," Kip said with a wave as he appeared from the kitchen. "Mal, this is Evelyn Brinkley."

Mallory immediately recognized the name, prompting a small smile onto her lips.

"It's nice to meet you, Mallory." Evelyn reached into her satchel for her wallet and removed a credit card. "Today must have been a crazy day for you."

And just like that, the delight Mallory felt vanished. She was sucked back into reality. And it must have shown on her face because Evelyn's green eyes clouded over.

"Oh, I'm so sorry. It's none of my business. I guess I'm trying to make sense of what happened. Maybe that's why no weed in my garden stood a chance today." Evelyn offered a chuckle, but it fell flat. "It seems unimaginable that my neighbor was murdered last night."

Mallory and Kip exchanged a look. It appeared her first opportunity to start investigating had walked right through the front door. Standing before her was the victim's neighbor, and she obviously wanted to talk.

"I'm sure it was a shock." Mallory rang up the sale and then prompted Evelyn to insert her card. "I know it was for me. Were you and Beatrice close?"

"We've been neighbors for nearly thirty years. She always came to me for gardening advice." Evelyn put her credit card back in her wallet after the card reader beeped. "I couldn't fathom what had happened when I first heard the sirens. I thought maybe she had fallen or something . . . but murdered?"

"Before you heard the sirens, did you hear anything out of the ordinary?" Kip stepped forward.

"No. Nothing out of the ordin . . . wait . . . I heard a speeding car driving away from Beatrice's house last night. I thought little of it because I assumed it was Daniel," Evelyn said.

"Her husband?" Mallory asked.

"Yes. They've been separated for a while, and when he visits the house, it usually ends in an argument and him storming off," Evelyn said. "Oh, listen to me gossiping."

"This isn't gossiping," Mallory assured. "You never know what may help the police find Beatrice's murderer."

"Perhaps you're right," Evelyn said. "Other than hearing the car, there's nothing else I can offer to help solve her murder.

Beatrice preferred to spend all her time in the kitchen. I choose to spend my evenings in my study, which is on the farthest side of the house, away from Beatrice's home."

"Did anything out of the ordinary happen during the day?" Mallory thought it could have been possible that an earlier encounter led to Beatrice's death later that night. Oh, right, like the one she had with Mallory at the bakery. *Shoot.*

"Other than the fight that happened here?" Evelyn's perfectly groomed brows raised.

Double shoot.

"Yes." Kip jumped in as he came out from behind the counter. "Anything you can recall would be helpful."

Evelyn thought for a moment. "I'm sorry. There's nothing else. If I do think of anything, I will definitely tell the police. Knowing that a killer is still on the loose here in Wingate is very unsettling."

Mallory couldn't agree more. Wait. Being suspected of being the killer on the loose was way more unsettling. At least to her.

"I can't wait to taste the cookies Beatrice had her panties in a bunch about." Evelyn flashed a wicked smile before turning and leaving the bakery.

Kip followed their last customer of the day and locked the door behind her. "Looks like we have a new lead in the case." He flipped over the closed sign and then turned to face Mallory.

"Beatrice's estranged husband." Mallory propped a hand on her hip. "It's always the husband, isn't it?"

"Hmmm . . . not always, but it would be helpful to us in this case. Come on, let's finish closing up." Kip returned to Mallory's side and slung an arm around her shoulder. "It's been a long day."

"You got that right. How about you tackle the register while I shut down the computer?"

Together, they worked in harmonious silence until everything was set for the evening and they could go home. Kip suggested takeout and a movie, but Mallory opted for leftovers and an early night. Being a person of interest in a murder was exhausting, and all she wanted to do was crawl into her bed with a book and Agatha.

But before she slid under the covers, she had one thing to set up. If she was going to investigate Beatrice's murder, she needed to be methodical and organized. It took a few hours, but by the time she went to bed, she had set up a system to help sort her thoughts and track her notes as she investigated. One way or another, she was going to solve this murder.

Chapter Nine

The crushing weight on Mallory's chest the next morning had her slowly opening an eye and groaning at Agatha, who sat mid-sternum staring at her. Ever since she was a kitten, Agatha liked to wake Mallory up in that fashion. When she was nothing more than a puffball, it was cute. But now, Agatha's lean frame had bloomed outward, causing Mallory to flinch every time the cat climbed on her.

"I know. I know. You want breakfast. Would it kill you to miss a meal?" Mallory stretched out her hand and grappled for her phone on the nightstand while Agatha's tail swished back and forth. "Okay. I'll get up." Mallory shifted her cat off her chest with her free hand and then raised her phone to check her notifications. Once she took over the bakery, she started setting her phone on sleep mode because she needed a good night's sleep every night. Having to be at the bakery bright and early meant she needed to be bright and alert. That was hard to do when her sleep was interrupted.

Agatha moped to the corner of the bed and sat stoically, waiting for her mom to rise and shine and feed her. Mallory shook her head and returned her attention to her phone. She wasn't sure why, but her first stop on the internet was the *Chronicle*'s website, and then with another tap, she scanned Dugan's post again. She should have stopped and closed out of the browser at that point. But no. She kept on reading right down to the comments.

For the second time already that day, she felt as if she couldn't breathe. Comment after comment, readers had left unkind words not only about Queen Bea but also about Mallory. Some even implied that she had taken criticism about her cookies to a fatal extreme.

First, Beatrice had never criticized the Almond Meltaways. No, she only accused Mallory's aunt of stealing the recipe. It took all her restraint and common sense not to start firing off rebuttals to those hateful commenters. To help make sure she didn't make the situation worse, though she had a hard time seeing how it could be worse, she closed out of the newspaper's website and checked her text messages.

Arrggh.

The only texts that had come after she climbed into bed were from Gil the Cheater.

Hey, heard about what's going on in Wingate. Just wanted to check on you and see how you're doing.

The next message from him.

How did you get caught up in that mess? Did she really accuse you of stealing recipes?

Oh, now it was recipes, plural? Mallory shouldn't have been too shocked to see the facts twisted and distorted.

There was one more from him.

Guess you don't want to talk to me. Understandable. I just wanted to make sure you're okay.

Suddenly he cared about her. If he did, then why had it taken him so long to reach out to her? And why had he done it by text? After what he did, he should have been at her front door groveling ASAP after she discovered him with Red. Wait. Not only groveling for forgiveness but also apologizing. Because of him, Red was now in her life. Her fingers tightened around the phone as she visualized his neck. No! She wouldn't go down that path of negative thoughts. Before she could second-guess herself, she deleted his string of texts and shut off her phone. She had to get her day started and find a murderer. Talk about a killer to-do list.

Downstairs in the kitchen, she filled Agatha's food bowl and set it on the mat along with her freshly replenished water bowl. She stepped to the side, leaned against the white farmhouse sink with her mug in hand, and sipped her morning coffee. The first cup was always the best. And it was the necessary jolt she needed to start her day so early. While Agatha chowed down, Mallory stared at the murder board she'd created last night while eating leftover pizza.

The modest kitchen had a choppy feel because of the three openings from the utility room, the living room, and the small dining room, which wasn't much larger than a dinette area. But from where she stood, she had a clear line of vision to the oval-shaped table where the board had been set up.

While eating dinner, Mallory had spent a couple of hours completing her arts and crafts project. She'd found an old bulletin board in the storage cubby beneath the staircase and scrounged up some push pins from her office supply stash, along with some index cards.

Smack dab in the center of the board was card number one with Beatrice's name written in black marker.

Anchoring that card were two others—one had the name Daniel written on it, and the other had the name Ernie Hollis. She'd done some online sleuthing and discovered that Daniel was a money guy. He'd provided start-ups with funding for nearly twenty years. There really wasn't much more she could find on him. He had no social media presence, and newspaper articles focused on his work rather than the man himself.

On the other hand, Ernie had a social media presence. His feeds were populated by yummy desserts he baked in his free time. He'd been featured in newspaper articles for winning baking contests and for participating in events at Abernathy College. There was also his late wife's obituary. Now, there was a baker. There was a photo of her in her kitchen, surrounded by all the ribbons she'd won over the years.

While Mallory didn't regret the time spent online, it really hadn't yielded her a smoking gun, so to speak.

A meow drew Mallory's gaze from the board to the butcher block island, where Agatha had perched, her tail swishing off the side.

"What have I told you about the island?" Mallory stepped forward and lifted her feline companion off. "Let's try to keep one surface cat-free, okay?" She set Agatha on the floor and returned to her mug while the cat pranced into the living room to find a spot for her after-breakfast nap. Mallory drained the last of her coffee and then quickly tidied up the kitchen before checking her phone one last time before heading out. The weather app predicted a seasonable spring day, so she'd be cycling to work. Her next check was her text messages. Still no reply from Darlene.

"That's going to change today," Mallory muttered as she walked into the utility room. "She can't avoid me forever."

* * *

In the bakery, Mallory checked her watch. Ten minutes to go before Luke Collins would arrive and do his photographic magic with her cookie bouquets. After arriving at the bakery, she got right to work creating the three bouquets for Luke to photograph. Bridal and baby shower season was in full swing and would continue through the summer, and Mallory had the perfect cookie bouquets for brides and moms-to-be. She'd set the three bouquets on the farmhouse table. Two were arranged in long flower boxes, and the third was arranged in a ceramic container. She rechecked her watch. Four minutes. Her stomach knotted at how much this photo shoot was costing. She prayed to God she'd be able to make back the fee and then some. At least a little *then some*.

Mallory's head swung up at the sound of the front door opening, and she inhaled a cleansing breath. Everything was going to be okay, she reminded herself as she stepped away from the table, ready to greet Luke.

Then she saw who entered, and disappointment stopped her in her tracks.

"What are you doing here, Aspen?" Mallory asked as she returned to the table and fussed with the tissue paper in one of the flower boxes. As if starting her day with mean comments and three texts from Gil wasn't bad enough, now she had to deal with Red?

"Is he here?" Kip appeared from the kitchen, and then he halted at the sight of Aspen. "Oh, it's you."

"Good morning." Aspen waved as she followed Mallory to the table. "I thought we could have a strategy meeting. You know, just in case Detective Hannigan officially brings you in for questioning."

"Wasn't that what he did yesterday?" Mallory asked.

"No," Kip said. "That was a voluntary interview."

"He's right." Aspen sauntered over to the counter and then propped a hand on her hip. Her body-skimming navy dress hugged her curves while loose tendrils from her updo framed her face. "You know something about law enforcement, don't you?" she asked Kip.

Kip gave a slight nod. "My father is the chief of police, and my sister is one of the officers who responded to Beatrice's crime scene."

"Then you have an inside track on what's going on." Aspen swung her head in Mallory's direction. "That could be helpful to you. Anyway, is there somewhere private we can talk?"

"Ah . . . sure. My office. But the thing is, Aspen, I'm not your client any longer. You gave me a referral to a criminal defense attorney if I needed one." Mallory checked her watch again. Time was ticking down. Luke would be arriving any minute, and she didn't want Aspen there when he did.

Aspen looked undeterred by the reminder. "There are a few pointers I can give you in case you have to go back to the police station. It won't take long. Is your office back there?" She pointed at the swinging door behind the counter.

"It is." Mallory set her coffee cup down as her mind raced for something to say. "But shouldn't we be careful?"

Aspen's head tilted, and she gave a questioning look at Mallory.

"Since you're not my attorney any longer, whatever I say to you regarding the case won't be considered attorney-client privilege. Even though I'm not guilty, even the most innocent comment could be construed the wrong way." Mallory shot a look at Kip, who replied with a thumbs-up.

"You're . . . you're right. Yes, a skilled prosecutor could twist any little thing to try to get a conviction. Where is my mind these days? I guess my spontaneous decision to shake up my life and move to a new town is clouding my judgment. Perhaps I should take a few hours for some *me time*. Help clear my head."

"Sounds like a good idea. See you later," Mallory said. Though she would have liked to have heard more about Aspen's spontaneous decision to shake up her life. Maybe find out why she had really moved to Wingate. However, now wasn't the time.

Aspen turned and left the bakery. Her departure was a welcome relief to Mallory, whose nerves were still skittering over too many things to list at the moment. She joined Kip behind the counter and looked for a task to keep her hands busy.

"How long do you think that will stave her off?"

Mallory shrugged. "I don't know. Right now, I'm just glad she left. Luke will be here soon, and my concentration has to be on getting the best photos for our promo."

Luke Collins arrived on schedule and wasted no time blowing up Mallory's photo shoot ideas. Sure, he nodded when she explained what her vision had been as she showed him the three products to be photographed. All was good, and she could step back and let him work his magic. Or so she thought.

The photographer trekked in his equipment from his truck in two trips after declining Kip's offer to help. Then he quickly set up the shoot. Because the front of the bakery had the most room and natural light, they agreed to work there. Plus, because it was early there wouldn't be many customers coming in. While he didn't have a problem with the location, Luke had one with Mallory's setup. He'd moved the table, placed a faux marble backdrop on top, and set up two softbox lights.

Mallory hadn't worked with photographers directly when she worked at the ad agency. Art directors and their teams had the most contact with photographers, directors, and stylists. But she absorbed as much insight as she could about working with creative pros. One thing she understood from secondhand knowledge was that creatives could be sensitive. So she had a decision to make—either trust Luke to do his thing or risk offending him. Based on his portfolio, she opted for trust.

A few customers trickled in while Luke was doing his thing. Since Kip was already out front in the bakery, he took care of the orders, leaving Mallory to observe Luke. His sandy blond hair needed a trim, especially his bangs that kept grazing over his blue eyes. Under the right circumstances, those pools of cool blueness could mesmerize a person. He removed his black leather jacket and dropped it on a hard case. His short-sleeved T-shirt revealed toned arms. No doubt, lifting and holding that camera with an enormous lens was a workout.

Mallory's gaze traveled from the camera in Luke's hands to his tanned, angular face. Two deep lines creased between his brows. It looked like he was trying to decide. He set his camera, fitted with an impressive lens, down and tweaked the setup. Then, appearing satisfied, he picked up the camera and started clicking.

Something about him looked familiar, though she couldn't place him. Until she did, it would gnaw at her.

"Come on and look at these." He lowered his camera and stepped back from the table.

Mallory glided past the equipment setup and stopped at Luke's side. She looked into the viewfinder as he clicked through the images. He'd only been shooting for a few minutes, and yet the photos were captivating. He'd pulled out six of the tulip cookies, each decorated pink with green leaves and stems, and set them alongside the flower box.

"Wow. These are amazing," she said, shifting her gaze from the camera to the photographer. Where did she know him from? Maybe it was from the advertising agency she had worked at.

He shrugged like a disinterested teenager. "Thanks." Click. Click. Click. Another flurry of photos snapped before he lowered his camera again. "Now, let's take some photos of that bouquet. I have another board to set up."

"Right." Mallory resisted saluting but was ready to spring into action. It made sense he wasn't into small talk since he was there to work. Also, it was crucial to stay on budget since she didn't have extra money to dole out.

Luke set his camera down and grabbed another marble board. Using brackets, he connected the two boards together. Then he asked Mallory to set the ceramic bowl that held a bouquet of assorted cookies with a woodland baby shower theme. Decorating the little foxes was the most enjoyable part of the process for Mallory.

The bakery's door opened, and Ginger Dupont entered. Her entrances were dramatic, her greetings lyrical, and her inquisitiveness endearing. She attributed her curiosity to being a fiction writer. Mallory had marveled at how Ginger got away with asking some pretty personal questions.

"Good morning, Kip. You look very bright and chipper this morning." Ginger approached and then set her satchel on the counter. "I need a treat. I've just finished writing my book! Time to celebrate." She clapped her hands together.

"I agree. What would you like?" Kip asked.

"Oh, I'm not sure." Ginger walked along the bakery case, her bejeweled pointer finger trailing along the glass. "So many yummy choices."

"Good morning, Ginger," Mallory said with a wave.

Ginger paused and set her hungry eyes on Luke. "Speaking of yummy."

Mallory stifled a chuckle while Kip clearly swallowed his laugh. Ginger Dupont was known for her insatiable appetite for gentlemen. She'd been married five times.

"I know you." Ginger abandoned the bakery case and walked toward Luke, extending her hand. "I'm Ginger Dupont, the romance author."

A mild irritation flashed in Luke's eyes, but it was gone in a second, and he shook Ginger's hand. "Nice to meet you."

"Luke Collins is a food photographer, and I've hired him to take photos for my advertising and promotion campaigns. We're in the middle of the photo shoot now." Mallory hoped Ginger would take the hint and return to choosing a cookie.

Ginger released Luke's hand. Good. It appeared she'd gotten the hint. Mallory was relieved.

"I've seen you around town. Give me a moment." She tapped her chin with her finger, and her hazel eyes studied Luke's face as she thought.

Relief lasted only moments for Mallory. She had to get Ginger moving.

"Yes! I remember. You worked for Beatrice. I remember her telling me about you." Ginger smiled triumphantly.

Luke moved the softbox lights and then grabbed his camera. "I did some work for her blog."

"You did?" This was news to Mallory. She hadn't known Beatrice had hired help for her blog. Though she'd known some bloggers outsourced the content writing for their sites. "How long did the two of you work together?"

He shrugged again. "On and off for a few months." He paused shooting and looked into the camera's viewfinder, his face etched in concentration. Then a slow smile slipped onto his lips, and he started shooting again. "I heard what happened to her. Tough break." Click. Click. Click. "You know, you are talented. Those tulips look unbelievably real, and the detail on these foxes and deer is off the charts. Now I know where I can go for unique gifts."

"Yes, she does marvelous work. Mallory is truly an artist. She's also an excellent baker. I really need a cookie." Ginger drifted back to the pastry case and selected her cookies with Kip's help.

"Thanks." Mallory enjoyed hearing the compliments, but she wanted to talk more about Luke's work with Beatrice. And she wanted to know what was up with that little smile when he said he'd heard about Beatrice's murder. "What exactly did you photograph for Beatrice? Did she have a digital cookbook?" Perhaps Beatrice had hired him for a project rather than the website.

Mallory had known two food bloggers who had hired photographers for their cookbooks.

"Not that I know of. I shot recipes for her blog posts." He pulled back from the camera.

"But you didn't work with her for long?" Mallory asked.

Luke shook his head and then went back to clicking photos.

"I doubt she could have had any qualms with your work," Mallory said. "Yet Queen Bea was very persnickety."

He straightened and gave a pointed look at Mallory. "Let's just say we had creative differences."

Actually, he was saying that Mallory should stop asking questions about him and Beatrice.

Interesting.

It was Mallory's turn to shrug. "Unfortunately, it happens. I'm going to get some water. Would you like a glass?"

Luke shook his head and continued taking pictures. Mallory turned and walked to the counter. She sent Kip back into the kitchen so she could keep an eye on Luke while he worked. She used the time to try and remember why he felt so familiar to her.

Before she knew it, Luke had packed up his equipment, and she was no closer to pinpointing why he looked so familiar. As he was leaving the bakery, he promised to send over the photos within two days. She'd attempted to ask again if they'd met, but he was on his cell phone confirming another shoot as he left.

"It seems to have gone well." Kip came out from the kitchen just as the front door closed behind Luke.

"It did. I got a sneak peek at the photos. A-ma-zing."

"Then why do you have that look on your face? What's going on?" Kip asked.

"Two things. First, he looks familiar to me, and I can't place him. He said he never worked with ad agencies, so I don't know him from there."

"Ahhh . . . that's going to drive you nuts."

"Yes, it is. Second, he did some photography for Beatrice, and when I asked why he stopped working for her, he shut me down."

"Most people wouldn't shut up about how much they disliked Queen Bea. Either he's very professional, or he's hiding something."

"My thoughts exactly." Her photographer was hiding something, and she intended to discover what it was.

"Mail call!" Mac O'Toole entered the bakery, holding a small stack of envelopes. She made a beeline for the counter. She'd chosen a floral silk scarf tied with a fancy bow around her neck that picked up the navy color of her headband. "It's a beautiful day, isn't it?"

"You're very cheery today." Mallory took the envelopes.

"Of course I am, because those aren't my bills." Mac laughed, dropping her hands to her side.

"That one never grows old," Kip chuckled.

"I ran into Ginger, and she told me Luke Collins was here." Mac gave the bakery a sweeping look and seemed disappointed to find the shop empty.

"Do you know him?" Maybe Mac could help pinpoint how Mallory knew him.

"Not really. But I know he worked for Beatrice," Mac said.

"We know that." Kip turned around and headed for the swinging door.

"Do you know they had a screaming match last week? Just outside of Bit of Britain. Saw it with my own two eyes." Mac made a V with two fingers and pointed them at her eyes.

Kip halted and returned to the counter. "Go on."

"What were they arguing about?" Mallory asked.

"I heard Beatrice say that he was making a mistake. She could ruin him. Then he said she'd regret threatening him," Mac said.

Mac's words hung in the air for a moment while Mallory digested them. Maybe Beatrice had the same déjà vu feeling Mallory had when she met Luke. Perhaps Beatrice sought out the answer and discovered a secret worth killing for.

Yes, it was conjecture. But it was at least a start for Mallory.

"I need to get back to my route. See you both tomorrow." Mac left the bakery.

Mallory propped a hand on her hip and looked at Kip. "What's the status in the kitchen?"

"We're on schedule. Why?"

"I'm going to do a little digging online to see what I can learn about Luke. And then I have to figure out a way to approach Ernie. I'll be in my office."

Mallory patted Kip on the shoulder as she swept by him. She had three suspects. It was time to start developing and using some sleuthing skills.

Chapter Ten

So much for her sleuthing skills, because Mallory came up with zilch, nada, nothing incriminating about Luke Collins. And she also hadn't figured out a way to question Ernie without coming across as nosy or confrontational. She could have asked her sister to arrange a meeting, but then Liz would want to know what Mallory was up to. She scratched that idea off the list. There had been a fleeting thought about delivering a bouquet of cookies and saying that he'd won a prize. Then she'd have to explain how he'd been selected and so forth. As a dull ache stretched out across her forehead, she couldn't think anymore. So she turned to an activity that always refilled her well—cookie decorating.

She removed a tray of sugar cookies in the shape of two intertwined hearts representing the bride and groom from the sheet pan rack. This was one of her favorite cookies to decorate because of the symbolism. She set the tray on her workstation. Alone in the kitchen, she could lose herself in decorating. The reprieve from reality would be appreciated. She double-checked her pastry bags and was ready to fill in the bride's heart when the swinging door opened and Kip burst in.

"I got it! I know how you can approach Ernie." Kip pulled out his phone and started texting.

"What are you talking about? Wait. What are you doing? Who are you texting?" Mallory's attention was torn between the cookie and her friend.

"Great!" Kip flashed a giant smile. "It's all set up. Now you have a cover for talking to Ernie. You're welcome."

"Cover?" Mallory set her pastry bag down and glared at Kip. "What did you do?"

"You're the chairperson of the Pie Baking committee for the Garden Tour." He dashed away from Mallory and zipped around his baking station.

"I'm the what? Are you insane? I don't have time to run the pie contest."

"Sure you do. It's only a meeting or two, and you're going to attend the contest anyway. There's no way you're passing up pie."

Darn. He knew her too well. She couldn't argue that point.

"My cousin, twice removed, is on the general committee, and I knew she'd need someone to handle the contest since it's been reinstated. And that's you," Kip continued. "It's a good way for you to strike up a conversation with Ernie. I'm sure you can come up with a reason to talk to him as the chair of the pie contest. Maybe set up a meeting to *discuss* his entry." He typed on his phone. "Just sent his address to you. Again, you're welcome."

"He works at Abernathy, and it's a weekday," she said.

Kip sulked. "I didn't think about that."

"We'll just call Abernathy and see if he's at his office." Mallory made the call and spoke to Ernie's secretary, who said he had the day off. Mallory thanked the woman for her help and ended the call.

Within an hour, Mallory had boxed up three decorated cookies for Ernie. She couldn't very well go empty-handed. Besides, cookies always made people happy, and happy people were more talkative. She selected them from her popular baking-themed collection. While she closed the box, she debated whether she should have thanked Kip or started plotting revenge against him for volunteering her to chair the Pie Baking Contest. There had to have been an easier way to find out Ernie's address and gain access to him. After all, he lived in Wingate. Perhaps she'd find a way to gracefully step down from the job. Until then, she'd do her best. But first, she had a suspect to bring cookies to and question. She secured the box in her bicycle's rear basket and headed for his home.

Kip had called him before Mallory left to make sure he was home.

While pedaling, she got a call from Liz. After her interview with Detective Hannigan, Mallory had sent her sister a text. She had left out the part about Aspen's legal background, so as she traveled along the winding back road, she filled her sister in.

"I should have known when Aspen said 'not too shabby' when we entered the interview room. She was comparing it to the conference rooms at her law firm where she took depositions." Mallory coasted along Peck Hill Road, toward number ten. Spring bloomed all around her, though she spotted the daffodils fading. They were ready to make room for eye-popping flowers that would blossom for summer. This lovely section of Wingate had undeveloped land with only a handful of homes.

"I hope you fired her," Liz said between breaths. She was cooling down after a four-mile run. That just sounded so brutal to Mallory.

"I did. What I can't figure out is why she up and moved to Wingate in the first place. Just a matter of days after she found out about me."

"It's weird. Do you think she's one of those crazy girlfriends?" Liz asked. "You know, like in *Fatal Attraction*?"

"Now there's an unsettling thought. Thanks a lot." Mallory's pedaling slowed as she noticed the numbers on the mailboxes. She was getting closer to Ernie's house. "Though it would explain why Aspen has inserted herself into my life. It's just that she doesn't seem to be the type."

"They never do," Liz said.

Finally, 10 Peck Hill Road came into view. Ernie's home was a tidy Cape Cod enclosed by a white picket fence with colorful garden beds.

"She seems harmless, but I'll keep my guard up around her, just in case. I have to go. Talk later." Mallory disconnected the call and guided her bike toward the fence. She got off and leaned the bicycle on its kickstand. She lifted the pastry box from the basket and then unlatched the gate. She spied Ernie walking along the stone path that led to the home's front steps with a handful of mail.

"Hello!" Mallory chased after his retreating form, heading toward the house, but then slowed down since she didn't want to seem too eager or suspicious. Who was she kidding? This whole idea was questionable.

Ernie looked over his shoulder and then stopped when he saw Mallory. He turned around to greet her, which seemed warm, but the look on his face suggested he was wary. She couldn't figure out why. Kip had told him she was coming over with news about the Garden Tour.

"Thanks for taking time to talk to me." When she reached Ernie, she opened the box, giving her suspect a glimpse of the cookies. "Would you like one?"

A big smile stretched from ear to ear on Ernie's face. "You're always welcome here with your cookies. They look too good to eat. But I'm going to force myself. Come on inside, and I'll make us some coffee."

Before Mallory could decline the coffee, Ernie had spun around and was marching to the house.

Inside, Ernie settled his guest at the kitchen table with the cookies after straightening the piles of paper and newspapers on the wood surface and shoved them aside. He then went for the coffee pot. From where Mallory sat, she had a view of his late wife's blue ribbons, which were displayed in a hutch.

"Please, don't go to any trouble because of me. I can't stay long," Mallory said, stopping Ernie from scooping out the ground coffee. "The reason I stopped by is to tell you in person that I'm the new chairperson for the Garden Tour's Pie Baking Contest."

Her words hung in the air for a moment while Ernie absorbed the news. At least that's what he looked like he was doing. Maybe she'd been wrong in thinking he'd be excited.

Ernie set the scoop back in the canister and rubbed his hands together. "The Pie Baking Contest is back on?"

She nodded.

Ernie expelled a big breath and smiled. This time it was bigger than the one he had flashed when she showed him the cookies. "Well, I'll be . . ."

"As surprised as I was." She laughed. "I guess with the change in leadership at the Garden Tour, some other changes are being made. I'd heard it was because of Beatrice that the contest had been sacked. That must have been disappointing."

"Life is full of disappointments." Ernie rubbed his chin. "It's a matter of perspective. However, I have to admit I was upset. The action was uncalled for."

"She accused you of cheating. I can't imagine that was something that could easily be brushed off. After all, your reputation is very important, given your position at Abernathy," Mallory said.

Ernie broke eye contact and then closed the lid on the canister and set it back in the row of matching containers against the tiled backsplash.

"Why did she accuse you of cheating?" Mallory asked.

"Because I was a better baker than her and she couldn't handle not winning." Ernie turned back to face Mallory. "She'd gotten used to pitching fits and getting her way. It was as if we were all living in Beatrice's world."

"Well, not anymore." Mallory looked at the hutch and then back at Ernie. "Who knows, you could win another first-place ribbon now that Beatrice is gone."

"I get the feeling there's more to your visit than just talking about the contest. I read that article about you on the *Chronicle*'s website." He approached the table, and he no longer looked like the welcoming host who had invited her inside. "I think you're trying to shift suspicion away from yourself. Let's be clear, there are dozens of people in Wingate who despised that woman. One of them being her husband. I've heard he's been having financial problems. Nothing solves a money crisis like an insurance payout."

Mallory jerked her head back at the callous yet intriguing comment. She let the remark sit for a moment before starting to say something but was interrupted by the back door opening. A reed-thin, bald man entered with gusto and then halted when he noticed Mallory sitting at the table.

"Oh, sorry. Didn't mean to interrupt." He glanced at his watch and then at Ernie. "You're still going, right?"

Ernie nodded. "Paddy, this is Mallory Monroe. She stopped by to tell me she's chairing the Pie Baking Contest for the Garden Tour. Mallory, this is my old buddy, Paddy Hannigan."

"Nice to meet you," Paddy said with a smile that seemed genuine.

"You also," Mallory said. "You wouldn't by chance be related to William Hannigan?"

"He's my nephew." Paddy glanced at his watch again. Now he seemed impatient. "I don't mean to break this up, but I'm feeling lucky, and I don't want to waste any time." He rubbed his hands together.

"Don't let me keep you." Mallory stood. "Where are you two heading off to?"

"Mohegan Sun," Paddy said.

"I took a personal day from work. Midweek isn't as crowded at the casino." Ernie's words were rushed.

"Thank you for speaking with me, Ernie. I'll be in touch." She offered a smile, which Ernie didn't return. Passing by Paddy, she gave him a nod and left the house through the back door. Outside, she walked around the meticulously cared for home and couldn't shake Ernie's comment about Beatrice's husband. Added to what Evelyn Brinkley had told her yesterday, it seemed the police would have a suspect with more motive than Mallory. As she climbed onto her bike, she mused that anybody would have a stronger motive than her.

Before she began pedaling, her cell phone dinged with an incoming text. It looked like Kip had given his cousin, twice removed, Mallory's contact information. She read the text. Yikes!

Sorry for the late notice. There's a committee meeting tonight. I'll email you with all the docs you need. Thanks for volunteering!

Talk about short notice. She wasn't on the job for twenty-four hours, and she was already behind. However, this new to-do item in her calendar meant she'd be face to face with Darlene. There would be no way her cousin could dodge her now.

* * *

Mallory entered the bakery through the back door. All was quiet from the kitchen, which she took as a sign Claudia and Kip were separated. One of them must have been out working the front counter. Maybe she shouldn't have been so skeptical since they seemed to have been getting along the past couple of days. As she dropped her backpack in her office, her mind wandered back to Daniel Wright. She wondered if his money troubles could have been resolved by his wife's death. Definitely gruesome thoughts. As was the idea of Mallory being tossed into a cell during the best years of her life. Or of her dream destroyed because her reputation was shredded into pieces.

If Daniel and Beatrice had been separated, she wondered if they were in a divorce process. If so, how far in were they? There would be court filings. She groaned. There was one person she knew who could navigate that world—Aspen.

"Up for another delivery?" Kip asked.

Mallory jumped, startled by his voice.

"Don't sneak up on me." She grabbed her bag and reached in it for her phone. She needed to call Aspen and ask a favor. "Delivery? To where?"

"The senior center. It's Senior Cookie Day."

"Gah." Mallory's head dropped backward.

She'd forgotten all about the delivery.

Once a month for two decades, the bakery had donated a platter of cookies to the center. For sentimental reasons, Mallory liked making the deliveries herself. It had started when Aunt Glenna wanted to encourage her mother to participate in the center's activities. Grandma Nettie could never turn down a cookie. That was another reason Mallory had decided to continue baking and selling her aunt's traditional cookies. They meant so much to the community.

Before she could say another word, Kip handed her the box of assorted cookies. Oatmeal raisin, chocolate chip, snickerdoodle, and glazed lemon drop cookies, which were both tart and sweet, with a burst of bright flavor when bitten into.

She shoved her phone back into her bag. She'd call Aspen later.

"Then when you get back, you can fill me in on your visit with Ernie Hollis." Kip tapped his nose with his finger. He had an obsession with old gangster movies.

Kip shooed Mallory out the back door, and she walked along the narrow walkway that paralleled the driveway. It was another beautiful spring afternoon in central Connecticut. The walk to the senior center would be pleasant if she could change the loop currently playing in her mind. It was all about murder. She'd really like to think about something more uplifting.

She reached the sidewalk and veered right, passing several shops, and she couldn't resist peeking into their windows. Ashley Bay Home Accessories, a housewares shop, displayed topiaries on a long antique table that was set for a spring celebration. She paused a moment and allowed herself to daydream. Maybe this year she'd host a spring brunch. For the first time since moving out of her childhood home and moving from apartment to apartment in the city, she felt the urge to entertain. And to offer more than just pizza or Chinese takeout. Gosh. She really was becoming an adult, complete with a business loan to pay back and a house in the 'burbs. Sure, it was a rental, but at some point she'd have to consider putting down roots and buying a place.

Whoa! Too much to think about at the moment. Her new address could be the state penitentiary if she didn't find Beatrice's killer.

She pushed forward and within a few minutes arrived at the senior center, which was located off Main Street on Maple Oak Drive. The one-story white clapboard building had been anchored between the back of the library and a Victorian house that now served as medical offices. She entered the center through the sliding front door.

Inside, the receptionist, who perked up when she saw the bakery box, greeted her. The young blonde, maybe a couple of years younger than Mallory, knew she'd be indulging in a treat within a matter of minutes. All Mallory had to do was deliver the cookies to the community room. On her way, she looked around for Gretchen Ford, the center's director.

Gretchen not only managed the hub of activity for Wingate seniors; she also oversaw the Garden Tour. It was the reason why Mallory wanted to talk to her. Gretchen kept track of every detail of the two-day event, from selecting the gardens to paying the expenses. This meant she had worked closely with Beatrice.

"Yoo-hoo! Mallory, dear!"

Mallory turned toward Ginger Dupont's voice. The novelist had called out from a small meeting room off the lobby.

"What brings you by?" Ginger asked as she filled her floral needlepoint satchel with a notebook, file folders, and a handful of how-to-write books. "Oooh, I see. It's Cookie Day!"

"Yes, it is. What are you doing here? Giving a class?" Mallory leaned against the doorjamb as Ginger zipped her bag close.

"A writing workshop." She pointed to the whiteboard behind her. The words *plot*, *twist*, *POV*, and *conflict* were scrawled in big, red letters. "It's been a while since I've given one. But I couldn't resist when Gretchen asked me to pull a class together. It gave me the nudge to finish my book a little earlier. And that makes my editor love me even more. Actually, having my book done allows me to go into next week without having it hanging over my head."

"What's happening next week?"

"The class comes back with their ideas and a few pages written."

"I'm sure they enjoy the workshop," Mallory said.

"Let me tell you, some people have the craziest ideas. You should have heard some of them." Ginger propped a hand on her hip. Her bright pink pantsuit with ruffled blouse was a stark contrast to the muted tones in the library. "Then again, people probably thought J.K. Rowling was crazy. Wizards and magic!"

"I think it's wonderful that people explore their creative sides," Mallory said.

"Amen." Ginger looked around the room before lifting her satchel off the table. "Though there are a few people I would never have expected to explore their creativity. Like Evelyn Brinkley."

"I met her yesterday. She was Beatrice's neighbor." Mallory walked with Ginger out to the corridor. "I got the sense she was a gardener. That's sort of creative."

"If she hadn't been involved in the Garden Club for decades, she'd be a hermit. Evelyn's always been a private person. Though today her mood seemed more upbeat, more talkative." Ginger paused for dramatic effect. "I'm certain it's because of Beatrice's death."

Mallory grabbed Ginger's arm and nearly toppled the bakery box. "Why do you say that? What do you know?"

Ginger's red lips slid into a mischievous grin. "The two of them had been going at it over their property line. I don't know the details, but it got bad between them . . . fast. Which isn't a surprise because they're both not exactly rays of sunshine." She chuckled, amused by her own character assessment.

"There you are, Mallory." Gretchen Ford approached with her hands out. The middle-aged woman was several inches shorter than Mallory, and she attempted to elongate her thick frame by wearing a column of navy. "I heard the cookies had arrived."

"I'm sorry. I got sidetracked," Mallory said sheepishly as she handed the box to Gretchen. She'd hoped to speak to the director privately in her office.

"No worries. We're grateful you've kept up your aunt's generous donation. I'll set these up in the community room. We know you have to get back to work."

"It's my pleasure," Mallory said. "Though if you have a moment, I'd like to have a word with you."

Gretchen's blue eyes grew wide. "Great minds think alike. There's something I want to talk to you about. I was wondering if you would consider teaching a class here. Maybe a basic decorating class. Nothing too fancy or too challenging. What do you think?" Gretchen looked expectantly at Mallory.

What did Mallory think? She thought she'd break into a happy dance. The invitation to do a class gave her a glimmer of hope—not everyone believed she had killed Beatrice. Her eyes watered as a warmth radiated throughout her body. If she didn't pull herself together, she'd break down in tears. Happy tears.

"Are you okay, dear?" Ginger nudged Mallory with her elbow.

"Yes. Yes. I'm great! Thank you, Gretchen. How about I follow up with you with some dates and times?" Mallory asked.

"Marvelous," Gretchen said.

"Your class will be a hit. I'm certain." Ginger gave Mallory a reassuring nod. "Sorry, but I must be off. I have a live event to do later today on social media. Tah!" And with that, Ginger floated away in her usual fashion, making her exits just as grand as her entrances.

"She's right, you know," Gretchen said. "I'd better get these into the community room. Thank you. Oh, and thank you for volunteering to lead the Pie Baking committee. With all you have going on, I'm both surprised and delighted you're making the time. I know you'll do a great job. You're going to make a lot of pie bakers very happy." Gretchen patted Mallory's arm and was about to walk away but then stopped. "I almost forgot. You wanted to talk to me about something."

"I wanted to ask you about Beatrice."

Gretchen's shoulders squared, and her jaw tensed. "What about her?"

"Was there anyone on the committee she had a problem with?" Mallory realized her question was way too broad. Beatrice had problems with practically everybody in town.

Gretchen's face closed off immediately. "Beatrice had a challenging personality, but she did a lot of good work for the center, and I will not talk disparagingly about her. And I expect that as member of the fundraiser, you will not either. The center relies heavily on the money raised from the tour. Am I clear?"

Mallory nodded.

"Good. Thank you again for the cookies." Gretchen walked away, disappearing into the community room. Then Mallory headed to the exit, waving goodbye to the receptionist at the front desk.

She replayed Gretchen's last comments. It sounded like she had threatened to remove Mallory from the committee if she kept poking around Beatrice's murder. It really wasn't much of a threat, since Mallory had only been on the job less than a day. Being tossed off the committee wouldn't devastate her.

By the time she stepped outside, her thoughts had shifted from teaching the class to what Ginger had said about Beatrice and Evelyn. And it reminded her she needed to reach out to Aspen about snooping around the courthouse filings. Slowing her brisk pace, she wrote a text and then sent it off.

"I can't believe I'm asking Red for help," she muttered as she picked up her pace and went back to the bakery.

*   *   *

The rest of the afternoon was unremarkable. Darlene hadn't replied to any of Mallory's messages, Hannigan hadn't come to arrest Mallory, and one new cookie bouquet order came in. All in all, not a bad day.

Though not a great day.

In hopes of winding down after so much activity, Mallory gathered the ingredients for her popular double chocolate walnut cookies.

As she poured the vanilla into a measuring spoon she inhaled its soothing aroma. The golden liquid was better than any aromatherapy she could buy. A few whiffs, and her mood lifted. Unfortunately, her phone dinged and interrupted her moment of Zen.

It was a text from Aspen.

Double checking. Are you sure about this? Aren't you worried about what we discussed? Attorney client confidentiality?

It looked like that excuse had come back to bite her.

Mallory started typing.

I've been thinking you were right.

She couldn't believe she was saying that. She continued typing.

Besides, nothing I'm doing could be used against me.

At least, she hoped not.

Thanks for your help!

After she got a thumbs up emoji from Aspen, Mallory set the phone down and went back to her cookie dough. As she combined the flour, cocoa powder, and other dry ingredients, she reviewed her conversations throughout the day.

She'd talked to a few people about Beatrice and received some very interesting reactions.

Luke all but shut her down.

Evelyn hadn't seemed bothered by a murder next door.

Ernie got a little hot under the collar.

Gretchen warned Mallory to back off and not rock her fundraising boat.

She made a mental note to add a couple more index cards to her murder board before she went off to the Garden Tour committee meeting.

With the dry ingredients mixed, it was time to add the wet ingredients. As the mixer whizzed, she shifted gears from investigating to the committee meeting later that night. She had to get herself mentally prepared for it. Not so much for the actual meeting, but for her face-to-face with Darlene. Because she wouldn't allow her cousin to avoid her. It was time for her to come clean about her plans and explain how they would impact Mallory's future.

Chapter Eleven

M allory closed the bakery and said goodnight to Kip and Claudia before getting on her bicycle. The ride home was relaxing despite having to pedal faster than normal. She wanted to have enough time to get ready for the Garden Tour's general committee meeting.

She burst into her house like the Tasmanian devil. Her whirlwind of activity confused Agatha, who had been woken from a deep sleep in the living room's window seat. Mallory attempted to soothe the ruffled feline with a gentle pat on the head, but all she got in return was a cold glare. She murmured an "I'm sorry" and then hustled upstairs to change out of her work attire. She hopped into the shower and then dressed in something more appropriate for the committee meeting in record time. An unexpected call from her mom put her behind schedule. The conversation lasted longer than she would have liked because she had to soothe her mother's nerves about the murder and her daughter's involvement in it. Finally, when there was a lull, aka her mother taking a breath, Mallory wrapped up the talk with a promise to be careful and to call soon. Her mom clarified that texting wouldn't count as calling. Mallory hated when her mom added stipulations to their agreements. But in order to get off the phone and out the door, she had no choice but to agree. Her next hurdle was Agatha, who stopped her halfway to the back door. The demanding meow had Mallory dropping her backpack on the counter and dishing out salmon paté for her feline. With dinner served, she could finally leave for the meeting.

Minutes later, Mallory pulled into a parking space behind Rusty's Grill. The restaurant was located at the north end of Main Street. It was a popular dining establishment among residents and tourists. In addition to serving lunch and dinner, the restaurant had three private dining rooms on the second floor. She made her way into the building, passing the hostess, who had just grabbed menus for the group of diners she was about to seat. Mallory walked to the elevator, which took her up to the second floor. When she stepped out of the elevator, all she had to do was follow the chatter to find the committee meeting.

The room was set up for the meeting, with rows of chairs facing the windows overlooking Main Street. Along one wall was a refreshment table, where several members mingled while pouring their coffees. As soon as she entered the room, all eyes were on her. The weight of the stares fell heavily on her, and she didn't know what to do. Her sister would have encouraged her to take on those stares directly, though she wasn't as confrontational as Liz. Those gawkers could be future customers. Was it really worth offending them just because they looked at her funny?

Though there was nothing funny about the way she felt at the moment. Her stomach clenched, sweat beaded at her temples, and her mouth went dry. Maybe coming here wasn't a good idea.

Then again, she'd have to face those stares at some point. Because until Beatrice's murder was solved, she was still a person of interest, not only for the police department but for Wingate as a whole.

Mallory decided she wouldn't confront anyone. But she wouldn't cower either. Instead, she'd find a middle ground, and it started with her finding a seat. She saw a friendly face gesturing to a chair.

Elana's eyes crinkled with a smile as Mallory sat. Before Mallory could offer her thanks for the seat, Darlene stepped up to the podium and opened the meeting. Her first remarks were about Beatrice and what a loss it was for the Garden Tour and her family and the town. Mallory had to hand it to her cousin; she sounded sincere. With that out of the way, she launched into the meaty part of the meeting—updates on various committees. One by one, committee heads took to the podium and read their reports. It appeared that the Garden Tour was a well-oiled machine. All the reports were positive, and not one chairperson had foreseen any problems on the horizon. Well, that was until Mallory was asked to come up and give her report. Then the well-oiled machine came to a grinding halt.

She'd barely had time to review the documents she'd received earlier, let alone read them and write up a report. Didn't her cousin realize she ran a business and was trying to solve a murder?

Mallory approached the front of the room with heavy steps. She was unprepared. And hated the feeling. Darlene stepped back, giving Mallory the podium. How very kind. Mallory tamped down the urge to strangle her cousin and sucked in a cleansing breath. She could ad-lib.

"Thank you, Darlene. Some of you may not know that I joined the baking contest committee this morning. Right now, I don't have a report to give you." She gave an apologetic smile and intended to continue with a promise to email the report within forty-eight hours. But a murmur of "oh's," several shakes of heads, and a whole lot of frowning had her wishing for a natural disaster to sweep in and end the meeting. Nothing too big. Just enough to evacuate. That would be so helpful. "However, I do intend to . . ."

A blaring siren had people jumping in their seats, confusion rumbling through the room as a man raced in screaming, "Fire! Fire! Use the stairs! Everyone get out! Now!"

Whoa. Did I manifest this?

Two years ago, she'd taken a manifestation course online. Three hundred dollars, a dozen printables, and ten videos later, she was still unconvinced of the power of manifesting, though she'd had a lovely vision board in her bedroom that year. Now she was scrambling with fellow committee members to exit the meeting room and escape the inferno. At least, that's what it felt like as she got caught up in a group of nimble septuagenarians. Within seconds, she stood outside the restaurant in the chilly night air after asking for a natural disaster to disrupt a meeting. And then there was a fire.

Coincidence?

Along with her fellow volunteers and restaurant diners, Mallory watched the drama unfold. It was like a scene out of a movie. Firefighters arrived, descended from their truck, and entered the building as the police officers secured the scene, keeping onlookers back.

"I can't believe there's a fire," one volunteer said to another, but within earshot of Mallory since she was standing next to her.

The other woman nodded. "Guess it's never dull when you're around," she said to Mallory.

"That's what our committee needs. Some excitement," the first volunteer said and then laughed.

Mallory offered a weak smile. She was gaining quite the reputation in town. And it wasn't the one she wanted. So perhaps she should manifest a new one.

"Looks like it's a kitchen fire," said a man weaving through the crowd. "They say it's under control."

Mallory looked around the crowd for her cousin. She'd caught a glimpse of Darlene when they'd first exited the building, but now she wasn't anywhere to be seen. Darn. Her cousin's refusal to look her in the eyes and address the information Mallory had learned was unsettling. It indicated that what Jake Lewis had told her about the sale of the building was true.

"There you are." Elana joined Mallory. "Talk about excitement. I heard the fire was snuffed out quickly. Thank goodness."

"What a relief. Though it was a little scary there for a few minutes," Mallory said.

"Yeah, but it got you out of giving your report. I can't believe Darlene expected you to give one since you only came on board today. Though I'm happy you're a part of the event. I've been a volunteer for years. I'm co-chair of the beverages committee."

Mallory chose not to air her grievance with her cousin publicly. Even though she was annoyed with Darlene, they were still family. "Darlene is juggling a lot. She probably thought I had time to catch up on everything. Anyway, I'm glad I volunteered." Okay, it was a fib, but it seemed to be the right thing to say.

"It's such a nicer atmosphere now that Beatrice is gone." Regret flashed on Elana's face. She cleared her throat and regrouped. "I know I sound harsh, but it's the truth. The Garden Tour is something I enjoy. I've been a part of it for years, but dealing with Beatrice has been very difficult lately."

"Why?" Mallory asked.

Elana chewed on her lower lip as she looked around the crowd still gathered outside Rusty's. "Not here. There are too many people. Since the meeting is over, why don't you come over to my house? I don't live far. Maple Oak Drive. Past the senior center. I can make us a pot of tea."

Mallory considered the invitation. Curiosity had gotten the better of her, so how could she refuse? "Okay. Should we leave now?"

Elana nodded. "It's number thirty-two. I'm parked up there." She pointed toward the curb.

A sudden movement from across the crowd caught Mallory's attention. *Great.* The last person she wanted to deal with was Dugan Porter. Time to get going before he noticed her.

"I'm in the parking lot. Meet you at your house." Mallory had barely moved when she heard her name shouted. Shoot. So close to a getaway.

Elana had already started walking toward her parked car as Dugan reached Mallory.

"Heck of a week. Murder. Fire. Do I dare wonder what tomorrow holds?" he asked.

"My advice would be not to wonder. Goodnight, Dugan," Mallory said.

"I get it, you don't want to talk to me. But I want to help." He slipped his hands into his pants pockets.

"Help yourself to another sensational story?" she countered.

He sighed and then leaned forward, his voice dropping. "My editor gave me notes for the article. He wanted it a certain way. Look, we all know Beatrice was a difficult, unlikable person, and she ruffled a lot of feathers. Not sure if this means anything, but I don't believe you were involved with her murder."

"What makes you so sure?"

"For starters, your Almond Meltaway cookie was way better than hers. Anyone who can bake like you do couldn't be a cold-blooded killer."

A shot of pride at the compliment worked its way through Mallory. "Then why didn't you say so?"

He shrugged. "I'm a reporter. I need to stay neutral."

"Fair enough." There was a nagging in her gut that told her not to trust Dugan. Editor notes or not, he'd written an article that had cast shade on her and left her innocence in question. But she needed allies, people who could help her find the truth. Dugan could be an ally. Of course, she'd have to be careful how much trust she put in him. "I could use a little information about Daniel Wright. What do you know about him?"

"Wright's been going through a rough patch lately with his investments. He's built a reputation for funding successful start-ups, but the last few have been duds. His investors haven't been happy." Dugan's phone buzzed. "I've got to take this and get back to work. We're good?"

Mallory nodded, and Dugan spun around and dashed away, taking his call. She had to get a move on. Elana was waiting for her, and she was dying to hear about her relationship with Beatrice. So, just to be safe, she texted Kip where she was going. You never knew what could happen.

*   *   *

A few minutes later, Mallory arrived at the Petersons' home. She reached the front door and was welcomed inside by Elana. The foyer opened through a columned entrance to a large, spacious room with a cathedral ceiling and fireplace.

"You have a lovely home." Mallory followed Elana to the seating area, which consisted of two deep-cushioned sofas and an oversized square coffee table topped with a tray of tea. "Have you lived here long?"

Elana perched on the edge of the sofa. She gestured for Mallory to do the same on the sofa across from her. Then she leaned forward and poured their tea.

"We've been in this house for ten years. Before that, we owned a larger piece of property on the edge of town. But the upkeep was too much." She handed Mallory a filled cup. "I much prefer not having to spend all my spare time tending to the garden or cleaning rooms we never use."

Mallory added milk to her tea and then took a sip. She wasn't sure if she should start the conversation rolling or allow Elana to take the lead and see where their visit went.

After Elana sipped her tea, she lowered the cup from her lips. "Thank you for accepting my invitation. It gives me the opportunity to apologize for what I said about the committee being more pleasant now that Beatrice is gone. It was unkind of me. I should have extended her kindness. Though that was a tough thing to do given Beatrice's personality. Then again, extending grace to those who grate on our nerves is what we're called to do. Don't you agree?"

Mallory took another sip of her tea and wondered what exactly Elana's purpose was in inviting her over. Recruitment? She already had a faith she believed in and had been praying nonstop since discovering Beatrice's body. She wasn't looking for a new team. So she simply nodded.

"Who am I kidding? Any grace would have been wasted on that horrible woman. I'm surprised somebody didn't do her in earlier."

Mallory nearly spit out her next sip of tea. "You are?"

Elana set her cup down on the coffee table and crossed her legs. "I can't tell you who, but a friend of mine made a big mistake last year."

An anonymous friend? Mallory couldn't help but think that whatever story Elana was about to share was really about her. And she was dying to know.

"My friend drove home after a party under the influence. She'd drunk too much but thought she was okay. Thank goodness there wasn't an accident. I know for a fact she only told a few of her closest friends, but somehow Beatrice found out about the incident."

"Sounds like there was a traitor in the friend group," Mallory said.

"Exactly what I thought. Are you familiar with the Mums, Merlot, and Mozart Festival?"

Mallory nodded. The annual event happened every fall in Wingate. Main Street would be decked out in colorful mums from end to end. Wine tasting events and tours of a nearby winery were set up. And the town hosted three nights of concerts. It was a much-anticipated long weekend for residents and tourists. During the festival, the year she was fourteen, she had her first kiss. The sweet memory flitted into her mind, and instantly she saw the boy she'd flirted with. Tall, lanky, with light brown hair and a big smile, wearing a baseball jersey. The kiss had sent a tingling from her lips to her toes until her mother had interrupted the kiss. Mallory had pulled away from him and reluctantly rejoined her family's picnic. She never saw him again. Whenever she thought of that kiss, she wondered what had become of that boy.

"Anyway, Beatrice used my friend's lapse in judgment to her benefit."

"How so?" Kelly asked.

"She blackmailed my friend to vote for her appointment to the Mums, Merlot, and Mozart Festival board. At first, I was shocked that Beatrice would blackmail someone to get on a stupid committee. I mean, it's a nice event and all, but resorting to blackmail to be a part of it? Insanity, right? Let me tell you, my shock wore off fast. I was so angry with her. I wondered how many times Beatrice had resorted to extorting people simply to get her way."

"Wait a minute. You're certain Beatrice blackmailed your friend to get onto the festival's board?" Mallory couldn't believe she was asking the question. It was a fundraiser that involved mums, wine, and some music. Why so cutthroat?

"Absolutely."

"I have to ask. Are you the *friend*?"

"No! No. I swear I'm not."

Mallory wasn't sure if she believed Elana. "Why did your friend do it? I mean, why did she agree to vote for Beatrice? It would have been her word against Beatrice's. Assuming the few friends she told stayed silent. I hope she didn't drive under the influence again."

"No, no, she didn't. She made a promise not to drink while out, and so far, she's kept it. She realizes it was a bad mistake that could have resulted in a tragic outcome. The reason she voted for Beatrice was that her actions embarrassed her. She didn't want to be gossiped about. Beatrice knew that."

Mallory could relate to the feeling of not wanting to be talked about. "I have to say this just sounds so unbelievable. Have you told anyone else about this?"

Elana shook her head. "I promised my friend I wouldn't. But here I am, breaking the promise." Her gaze drifted off to the two large front windows.

"The police would probably like to speak with your friend."

Elana's gaze whipped back and landed on Mallory. "She's not a murderer."

"I didn't say she was. But, as you said, Beatrice might have blackmailed other people. The police should know that." Was that what had happened between Beatrice and Luke? Had she been blackmailing him?

"I can't betray her. I won't. I've said too much already." Elana folded her arms as a determined look settled on her face. She wouldn't spill the beans.

"I understand." Mallory set her cup on the coffee table. "But there's more, isn't there? Something to do with your marriage. You were upset the day of the cookie decorating class at my bakery and asked if I had any marital advice to offer. Remember?"

"My husband and I had an argument. One of many lately, I'm afraid. He's run into some financial troubles." Elana stood and walked over to the fireplace. She adjusted the accessories on the mantel. Moving the blue and white vase an inch, straightening the framed photo of two teenage boys, adjusting the spacing between the three candlesticks. "He invested in a sure thing based on Daniel's recommendation, and it tanked."

"Daniel? Beatrice's husband?" Mallory asked.

Elana turned to face Mallory. "Yes. Daniel had been so confident, so sure the app would take off. I don't know if it even got fully developed."

What Elana was telling her confirmed what Dugan had said earlier. It sounded as if Daniel had gotten Elana's husband to invest in a dud.

"Investing is a risky proposition, but it wasn't Beatrice's fault the investment failed."

"I know. Yet, knowing she was conniving and manipulating people to get what she wanted, coupled with her husband's horrible investment advice, just chafed me. It made me so angry." Her hand flew up and pressed on her chest, over her heart. "Not angry enough to kill her, I swear."

"I should get going. Thank you for the tea." *And for the information.* Mallory stood, grabbed her backpack, and walked to the door with Elana following. She stepped out into the night air, now cooler than when she was standing outside the restaurant. Spring in Connecticut brought a wide range of temperatures. There could be nights when the temps were hovering around freezing, while other nights it would be a balmy seventy degrees. It was one reason

123

why she layered her bedding and why she kept a cardigan in her car. She needed to slip that on ASAP.

She descended the porch steps and walked toward her car. As her wedge heels hit the pavement, an eerie feeling of being watched fell over her. She glanced over her shoulders and saw no one. She chalked it up to her imagination working overtime.

Then she heard it.

It sounded like a twig breaking, and it took her back to the night she had found Beatrice's body.

She'd heard a similar sound just before she reached the kitchen door.

How had she forgotten that?

Now, she did a complete 360-degree turn.

No one.

No sound.

At least not at that moment. With her heart pumping a little faster and her internal warning system on high alert, she hurried to her car. Safely inside her vehicle, she started the ignition and pulled out of the Petersons' driveway.

Mallory reached the intersection and waited for a break in traffic before turning onto Main Street. Her impromptu tea date with Elana had given her some new information about Beatrice. Could it be true? Had Beatrice sifted through people's lives for a whiff of scandal and then used it to get something she wanted? What kind of person had Beatrice Wright been? If what Elana said was true, then Beatrice had been a horrible person. Mallory needed to find out who the anonymous *friend* was. Elana might have refused to name the person, but she had let a detail slip that Mallory could use to begin her search—the person was involved with the Mums, Merlot, and Mozart Festival. And to narrow down the search even more, the *friend* was someone who had been on the board. There was also the matter of turning over this information to Detective Hannigan. By the time she arrived home, she had decided that she'd share with the detective once she had identified the person. After all, she didn't want to waste his time if her new lead turned out to be a bust.

Chapter Twelve

T he next morning at the bakery, Mallory secured the lock on her bike. The ride from her cottage to the bakery seemed to take forever since her legs were pedaling at the minimal speed. She probably should have driven that morning.

"Yoohoo! Got a sec, Mallory?" Aspen called out.

The perky voice cut right through Mallory. She'd barely slept a wink last night. The events of the past days had replayed over and over again in her mind, keeping her from slipping into and staying in her deep sleep cycle, according to her smartwatch. And she felt it. Heavy eyelids, sluggish gait, and the need to infuse caffeine into her body. It was going to be a long day.

"Not really," Mallory muttered to herself.

Aspen scooted toward Mallory in her bubble-gum pink velour hoodie and matching jogger pants, holding two travel mugs. She looked bright and energetic with her hair swept up into a high ponytail and a full face of makeup. Mallory, meanwhile, had gathered her hair up into a loose bun and barely swept a coat of mascara on her lashes.

"Oh, honey, are you okay? You look like something the dog dragged in. Rough night?" She giggled. "Oops. See what I did there? Dog, rough?"

"Hilarious." After double-checking her bike's chain lock, Mallory plodded toward the bakery's back door with Aspen trailing behind her. "After work, I had a committee meeting. Kip got me involved with the Garden Tour, and there was a fire."

"A fire? Is everyone okay?" Aspen asked.

"Yes. It wasn't a big deal. Anyway, I ended up at Elana Peterson's house afterward."

"To think, I thought Wingate would be dullsville when I moved here." She shrugged. "Oh, this one is for you." She handed one of the thermal mugs to Mallory, who looked at it skeptically as she recalled her conversation with her sister about Aspen. The big question mark hanging over the curvy redhead was her motive for befriending Mallory. So could Mal trust what was inside the mug?

It seemed unlikely that Aspen would poison her in public. Instead, if the woman had any smarts, she'd slowly poison Mallory with something that would be untraceable in a standard autopsy. So she'd only take one sip to placate her upstairs neighbor.

"Thank you." Mallory took the mug and then grasped the doorknob. The knob was tarnished and scratched from years of use, like the worn door. She entered, slinging off her backpack as she walked into her office. There she dropped the bag on the desk. After taking one sip of Aspen's coffee, she smiled and set the mug down next to the bag. "Bold. I like it." She slipped out of her coral denim jacket and draped it over the chair.

"I grind my own beans," Aspen said proudly. "What have you been up to?"

"Last night, I had a conversation with Dugan Porter." Mallory yawned. She knew it would be one of many to come. She glanced around her office. She had to find a spot for a coffee maker. Better yet, she should add coffee to the bakery's menu. The coffee station she had set up for the day of her interview with Dugan had gone over well with her customers. She made a mental note to follow up on that idea.

"Do you think that was a good idea?" Aspen stood in the doorway. "Kip doesn't trust him. What did he want to know?"

"Actually, he offered to help me."

Aspen snickered.

"I think he was being sincere. He told me that Daniel Wright is having money problems. And from what Elana later told me, it sounds like he was right." Mallory walked out of the office and into the kitchen. She flicked the light switch, and the space lit up. The three workstations were ready for a day's work. There were orders to fill, cookies to decorate, and she had a class to prepare for the senior center. Together, they were all positive things. Claudia would be in soon, and Kip would arrive a few hours later. He'd be closing the bakery today. "This kitchen is so small. How do all three of you work in here?" Aspen inspected the room and seemed fascinated by the stand mixer. It was a KitchenAid on steroids. That old gal had made a lot of cookie batter over the decades, and despite a few dings and the dullness of its stainless steel, it was still going strong. With regular maintenance and a little TLC, Mallory hoped the mixer would last another decade. Replacing the machine would cost her a fortune.

"We make do." Would Mallory have liked a bigger space? Absolutely. But the kitchen had been good enough for her aunt. Glenna had started thirty years ago with a dream, a small bank loan, and had grown her home-based business into a thriving retail shop. Albeit with a small kitchen.

"I poked around the court documents and found numerous filings between Daniel and Beatrice. They were battling over their assets." Aspen looked away from the mixer and back at Mallory. "It seems Dugan was on point with his theory about Daniel having money problems. Especially since it appeared Beatrice had been dragging out the divorce."

"Interesting," Mallory murmured as she tied on an apron.

"Get this," Aspen said as she walked to the workstation. "I also discovered it was only Beatrice's name on the deed to their home."

"Isn't that unusual? They were married. Wouldn't both names be on the house?"

"It's not as uncommon as you think. He could have had money troubles that precluded him from getting a mortgage when they purchased the house. Also, it's a way to protect assets. Being an entrepreneur, Daniel is always taking risks, leaving him vulnerable to bankruptcy or legal actions. He probably didn't want to risk losing his home, so it was put into Beatrice's name."

"Which meant it couldn't be taken away if he went belly up or got sued," Mallory said.

"Exactly. It was a prudent thing to have done. However, it came back to bite him because in the divorce settlement he wouldn't get half of the house."

"Ouch. That had to sting." It sounded as if Daniel's plan had gone awry. "Didn't you say they were fighting over assets?"

"They had more than the house. There are retirement accounts, bank accounts, vehicles, and investments." Aspen stepped back from the table, leaned against the opposite counter, and sipped her coffee. "Divorce can get ugly. From what I've learned about Beatrice in the last few days, she sounded like a bitter person who made it her mission to make her husband's life miserable. Let me tell you, a divorce can bring out the worst in people."

"I don't doubt it. Hopes and dreams and trust are shattered. It's hard not to hate the other person."

"It's probably for the best we found out who Gil really is before we got serious with him," Aspen said.

Mallory dipped her head. She didn't want to share that she'd already gotten serious with Gil. She'd thought their next step would be getting engaged, not breaking up. It wouldn't do her any good thinking about Gil the Cheater. She looked back up at Aspen. "Killing Beatrice would speed up the divorce. Daniel would get everything."

"Not necessarily," Aspen said. "It all depends on what Beatrice's will says. He could be the beneficiary. Or someone else could have been."

"Wills are private until the person's death, correct?"

"Yes. I'm sure Beatrice's attorney is arranging for a reading of her will. That is, if she had one. Wills are often something people put off. They don't like to think about their own mortality. Do you have a will?" Aspen asked.

Mallory walked to the refrigerator and took out a block of unsalted butter and a carton of eggs. "Ah . . . sort of. It's not finished yet." When she had purchased the bakery, her lawyer had urged her to write a will. But being bogged down with all the paperwork for the purchase, finishing the will had fallen to the wayside.

Aspen's phone chimed, and she pulled it out of her hoodie's pocket. "Got to take this call. Don't forget your coffee. You left it in the office." Aspen was out of the kitchen with that reminder, and Mallory would be dumping the rest of the beverage later. While the butter and eggs got to room temperature, she started mixing up a batch of royal icing and devising a plan to pay a visit to Daniel Wright. She wondered how much trouble he was in financially and if the marital assets could have helped resolved his problem.

Mallory spent the next couple of hours decorating cookies for special orders. They'd come in after the news of Beatrice's death broke. She was grateful those customers hadn't paid attention to the rumors, innuendo, or gossip circulating through Wingate. Granted, two of the orders were from customers in nearby towns, so maybe the details of Beatrice's murder hadn't reached them. It didn't matter. All she knew was that she would enjoy making the deliveries and seeing the joy on the faces of the lucky cookie recipients.

Once her cookies were done, and the bouquets arranged, she packed up a box to take on a trip she'd been plotting all morning. She'd come up with a plan to talk with Daniel Wright. She prayed he'd talk to her.

She checked her watch. Time to get the information she needed. Mallory dashed out of the kitchen, through the hall, to the back door. Outside, she jogged down to the sidewalk. She shielded her eyes from the sun with her hand and looked up the street.

Right on time.

Mac approached, pushing her mail cart. She had a big smile on her face and her head bobbed up and down. Mallory guessed she was listening to her favorite music channel—pop hits from the '80s.

Mallory waved and rushed to meet her halfway.

"Hey there, Mal. You're eager to get your bills today, aren't you?" Mac pulled out her ear buds and then dug into her cart for the small stack of envelopes addressed to the bakery. "Here you go."

"Thanks. But there's something I need. An address. I'm hoping you can help me," Mallory said.

"If I can. Whose address?"

"Daniel Wright."

"Weren't you at his house the other night?" Mac grinned.

"His other house. They were separated."

"I know. I'm just teasing."

Mallory leveled a flat stare on her mail carrier.

"Too soon?"

Mallory nodded.

"Daniel's rental is 9 Graystone Way. Anything else?"

"No. Thank you." Mallory rushed back inside the bakery. With the address, she was set to put her plan into motion once Kip arrived for work. She dropped the mail in her office on her way back to the kitchen.

"I hope you know what you're doing," Claudia said as she marched across the kitchen to the oven. She'd arrived right after Aspen left and got to working making cookie dough for the day's baking. She removed a tray of giant oatmeal raisin cookies from the oven and then set them on the cooling rack. "Do you think he'll be receptive to your visit?"

"Who are you visiting?" Kip entered the kitchen in the middle of Claudia's question. He gave Mallory a curious look.

"Daniel Wright. Mac gave me his address." Mallory finished tying the bow on the pastry box and then set aside the spool of white and red ribbon. Inside the little white box was an assortment of cookies, minus the Almond Meltaways. She didn't think they were a good choice under the circumstances.

Kip's eyes bugged out. "You're going to see the widower? I definitely missed something. This is why I don't like working the late shift." His shoulders drooped as he pouted on his way to his workstation.

"Meddling in a police matter is asking for trouble. Mark my words." Claudia walked over to the sink, where she washed and dried her hands. "Look what happened last time when you just popped over to someone's house uninvited. You found a dead body."

"What's she supposed to do? Sit by and do nothing?" Kip tightened his apron before he started measuring flour.

"It would be the prudent thing to do," Claudia countered.

"Well, you would know about being a pru—"

Mallory held her hands up. "Enough. I'm going to take these cookies to Daniel. You," she pointed at Kip, "will take over in here while Claudia works the counter until her shift is over. Sound good?"

Kip nodded.

"I'll just finish up here, okay?" Claudia asked.

"Yes. I'll be back soon." Mallory swiped up the box and headed toward the doorway. In the hall, she grabbed her backpack and then made her way out of the bakery. She set the box in the bike's rear basket and then checked her phone's map app. Graystone Way sounded familiar, and the map confirmed she knew where the street was. It would be a quick ride.

* * *

Mallory slowed her bicycle as she reached Daniel's rental house. And what a house it was. Rising from the ground like a monument, the brick Federal-style house was as stately as they came. But its simple design kept it from being too ostentatious. There was nothing flashy about it, from its symmetrical design to the sturdy white columns holding up the pediment over the front door. Yet it gave no hint of the money woes people said Daniel had. Then again, as a venture capitalist, he needed to maintain a perception of success, no matter if his checking account was bleeding out.

And the sleek Mercedes parked in the driveway was a nice touch for Daniel's successful image. Mallory parked her bike, lifted the cookie box from the basket, and treaded along the brick path to the front door. The focal point of the long, narrow front lawn was a graceful weeping willow. The tree's silvery-green foliage was perking up for the season. As was the sweeping garden that bordered the lush green grass. Pops of yellows and oranges burst against the neatly manicured shrubs. She couldn't fathom how long it must take to trim all those bushes.

She climbed the steps to the black front door embellished with a brass knocker.

Her nerves were firing off little missiles of doubt, making her question whether Claudia had been right about this being a bad idea. Then, before she could use the knocker to announce her arrival, the door swung open, catching her off guard.

"I have no comment," the towering man said as he was about to shut the door.

The jarring comment reverberated through Mallory and reinforced her doubt about visiting Daniel Wright. She held out a hand and said, "I'm not a reporter. I'm Mallory Monroe. I knew your wife." Barely, though; she didn't think it was the time to nitpick.

"Why are you here?"

"I wanted to pay my condolences. Here, I baked cookies." She offered the box and received a scathing look. He knew who she was, and he knew how she knew his late wife. She lowered the box.

"You have a lot of nerve showing up here."

"I probably do, but I'm very sorry for your loss. Beatrice and I argued the day she died, but I didn't kill her. I went to your . . . sorry . . . her house because I wanted to work things out with her. Instead, I found her lying on the kitchen floor."

Mallory squeezed her eyes shut as the image flashed in her mind, causing a sharp pain in her head. A bout of dizziness swept over her, and her body swayed. In an instant, she was being supported by Daniel.

"Are you okay? Come, come on inside." Daniel helped Mallory into the house and led her into the first room off the foyer. He settled her on a sofa, taking the pastry box from her. "Would you like something to drink? Water, perhaps?"

What she'd like was to shrink out of sight. How embarrassing. She'd nearly fainted in front of Daniel. That was something Nancy Drew or Miss Marple never did.

"I'm sorry. I don't know what happened there." Mallory pressed her palms into her thighs and dragged in deep breaths.

"You got really pale there. Like you saw a ghost."

It wasn't a ghost, but Mallory wondered if the murder scene would haunt her for the rest of her life.

"Are you sure you're okay? Should I call someone for you?" Daniel stood with his hands in his pants pockets, keeping his eyes on her, his wife's murderer.

"I appreciate the offer." She straightened and looked around the room. The front windows were framed with floor-length drapes. The bookcase was filled with hardcover books and small decorative objects perfectly arranged in groups of threes. The sofa she was settled on was upholstered in a luxe floral fabric. "This is a nice place. Have you been here long?"

Daniel pulled his hands from his pockets and stepped forward. "Why exactly are you here? And don't tell me it's to express your sympathy for my wife's death."

A knock at the front door postponed Mallory's response.

"I'll be right back, and I expect an answer." He turned and walked out of the room.

Mallory remained seated and listened as Daniel opened the door. She craned her neck forward, hoping to make out the muffled conversation. Then the door closed, and footsteps headed back to the living room.

Behind Daniel was the one person she didn't want to see there. As Detective Hannigan entered the room, she jumped up from her seat and plastered on a friendly smile. Panic stirred inside her. How would she explain her presence there? Oh, wait. She'd tell him she was paying a condolence call, just like she'd told Daniel.

Hannigan came to a halt and gave a slight shake of his head. She suspected he wouldn't buy her condolence call story. "Miss Monroe. I thought that was your bicycle out front. What brings you by Mr. Wright's home?"

"I came by to express my condolences. I brought cookies." She pointed to the pastry box on the coffee table.

Hannigan gave a dubious look. "Very considerate of you. I'm here on official business and need to speak with Mr. Wright . . . in private."

"Miss Monroe was leaving," Daniel said as he stepped forward to pick up the box of cookies and handed it to Mallory. "Please don't come back."

Mallory's gaze fell on the box, and she swallowed. Her cookies had always seemed to smooth things over. She believed there was nothing cookies couldn't mend, from heartaches to hurt feelings, until now.

Daniel's animosity was palpable, and it was directed solely at her. So she cautiously passed by the widower and headed toward the doorway.

"Let me escort you to your bicycle," Hannigan said to Mallory, guiding her out of the room. "I'll be right back, Mr. Wright."

They walked in silence through the foyer and out of the house. She wasted no time in putting space between herself and Hannigan. "I don't need an escort. My bike is right over there."

"Why did you really come here?" he asked.

"Have a nice day, Detective." Mallory started walking away from him.

"I'm not buying the sympathy call."

Mallory reeled around, facing the detective once again. "Do you know he's having money problems? He and Beatrice were fighting over assets in their divorce. Also, Beatrice was blackmailing people. Can you believe that? She even blackmailed someone to get her on the Mums, Merlot, and Mozart Festival committee."

Hannigan's head cocked to the side as his eyes brightened, but only momentarily.

"Mums, Merlot, and Mozart Festival?"

"It's a three-day—"

He raised his hand, signaling to her to stop talking. "I know what the festival is. What I want to know is, how do you know all this? Are you meddling in my case?"

"No! I'm not meddling. People talk to me, and I listen." She didn't see any sign he was buying her explanation. "Does it really matter how I know this stuff?"

And there it was again. That glint of amusement in Hannigan's eyes that she'd seen the other morning at the bakery. "A murder investigation is no place for a civilian. You're a baker. Not a detective."

Mallory knew exactly who she was, thank you very much.

"Then you probably should detect the reason why Beatrice blackmailed someone to get on a festival committee. I'm guessing the reason could lead you to a motive for murder." She whipped around and retraced her steps back to her bicycle . . . with the occasional glance over her shoulder. The nerve of him.

You're a baker. Not a detective.

She was also a person of interest in a murder. She still couldn't wrap her head around how that had happened. But she knew, one way or another, she would clear her name. Another glance over her shoulder, and he was still there. When she reached her bike, he finally retreated into the house. She set the cookie box in the rear basket and then walked the bike down the driveway. The visit hadn't gone as she'd planned it. Daniel had been unreceptive, she had almost fainted—talk about embarrassing—and then

Hannigan arrived. All in all, the outing had been an epic failure from a sleuthing perspective.

She looked back at the house. She should get on the bike and ride back to the bakery. But if she did, she wouldn't be able to talk to Daniel and convince him she hadn't killed his wife. When she'd set out to visit the widower, her intent was to find out if he had an alibi for the night of Beatrice's murder. But after feeling the weight of his anger when he looked at her, she couldn't leave without one more attempt to make him believe she wasn't the murderer.

But she couldn't stay there and wait until Hannigan left. Daniel would probably instruct the detective to arrest her for trespassing.

So I have to hide.

Daniel's rental house was set on a corner lot, and a row of mature rhododendrons bordered the property line. She could simply hang there, out of sight, for a while. The bakery was slow, and she was confident Kip and Claudia could survive a little longer without her.

Just in case Hannigan was keeping an eye on her from the front window, she climbed on her bike, cycled to the stop sign, and turned left. That's where she stopped, turned the bike around, and inched to the edge of the row of rhododendrons. She got off the bike, engaged the kickstand, and peeked through the greenery. Not the best view, but it would do the job. She'd be able to see Hannigan leave.

It didn't take long for Mallory to realize the stakeouts she'd seen on her favorite crime shows were far more interesting than the one she was currently on. She was bored, tired, and hungry. She hadn't eaten since breakfast, which had been only a slice of multigrain toast with almond butter. She pulled back from the shrubs, ready to wrap up her surveillance and go back to the bakery, when she caught a glimpse of Hannigan at the front door.

He was leaving!

She nestled back into her spot, pushing away branches to get a better look. He was indeed heading for his vehicle. At the driver's side, he hesitated after opening the door. He pulled out his cell phone from a pouch on his belt, tapped the screen, and then read. She sighed. Couldn't he read his texts later?

Finally, he secured his phone back in its pouch and slid into the vehicle. It didn't take much time for him to reach the top of the driveway. And her breath caught. What direction would he be heading? She waited. When he turned in the opposite direction, she let out her breath.

Her immediate reaction was to hop on her bike and head back to Daniel's driveway, but she waited. The last thing she wanted was for Hannigan to backtrack because he forgot to ask a question. No. It would be better to wait a few minutes.

Minutes ticked by on her watch, and feeling confident Hannigan wouldn't be back, Mallory was about to pull herself out of the shrubbery and get on her bike. Until another car turned into the driveway. Mallory remained in place, trying to get a look at the driver. The driver's side door opened and the person got out. It was a woman, but the floppy hat she wore obscured her face. Until she walked around the front of the car and looked in Mallory's direction.

Mallory dropped down, praying she hadn't been seen. Then, after waiting for a beat, she slowly inched back up and watched the visitor approach the front door. What on earth was *she* doing there?

Chapter Thirteen

Natalie Kellogg strode purposefully along the walkway dressed in a pair of wide-leg pants and a white ruffled blouse. She unzipped her purse, pulled out a key, and let herself into the house when she reached the door.

Mallory's jaw went slack.

Why did she have a key to Daniel's house? What was going on between them? There was one obvious answer to that question, since Natalie had a key. Though jumping to conclusions was a bad habit to get into. Mallory needed to confirm her suspicions. But how?

Mallory thought for a moment. The only thing that came to mind seemed so out of character for her. But then again so was hiding in the shrubbery. She poked her head through the rhododendrons to ensure that neither Natalie or Daniel was at the front door. Then, with the coast clear, she emerged from her spot and inched her way up the front lawn, staying as close to the shrubs as possible.

Her heart thumped against her chest as she continued along the shrub border. If caught, how would she explain being there? She gave herself a mental shake. She couldn't think about being seen. Those were negative vibes she was sending out to the universe, and they'd boomerang right back at her. Which would be a terrible thing.

When she reached the spot perpendicular to the corner of the house, she sucked in a breath and summoned the courage to dart across the lawn to the house.

One. Two. Three.

And she pushed off, scurrying across the grass and leaping into the mulched garden bed alongside the home's foundation. She stayed low as she skirted toward a window.

Slowly, she eased up and peered into the window. And her eyes nearly bugged out of their sockets.

Daniel and Natalie were in an embrace, kissing.

Whoa! She pulled herself down and rested against the brick. Her thoughts tumbled over each other as she tried to understand what she'd seen. Daniel and Natalie were romantically involved. Suspicion confirmed.

Giving them both a motive for murder. Daniel had a financial motive for killing his wife, and Natalie had a personal reason for killing Beatrice—she had been dragging her feet with the divorce. Murdering the estranged wife was one way to speed up the process.

Her cell phone vibrated, startling her. She grappled for the phone, pulling it from her back pocket. It was a toll-free number. Great. A telemarketer almost gave her a heart attack.

It was time for her to leave. Now she had to make it back to her bicycle without being seen. Since the sneaky couple was otherwise engaged, as long as she stayed low and quiet, she should be able to make it across the lawn undetected.

Mallory retraced the path she'd taken to get to the house, and when she arrived back at her bike, she took a moment to decompress. She couldn't believe she'd been peeping through somebody's window. It felt like she'd violated their privacy. Though she might have obtained a new lead for Detective Hannigan. She'd have to figure out how to let him know what she had discovered without incriminating herself. Her phone buzzed, and she checked her messages. A new voice mail from Gil had come in while she was hightailing it from the house.

She would not risk checking the call at the moment. No. She wanted to put some distance between her and Daniel's love nest. She pedaled like the wind until she felt it was safe to stop and check Gil's message.

She opted to take a quicker route back to the bakery, but it had her riding on Blueberry Ridge Road. This heavily traveled two-lane road connected Wingate to several bordering towns. There was a spot where she could safely pull over. That section was bordered by a guardrail with a backdrop of blooming wildflowers.

With her bike pulled off to the side of the road, she took out her phone and was ready to hit the delete button as Gil started talking, but he hadn't called to ask for forgiveness or another chance. Instead, he'd called to tell her that his boss had heard about the murder and Mallory's connection to it, and he wasn't happy. In fact, he had been so unhappy he told Gil to cancel the order. The news was devastating, and tears stung her eyes. Losing the order was a financial blow, and she couldn't help but wonder if Gil had made any effort to talk his boss out of canceling. He knew the bakery needed the money. She wiped her eyes with the back of her hand and slipped the phone into her backpack. Frame & Brewster, like Gil, was now in her past. She had no choice but to continue moving forward. She was confident she could weather the loss if she could turn the PR page on the bakery and get some positive publicity. Teaching the cookie decorating class at the senior center was a start. But she needed something else.

And there was only one other person who could help her with that.

* * *

How the Murder Crumbles

Darlene's quintessential New England farmhouse came into view as Mallory glided her bike up the driveway, cracked in spots with weeds springing up, and pitted in other areas where Darlene's husband's big, old pickup had been parked for years. The driveway needed a makeover. But that was to be expected thanks to harsh winters and heavy use. There were also other expenses that were higher in priority. There always seemed to be a big-ticket item to repair or replace when you owned an antique home.

The dreamy farmhouse had sheer curtains fluttering in the spring breeze, hanging pots of fragrant geraniums, wicker furniture set up for reading or casual visits with friends.

A sudden burst of cackling had Mallory looking over her shoulder in the direction of the chicken coop. A dozen chickens provided fresh eggs for Darlene's baking. Near the pen was the greenhouse. Finishing off the outbuildings was the three-car garage and carriage house Darlene's husband had turned into a woodshop.

Mallory parked her bike and then grabbed the pastry box before heading around to the back of the house. Why let those cookies go to waste? Hazel would love them. She climbed the back deck steps and walked across to the door. Its window gave her a glimpse into the mudroom. Tidy, as usual. Six cubbies were organized for coats, bags, and shoes. Darlene lived by the motto: a place for everything and everything in its place.

She jiggled the knob, and it turned. Wingate was still one of those places where residents didn't lock their doors. While Darlene and her husband were trusting, they weren't foolish. Mallory knew she was being viewed on her cousin's phone right now thanks to the security camera discreetly hung above the door.

As soon as she pushed the door open a crack, the fragrance of apples baking lured her inside. Fresh apples mingled with just the right amount of cinnamon and nutmeg had her nose twitching.

Her mind churned over childhood memories of baking with her aunt. She moved through the mudroom and arrived at the kitchen doorway, where she caught sight of her cousin. Darlene stood at the island with her daughter, dusting the apple cake with powdered sugar. She tapped the strainer gently, just like her mom used to do, making it snow on the cake. All the while smiling just like her mom. Until she glanced in Mallory's direction. That smile turned upside down in a heartbeat.

Though Hazel's eyes brightened as she leaped off the stool. Then, with her arms wide open, she rushed to Mallory and flung herself into her embrace.

"Hey there, moppet." Mallory squeezed her little cousin and then opened the space between them to get a look at Hazel. After all, she hadn't seen the girl in over a week. Her dark ringlets had a shininess to them Mallory could never get with all the fancy hair products she bought, so she chalked it up to youth. Was it wrong to be envious of a five-year-old?

"We baked a cake." Hazel took Mallory's hand and led her to the island. Unlike Mallory's kitchen, this one was spacious, with a proper eat-in space complete with a hutch displaying Aunt Glenna's china. "It's my favorite."

"I know. Apple cinnamon cake." Mallory scrunched down and tickled Hazel's belly, and her heart melted at the giggles. "You always asked your grandma to bake it." There was nothing fancy about the one-layer square cake. She always believed all the love her aunt poured into her baked goods made them five-star desserts.

"I helped this time," Hazel said proudly as she hopped back up on the stool and set her gaze back on the cake.

With Hazel there, Mallory wouldn't be able to discuss the issue of the bakery's building because she couldn't guarantee she wouldn't lose her temper with Darlene. Yet again, Darlene would get to avoid that confrontation. At least for the time being.

"What brings you by on a workday?" Darlene gathered up the stainless steel bowls and strainer and set them into the sink. A large window over the sink offered a spectacular view of the two acres she and her husband, Billy, owned. Only about a third of the property had been cleared. The rest had been left untouched, leaving space for deer to bed down in the winter and wildflowers to bloom for butterflies in the spring.

Mallory set the box of cookies on the counter.

"I've been thinking about the Garden Tour. Since I'm more involved now, I'm reminded of how important the event is to the town, and I'd like to do more." Mallory couldn't believe the spin she'd put on her desperate need to get more positive PR for the bakery. And now, with her big corporate order canceled, she needed sales to fill that lost revenue.

Darlene turned around and propped a hand on her hip. "Don't you think you have enough going on? Have you even read the files about the committee you're chairing?"

"Not yet." She held her hand up to stave off any further objections from her cousin. "I will. Tonight. It's tops on my list to do when I get home. I'd like to host a cookie decorating workshop as a fun activity for kids." Yes! Kids! So far, her classes had been geared toward adults, but offering one for the littles would attract more families to the tour. Finally, she might be on to something.

"Can I go? Can I, Mom?" Hazel asked from her perch at the island. Now she was practically standing on the stool. And that earned her a warning look from her mom, which she heeded.

"See, it'll be a hit." Mallory flashed her little cousin a grateful smile. "What do you think, Darlene?"

Darlene returned to the island, her slippered footsteps heavy. She exuded a perfect, blissful domestic life in her hundred-year-old-plus farmhouse with carefully designed gardens and sourdough starter on the counter. Still, she was real about what her days included. For that reason, she favored leggings, tunics, and fuzzy slippers as her go-to uniform when home.

At the island, she lifted the bowl of multicolored eggs gathered from her hens and set them in the refrigerator. Then, after closing the door, she faced Mallory.

"Do you really think you can handle the cookie decorating workshop and everything you have to do? And I mean *everything*."

"What do you mean, *everything*?" Mallory asked, stepping closer to the island and inhaling the sinfully delicious fragrance of the cake. She hoped her cousin would offer her a slice before she left.

Darlene's gaze darted toward her daughter, and then she chose her words carefully. "The situation with Beatrice Wright. I've heard you've been inquiring about what happened to her."

"I don't have a choice since I'm involved with what happened to her . . . even though I didn't do it. I'm doing fine juggling that situation and my responsibilities as a business owner. Though there is a matter relating to the business I haven't been able to fully explore. It's about the building. I keep hitting a wall." Mallory tilted her head sideways. She was proud of herself for not losing her cool in front of Hazel.

Darlene cast her gaze downward. "Fine."

"Does this mean I can do the workshop?" Mallory asked.

"Yes. But I need all the information about it ASAP to add it to the schedule and work on promo for it," Darlene said. "ASAP, like tomorrow."

"Yay!" Hazel's arm shot up in victory. "It's going to be the best ever!"

Back at the island, Darlene set the cake aside and wiped the granite countertop. "I'm sure you have to get back to the bakery."

She shot Mallory a pleading look. She knew her cousin wanted to discuss the building's pending sale, but she didn't want to discuss it in front of Hazel.

"First, there is something I need to ask you about." Mallory leaned her hands on the island. The fear that sparked in her cousin's eyes was priceless. She knew she shouldn't taunt her cousin like that, but the woman was going to sell the building where her business was located. She deserved to feel a little unsteady, as Mallory had when she heard the news from the real estate agent. "Do you know who is on the Mums, Merlot, and Mozart board?"

Darlene's head bowed slightly. It wasn't the question she'd expected, and when her gaze returned to Mallory, she looked grateful.

"Are you thinking of joining another group? You're becoming very civic-minded," Darlene said. Then she quickly checked herself. "Which is a good thing for Wingate. Let's see . . . there are six people on the board . . . Triple M, as it's called, is run by Emerson Lewis. It's one of the fundraising activities that her mother started when she formed her nonprofit. The funds raised are distributed by the nonprofit to charities. Emerson has culled her own A team, so to speak. Triple M is amazing and raises so much money every year."

"Do you know who works with Emerson on Triple M?" Mallory asked.

Darlene rinsed out the cloth in the sink and then set it aside. She gathered plates, forks, and a cake knife. Back at the island, she cut three slices of cake. She slid one plate to her daughter and handed her the fork. Then she slid a plate and fork to Mallory.

"There's Emerson's brother-in-law, Marcus. He owns the Cork and Barrel liquor store. Then there's Jonah, Regina, Caitlyn, and

Annalee. Oh, poor Annalee." Darlene took a bite of the cake, and her eyes rolled in a good way.

"Yummy," Hazel proclaimed.

"Oh my goodness, this is delicious. Just like your mom's," Mallory said between bites. Her cousin was as good a baker as her mother but never had an interest in taking over the bakery. So her attitude about the changes Mallory had made to the business puzzled her. She stopped eating to follow up on Darlene's comment about Annalee. "What happened to her?"

"Her husband had a stroke and she had to resign. It's a shame. She loved the festival."

So it was Annalee's spot Beatrice had been after. Of the five others, who had she blackmailed to get it?

"And I think Caitlyn may be leaving Triple M too. When I ran into her last week she was really upset about something," Darlene continued.

"She didn't say what upset her?" Mallory asked.

"No. But I think it had something to do with losing her job. She worked for Beatrice as a server and Beatrice decided to close the business down to focus on her blog."

Caitlyn must have been the friend Elana had been talking about. Being employed by Beatrice would explain how her indiscretion could have been discovered. But why had Beatrice wanted to get onto the Triple M committee? Mallory was missing something.

After finishing her last piece of cake, she carried the plate and fork to the sink. "Do you know Caitlyn's last name?" She hoped the question sounded innocent.

"Baxter. Why?" Darlene joined Mallory at the sink with her and Hazel's plates and forks. "What are you up to?"

What are you up to? It seemed Mallory could have asked her cousin the same question. Instead, she shrugged it off and murmured, "Just curious." Then she returned to Hazel and gave her a kiss and hug goodbye. "Great job on the cake, moppet. And we'll talk later," she said, passing Darlene.

Mallory stepped outside, hurried down the deck stairs to her bicycle, and climbed back on. This time she really was going back to the bakery. She hadn't pedaled far when she spotted a familiar car in her cousin's driveway.

What the devil was Hannigan doing there?

She halted as Hannigan closed his car door and shook his head. The look on his face indicated that that he wasn't surprised to find her there. But he shouldn't have been. She and Darlene were family. Sure, their relationship was complicated, but they were cousins, and cousins visited each other.

"Is the bakery closed today?" he asked.

She gave a half-hearted laugh. "Kip and Claudia can hold down the fort for a little while. So why are you here at my cousin's house? Oh, no. Is Billy okay?"

"I'm not here about Mr. Hughes. I'm here to talk to Mrs. Hughes. Have a safe ride back to the bakery." He started walking toward the front porch.

"Wait! Why?" She climbed off her bike in a hurry and got her legs tangled up in the pedals. When she finally straightened herself out, she followed after the detective. "Are you here to question her about Beatrice's murder?"

"I cannot comment on an ongoing investigation."

"Oh, come on. Do you really think my cousin wanted to be the chairperson of the Garden Tour committee so badly that she murdered Beatrice? Sure, Darlene is competitive, but she's no killer."

"How long had Darlene wanted to take over the Garden Tour?" he asked, breaking his stride and turning to face her.

"It's not that she wanted to take it over . . . wait, no, don't twist my words."

Again, there was that glint of amusement in Hannigan's brown eyes. She had to wonder if he had intentionally flustered her to get that reaction from her. Now, that set her blood boiling.

"Have a nice day, Miss Monroe." He turned and continued toward the front porch.

Her gaze lingered on his retreating form. His fitted navy blazer skimmed over his strong shoulders and lean body while his pants hugged his taut backside. Instantly, she chided herself for objectifying him. *Wrong, Mal. So very wrong.* But it had felt so right. She suppressed a giggle and then hurried back to her bike. She had a bakery to run, cookies to decorate. And Caitlyn Baxter to track down.

Chapter Fourteen

Mallory pulled open Heavenly Roast's door and stepped inside, and the aroma of freshly ground coffee brewing greeted her. Her eyes fluttered closed as she inhaled. It took only two seconds to switch from her usual pick-me-up in the afternoon, iced matcha tea, to something hot and packed with caffeine. A double shot latte was what she was craving. Crossing the café, she paused a moment when she heard her name. She looked around and found Lauren seated at one of the tables. Changing course, Mallory approached her friend.

Lauren, dressed in her police uniform, sat with a large iced coffee. She gestured for Mallory to take a seat.

"Just the person I wanted to run into." Mallory slung her backpack over the back of her chair. Once settled, she clasped her hands together on the table. "Do you know why Detective Hannigan is talking to Darlene?"

Lauren looked away and chewed on her lower lip. She didn't have a poker face. She knew something—something about Mallory's cousin and Beatrice.

Mallory unclasped her hands and rapped the table with her fingers. "Spill. What do you know?"

Lauren swirled her coffee. She looked conflicted. Mallory suspected there was a professional line she wanted to make sure she didn't cross. Finally, after gulping a drink, she pushed the cup aside and leaned forward. Her voice was hushed. "I'll deny telling you this. Understand?" She waited until Mallory nodded. "Two days before Beatrice's murder, she and Darlene argued."

Mallory was underwhelmed and sank back in her seat. "So? You've met both of them. Neither one ever met an argument they didn't enjoy. And it was probably about the Garden Tour. Is that why he's questioning her?"

"I'm not in the detective unit's inner circle," Lauren said. Her words had a hint of bitterness, but she hadn't expressed an interest in going after a promotion. Though she was pushing thirty and had good instincts that came from years of experience. She'd make an excellent detective.

"Do you know Caitlyn Baxter?" Mallory asked.

Lauren shook her head.

"How about Emerson Lewis?"

"I know of her. Why are you asking about those women?"

"Darlene told me Emerson oversees the Mums, Merlot, and Mozart Festival. And Caitlyn is involved with it too."

"What's going on?"

"Nothing. I'm thinking about the bakery's marketing for fall. I could make cookie bouquets to raffle off. Ooh, a basket of mum cookies!" Mallory clapped her hands together at the thought of an arrangement of multicolored mum-shaped cookies. And she could do a wineglass cookie bouquet. Ideas for cookies started popping up, and she reached for her backpack to grab her phone to make a few notes so she wouldn't forget.

"Ah-ha." Lauren sounded like she wasn't buying Mallory's explanation.

"Thanks for the intel, and my lips are sealed." Mallory stuffed her phone into her backpack. Time to get her coffee and head back to the bakery.

"I saw on social media that you're working with Luke Collins. You know, he worked with Beatrice."

A smile slipped onto Mallory's lips.

"Don't tell me you hired him because he worked with Beatrice?"

Mallory waved off the suggestion. "I didn't know until *after* I hired him. Though he looked familiar to me and not from seeing him around town."

"He has a familiar face. I can't pinpoint where I've seen him before either." Lauren raised her coffee cup.

"Guess he has one of those faces."

Lauren shook her head. "No. I don't think so. It'll come to me."

"Let me know when you figure it out. Have a good day." Mallory stood and went to the counter. While waiting patiently for the couple in front of her to place their order, she couldn't help but overhear the conversation happening at the table closest to her. The three women gathered around the table were Dee, Mac, and Ginger.

"Junk mail," Dee Marshall complained as she sorted through a short stack of envelopes. Her dark hair was pulled back into a severe bun that only a former runway model could get away with. "This one is addressed to Mason Brinkley. You'd think after thirty years any mail for him would stop."

"Guess he never filled out a forwarding address card." Mac set her cup down and grinned.

"Well, if Evelyn had given him the same amount of attention she gave her garden, he would have never left." Ginger sipped her coffee, leaving a bright red lip print on the cup.

"We don't know what went on behind closed doors. Let's not judge," Dee cautioned, waving a finger.

"Good riddance was all I had to say when he left. From what I heard the man was nothing but trouble," Mac added.

Ginger leaned forward. "You know, I used his mysterious disappearance in one of my books years ago. I gave him a whole new life . . . probably better than he deserved, but it was a fascinating story."

"Does Evelyn know?" Dee asked. "She'd have a cow. You know how private she is."

"It's ancient history. Did you know that Susan Pritchard is dating again? Saw her with her new boy toy last week," Mac said.

Mallory side-eyed them. And then shook her head. While she adored each woman, she detested gossip. Perhaps a slight interruption would sidetrack them from speculating on idle rumors.

"Good afternoon, ladies," Mallory said after stepping off the line and approaching the table.

"Mal, how are you holding up?" Dee asked. "Come, join us. I have a few minutes before I need to get back to work." As the owner of Heavenly Roast, Dee was in the café from morning to closing, working behind the counter, cleaning the tables, and ordering supplies. And yet she still found time to sit and chat with her customers and friends.

"Yes, dear, do sit and visit with us." Ginger gestured to the empty chair across from her. "I can't imagine how dreadful it must have been finding a dead body. Especially after having harsh words with Beatrice only hours before."

Mallory pinned a scowl on Ginger. Whose side was she on?

"It's an ongoing investigation, and I shouldn't discuss it." Mallory's reply was met with disappointed looks and murmurs of fake understanding from the ladies. And she didn't feel one bit upset about it.

"Hey, Mal, you're next! Do you want the regular?" Cherie called from behind the counter.

"I have to go. Enjoy your coffees." Mallory dashed back to the counter and gave her latte order. While waiting she checked her phone. She hoped there would be one from Darlene with a message to meet and talk. Or one from Gil saying his boss had changed his mind. Or one from Hannigan saying that he'd made an arrest and she was free and clear.

"Here you go, Mal. Have a nice day." Cherie flashed a smile before taking the next customer's order.

Have a nice day? If only it were that simple.

* * *

The rest of Mallory's day actually wasn't so bad. There were a few walk-ins, and a couple more online orders came through. Still, nothing came in that matched what the bakery had lost with Gil's company's order cancellation. Just thinking about it made her stomach knot.

She'd broken the news to Claudia and Kip when she returned from Heavenly Roast. Then she sulked in her office while she drank her latte and got to work finding a bright spot in the disaster of what was currently her life.

When she emerged from her office, she had a promotion plan to capitalize on the upcoming national holiday celebrating nurses. The news was received lukewarmly by Claudia. As was most everything Mallory shared with her. Meanwhile, Kip started rattling off design ideas. They put their heads together and sketched out a few cookie designs, and high-fived each other when they finished.

By the time she closed the bakery, she was wiped out—physically and emotionally.

Thankfully, Kip offered to come over and make dinner for them. She never turned down an offer for someone else to cook.

* * *

Kip stood at the stove, stirring the quick marinara sauce he whipped up after arriving at Mallory's cottage with a bag of groceries for

155

their dinner. After handing the canvas bag to Mallory, he got to work on the sauce. He emptied cans of tomatoes, crushed and whole, into a saucepot, added chopped garlic, and then sprinkled in spices he found in the lazy Susan cupboard. He worked at warp speed because they had both declared they were starving.

Boiling in the larger pot was their spaghetti, and heating in the oven was their garlic bread. And in Mallory's hand was her wineglass. Leaning against the counter, she admired Kip's culinary dance in her kitchen. He loved to cook and took pleasure in preparing meals for family and friends. She, on the other hand, didn't enjoy cooking and happily let Kip fuss over dinner.

She preferred to bake cookies and then make them pretty. Of course, she did bake cakes occasionally. Like the apple-cinnamon one Darlene and Hazel made earlier. But cookies were her passion, and she had a canister of old-fashioned oatmeal cookies on the counter for dessert.

"When I stopped in Heavenly Roast, Ginger, Dee, and Mac were huddled together, sharing information." She swirled her wine and then sipped. In the canvas bag with the groceries had been a bottle of red wine. While she had limited cooking equipment, she had a wine bottle opener.

"You mean gossiping? It's a wonder the mail gets delivered. Or how Ginger writes her books between gossiping and getting married," Kip said.

Mallory laughed. "It must be eating them alive."

"What is?"

"They know all the goings-on in town, yet they don't know who the killer is. If anybody can solve the murder, it should be them. Right?"

"Always said my dad should hire those three as consultants for the department." Kip taste-tested one of the noodles. "Almost done."

And just in time. Mallory's nose twitched at the aroma coming from the oven, and she proclaimed the garlic bread done. Then, quickly, she set her glass down, grabbed a potholder, and opened the oven door.

The stove and the other major appliances were old and finicky. It wasn't the first time she'd had to work with subpar equipment. Most of her rental apartments in New York City had less than ideal kitchens. She'd learned to rely more on her nose than the timer when using the oven. Baking was no easy feat. There was a very narrow margin of time between the cookies smelling like they'd been perfectly cooked to being sadly burnt. She used two oven thermometers to ensure she was cooking at the right temperature.

Since she expected to stay in the cottage for longer than a year, she had contacted the cottage's owner about replacing the oven. Mr. Winchell had no problem with replacing the out-of-date appliance. She'd been ecstatic. However, he did have a problem paying for it. They'd come to a compromise. A basic, no-frills oven that worked would do, and it would be delivered in a couple of weeks.

She grabbed the edge of the baking sheet, pulling it closer to her, and she inhaled deeply. Her tummy grumbled. When she set the tray on the cooling rack, she caught a glimpse of Agatha seated on a chair at the table. The feline's belly was full from a big dinner Mallory had served after she'd gotten home. After a quick shower and changing into her beloved leggings and a tunic, she'd returned to the kitchen to set the table for dinner. And now she'd taken the bread from the oven. Her job was done. She swiped up her wineglass and sipped.

"It's almost ready," Kip proclaimed as he lifted the strainer insert from the pasta pot and shook. Next, he dumped the spaghetti into the saucepot and turned off the burners.

"It smells so good in here. I'm starving," Mallory said.

"You worked up an appetite today." Kip coated the spaghetti with the sauce, and then he playfully snapped his fingers. Mallory scooted to the table and retrieved the plates. She held them out at the stove for Kip to fill with spaghetti. "Chasing down suspects, peeping into windows while I was stuck at the bakery with Claudia." He made a face and visibly shuddered.

"Oh, stop. It wasn't so bad." Mallory returned to the table with the plates and set them down. Back at the island, she sliced the bread and took a bite as she carried the basket to the table. "Was it?"

"I don't want to spend my off-hours talking about Claudia. I'd rather talk about what you learned today. And work on the murder board." Kip settled at the table and unfolded his napkin, draping it over his lap. He then pointed at Agatha. "Does she have to sit there while we eat?"

"Don't worry, she won't eat any of your pasta. She already had dinner." Mallory didn't waste any time twirling spaghetti onto her fork.

He shook his head. "She's staring at me. It's creepy."

"And eating dinner next to a murder board isn't?" Mallory glanced at the bulletin board.

While Kip had unpacked the groceries, she'd added more index cards with the names Caitlyn, Natalie, Elana, and Evelyn written on them. The one index card she couldn't bring herself to add to the murder board was one that named Darlene as a suspect. Whatever issues they were having, she knew her cousin wasn't a murderer. Which was the rationale she used for not telling Kip about Darlene's argument with Beatrice before the murder or Hannigan's visit.

"You're asking a guy who spent his whole life listening to cop stories at every meal? Trust me, the board is kind of lightweight."

"Lightweight?" Mallory looked at the board again. "There are six suspects on it."

"Pffft." Kip helped himself to a piece of bread. "Where should we start? With Ernie?"

"You know, I don't see a powerful motive. Sure, he benefited from Beatrice's death." Mallory sopped up some sauce with her garlic bread. "But is reinstating the baking contest enough of a motive? Besides, there wasn't any guarantee they would reinstate the contest."

"True." Kip sipped his wine, then said, "I agree with your assessment. Let's move on to the next suspect."

"At first, I thought Daniel only had a financial reason for murdering his wife, but now it appears he might have another reason. Which also gives Natalie a motive," Mallory said. "Then there's the dispute Beatrice had with Evelyn over the property line."

Kip wrinkled his nose. "Seems kind of weak, like Ernie's motive. Killing Beatrice wouldn't resolve the property issue. It is what it is."

"I agree with your assessment. Let's move on. Elana Peterson?" Mallory realized her board was missing a name. "I should add Elana's husband up there, too. They blame Daniel for their money troubles."

"Then why kill Beatrice?" Kip topped off his and Mallory's wineglasses.

"Misplaced anger?" She stood and walked over to the board with her glass in hand. She tapped on Caitlyn's card. "If she's the *friend* Elana was talking about, she has a strong motive. She was being blackmailed."

Kip pushed back his chair and joined Mallory at the board. "And blackmailers rarely keep their word. What if Beatrice tried to get Caitlyn to do something else and used her secret as leverage? The only way to stop it would be to come clean and admit her bad choice, or . . ."

"Get rid of the blackmailer."

They both nodded. She was always amazed at how good it felt when they were in sync, on the same wavelength, simpatico.

A knock on the door interrupted their simpatico moment, and Mallory stepped through the kitchen into the utility room to answer the door. Grabbing the knob, she caught a look through the glass. What was Aspen doing there?

"Hey, Aspen. What's up?" Mallory asked with the door wide open. "It's kind of late."

Aspen glanced at her blinged-out watch and then back at Mallory. "You think so?"

"Who is it, Mal?" Kip called out from the kitchen.

"You have company. I should have called before dropping by. My bad." Though Aspen didn't look too apologetic.

"It's only Kip," Mallory said.

"Hey, I heard that!" Kip said.

"He cooked dinner. Actually, we're finished, so come on in." Mallory stepped aside and let her unexpected guest enter. After closing the door, she led Aspen into the kitchen. "Look who dropped by."

Kip swung around on his chair and smiled. "Hey there, Aspen. What brings you here?"

"I wanted to check in with Mallory. Have you heard anything else from Detective Hannigan?" Aspen looked around the kitchen as she slowly made her way to the table.

This was the second time she had used the excuse of a follow-up interview to talk to Mallory. It seemed more and more that Aspen wasn't a stalker but someone who was lonely and wanted a friend. Then why on earth had she moved to Wingate, where she knew no one? Could Gil's betrayal have been too much for Aspen? Maybe she wasn't a stalker, but she might be unstable, which could be worse.

"Mal? Aspen asked you a question," Kip said, bringing Mallory out of her thoughts.

"Sorry. No, Hannigan hasn't asked for another meeting." Though she wouldn't have been surprised if he did so shortly. Running into him when she was out attempting her own interrogation of Daniel had been unsettling. She wasn't sure if it was because his nickname should be Detective Hottie—gosh, how she hated to admit she found him attractive—or because he saw right through her blatant lie. Either way, she needed to keep a low profile where he was concerned. "Was there another reason you came by?"

"Here, sit." Kip pulled out the other chair for Aspen. "There's some spaghetti left. Would you like a plate?"

"Oh, no, thank you." Aspen sat, placing her bag on the chair that Agatha had vacated sometime during dinner. "There's another reason why I stopped by tonight. I've found out Beatrice's will has already been read. Unless someone contests it, the likelihood of it becoming public is slim."

"That's not helpful," Mallory said as she walked to the cookie jar and plated some oatmeal raisin cookies. She carried the dish to the table and joined Kip and Aspen.

"What is going on with this?" Aspen pointed to the murder board.

Mallory hastily cleared the rest of the table. Then she and Kip filled Aspen in on the murder board over cookies and tea. Aspen listened intently as Mallory went through the suspects so far.

"One thing we should consider is that Caitlyn may not have been the only person Beatrice blackmailed. She could have leveraged secrets to get her way in many situations over the years," Kip said.

Mallory's thoughts flitted back to her cousin. Could the argument she'd had with Beatrice have been about blackmail? If so, what kind of secret could her cousin have? Secrets . . . on the table at Ernie's house he had a stack of papers.

"I remember seeing something at Ernie's house. He cleared off the table when I arrived, and in a pile were racing forms. Then his friend showed up. They were going to Mohegan Sun."

"In the middle of the workday?" Kip took a bite of his second cookie.

"He had the day off. Maybe he has a gambling problem?" Mallory shot up and added the possibility under his name. "Do you think he was embezzling money from the university?"

"What does he do there?" Aspen stirred her tea and then took a sip.

"Admissions director," Kip said.

"My guess is that he wasn't embezzling. More like an admissions scandal." Aspen set her cup down. "If he's a hardcore gambler who isn't any good at it, he needs a steady cash flow to chase his next big win. Parents will pay big bucks to get their kids into college."

Mallory and Kip stared at each other. Aspen's theory made sense.

"Somehow, Beatrice found out. She wanted something in return for staying quiet, but Ernie couldn't take the risk, or she wanted something he couldn't give her." Mallory returned to her seat at the table. "Though he doesn't seem like a killer."

"They never do," Aspen said. She pushed her teacup aside and leaned forward. "You know, this is fun! And I haven't had fun since my weekend away with . . ." Her words trailed off as she caught Mallory's gaze.

Mallory knew what weekend Aspen was referring to and she did her best not to react. Gil and his lies were in her past.

"Anyway, I'd love to join your investigation," Aspen said.

Mallory's gaze drifted to Kip, and he shrugged.

"I can be an asset because I have superb people skills," Aspen said.

Oh, that's what you call it? Mallory couldn't help herself. She still harbored some bitterness toward Aspen, but she was rational enough to know the redhead had been duped by Gil just like Mallory had. Then there was the big question about why Aspen had relocated to Wingate so quickly.

Kip nudged Mallory. It was that *come-on-give-it-a-try* prod.

"It can't hurt to have another ally," he said before finishing his cookie.

Aspen beamed. She had one vote to join the team.

Mallory sighed. She didn't completely agree with Kip's assessment, but since Aspen didn't appear to be going anywhere, she might as well make the best of it. Who knew? Maybe Red could actually help.

"Fine. You're in." Mallory buried her apprehension in another cookie. Eating her feelings was a path to self-loathing and pull-on jeans, but she had a possible arrest hanging over her, and she needed all the help she could get.

* * *

After saying goodnight to her guests, Mallory cleaned up the kitchen before bed. When she was finished, she walked through the living room. The house was silent except for the tick of the wall clock hanging opposite the sofa. The furnishings and accessories that had come with the house were on the old-fashioned side, but they had a quaint charm to them, and each day she was becoming more attached to them. The clock was one of those items she'd like to buy if she took a leap and purchased the cottage. Though becoming a homeowner was a long way down the road. She couldn't imagine taking on more debt at the moment.

On her way to the staircase, she did a quick tidy-up of the old chest in front of the sofa, and she looked around for Agatha. Nowhere in sight. Mallory guessed her furry companion was already upstairs in bed, snoring peacefully. And she intended to join her in a matter of minutes.

She picked up her current read, a psychological thriller about two friends who realize they never really knew each other. One had successfully hidden her envy of her college bestie. The story was a roller-coaster of deceit, betrayals, and lies. She guessed the author had been examining the question of how well we really knew the people in our lives. Tempted to sink into the sofa and read a chapter or two, Mallory glanced up at the clock. Being a baker meant her lifestyle was early-to-bed, early-to-rise. So reading would have to wait. Oh, shoot. She forgot she'd promised Darlene she'd read all those files on the baking contest. Stifling a yawn, she accepted the fact she would break the promise. She tossed the book down and moved to the staircase.

An uncomfortable chilliness worked its way through her body, and she wrapped her arms around herself as she climbed the stairs. The hair on her arms pricked, as did the ones on the back of her neck. She stopped and looked back down at the living room.

Only the tick-tick-tick of the clock.

She was being foolish.

Then again, she'd been seated around the kitchen table discussing suspects and motives casually over dinner.

Her mind ran through the list of names as she continued up the stairs. Then her breath hitched at a sudden, unsettling thought. The murder had happened after she found Gil and Aspen together.

How the Murder Crumbles

She had only Aspen's word that she had broken up with Gil. Heck, she vetted cell phone providers with more scrutiny.

What if *he* had broken up with Aspen? What if she knew about Mallory weeks ago? She knew nothing about the woman, yet she let Aspen into her life so easily. What if she had murdered Beatrice with the intent of framing Mallory?

Chapter Fifteen

The following morning, Mallory arrived at the bakery ten minutes earlier than Kip and Claudia. She parked her bike, grabbed her backpack and went to pick up three hot beverages. Today, the bakery closed an hour earlier than the other five days, which meant all three of them started at the same time. It'd become her tradition to treat Kip and Claudia to their favorite caffeinated drinks. Kip requested a cinnamon dulce latte, Claudia asked for a bold black coffee, and Mallory was torn between a caramel macchiato or a chai tea latte. Her pace was quick, and she reached the Heavenly Roast before another rush of caffeine-depleted Wingaters converged. As she made her way to the counter, she spotted Detective Hannigan seated at a table with a woman. They each had a coffee and looked deep in conversation. She couldn't help but wonder who the woman was. Girlfriend? A flush of warmth hit her cheeks as her muscles tightened. It was none of her business.

"Mallory, do you want to place an order?" Cherie, the barista called out from the counter.

"You're next," the person behind Mallory said.

Mallory murmured an apology and then moved forward to place her order. While the barista prepared the drinks, Mallory's gaze slid back to Hannigan and his coffee companion, who had just let out a laugh, her shoulder-length brunette hair bouncing as her head tipped back.

"All the good ones are taken," Cherie said as she set the drinks in the to-go tray. Her gaze traveled to Hannigan. "It's the third time I've seen him with her."

"Do you know who she is?" As soon as she asked the question she regretted it. When Cherie shook her head, Mallory swiped her credit card and then left the coffee shop. She managed not to look back at the couple on her way out.

Still distracted by her annoying interest in Hannigan and the woman with him, Mallory wasn't paying attention to where she was walking when she exited Heavenly Roast. And because of that, she bumped into someone.

"Oh, I'm so sorry." Luckily, she didn't spill the hot drinks; they only sloshed around a bit and soaked the napkins stuffed into the empty cup holder. When she finally looked up, she recognized the man immediately. Paddy Hannigan. Will's uncle. "I wasn't looking where I was going."

Paddy hooted a laugh. "No harm done. You need to be more careful. You're carrying precious cargo there." He pointed to the coffee tray.

"I am. And I will be," she promised.

"I know you, don't I? I never forget a face." He went silent for a moment, and then there was flicker of recollection in his deep-set eyes. "You were at Ernie's house the other day. Something to do with the Pie Baking Contest. Let me tell you, he's been talking nonstop about it. I still can't believe there was such a fuss about it. For goodness sakes, it's only pie." He stepped around Mallory, heading for the coffee shop's door.

"That's right. I'm Mallory Monroe. You were there picking Ernie up to go to Mohegan Sun. Tell me, did the house win?" Mallory asked.

"The house always wins. Well, at least where Ernie is concerned. I did okay at the slots." Paddy grabbed hold of the door handle.

"Does Ernie go to the casino a lot?" Right away, Mallory realized she should have been less direct.

Paddy shrugged. His friendly eyes clouded over a bit, and his smile slipped. "Nothing wrong with having a little fun at the blackjack table. Or betting on horses."

"Or baking pies." She forced a laugh in hopes of lightening the mood in their conversation. "I was asking because I've been thinking about going to the casino. And since we'll be working together on the pie contest, I thought maybe he could give me some tips."

Paddy leaned forward and lowered his voice. "Ernie's your guy to go to for help with pie baking. But trust me, he's not your guy for tips on betting."

"No?" She puckered her lips and did her best imitation of being disappointed.

"I could give you a few tips." His eye contact intensified. "I have a slot machine system that never fails me."

"Oh, really? How come Ernie doesn't use it? I mean, you said the house always wins where he's concerned."

"It's because he plays blackjack," he said with a shake of his head.

"And he bets on horse racing."

"Yep."

"But he loses a lot," Mallory said.

"Yep. So when you're ready, let me know." He hitched a thumb toward his chest. "I'll teach you a few things." Paddy suddenly reached into his back pocket and pulled out his phone. He squinted to read a message and then looked at Mallory. "I have to meet my nephew. Have a nice day, Miss Monroe." Paddy tipped his head and then entered the coffee shop.

Mallory lingered for long enough to see him approach Will's table and greet the woman with a hug. While she was still curious about who the woman was, Mallory was more curious about what she'd learned from Paddy. It sounded like her theory about Ernie taking money to get unqualified students into Abernathy to cover his gambling losses could be true. Had Beatrice found out? If so, how?

The first person who came to mind was Liz, since she worked at Abernathy. But another name popped into her mind. Chad Bellamy. The student Liz had said had no business getting into the college. He appeared cocky, and he'd razzed Ernie, calling him Mr. Pie-Pie. Clearly the student had no respect for the admissions director. Which he wouldn't if he knew Ernie had sold his integrity for a price.

Mallory started her walk back to the bakery, and her pace quickened because she needed to contact Dugan. With his investigative skills, he should be able to get some intel on Chad. Her footsteps faltered. Bringing in the reporter on only a theory with no proof to back it up could be a mistake. What if she was wrong about Ernie taking money to get students into Abernathy? No. She wouldn't destroy an innocent man's life to clear her name. She'd find another way.

By the time Mallory returned to the bakery, Kip and Claudia had arrived and were getting out of their respective vehicles. Kip drove a hybrid, while Claudia relied on her ten-year-old station wagon for transportation. Mallory sighed. They still kept an empty space between their cars. Hope was fading that the two of them would ever become friends.

"Good morning," Mallory said in her most chipper voice. "I got our drinks."

"Obviously," Claudia said. She clumped along to the back door with her black satchel in her hand. She had on a lavender jacket that added a touch of brightness to her face. Beneath the jacket, she wore her standard black pants and white shirt.

"Well, *I* appreciate the gesture, Mal." As Kip approached the door, he slid off his shades and set them in the messenger bag he had slung crossbody. "Let me take the tray."

Mallory handed over the drinks tray to Kip as she went to unlock the back door. But it was unlocked. She twisted the knob and pushed opened the door. She looked over her shoulder at her employees, who looked as confused as she was. "This is strange. I locked the door last night," she said.

"Are you certain?" asked Claudia.

"Of course I'm certain. I wouldn't leave the bakery unlocked." Mallory took a moment to decide whether to enter. Maybe she did forget to secure the door last night. It was possible. She'd had a lot on her mind lately. She hesitated for another moment and then decided. She was going in . . . with Claudia and Kip. There was safety in numbers.

She pushed the door open cautiously and stepped over the threshold. Then she flicked on the light switch, and the hall where they deposited their outerwear and bags was illuminated. Everything looked okay. She continued, with her employees behind her. All three were silent as they peered into her office.

Nothing appeared out of place.

It was looking more and more like she had forgotten to lock the door. Claudia would never let her live it down. Their next stop was the kitchen. She opened the door and entered their work hub, and she gasped.

"What the . . ." Kip's voice trailed off as he looked over Mallory's shoulder.

"Look at the mess!" Claudia whipped around Mallory. "Who did this? And why?"

How the Murder Crumbles

Mallory swallowed the lump in her throat as she stepped closer to inspect what appeared to be a flour outline in the shape of a body with a marble rolling pin next to it.

"It looks like a body." Kip came up behind Mallory.

"What does it mean?" Claudia asked, pulling out her cell phone. "I'm calling the police."

"This is how I found Beatrice. Her body was outlined by flour and there was a bloodied rolling pin near her body," Mallory finally said. She looked back to Kip and Claudia. "It's a message to me."

This time, Mallory hadn't missed the two letters written in the flour—LL. The next two letters in her name.

"The letters MA were written in flour besides Beatrice's body," Mallory said, staring at the two cryptic letters.

Claudia lowered her phone, her head shaking and her gaze fixed firm on Mallory. "What on earth have you gotten yourself caught up in?"

*　*　*

Mallory's chai tea latte cooled as she sat at one of the café tables by the bay window. The closed sign still hung on the front door, and passersby glanced in with curiosity. Having two Wingate police cruisers parked in front of the bakery would pique anyone's interest. Her shoulders slumped and her spirit tanked as she calculated the cost of having the bakery remain closed. Sure, business had been down the past few days, but there had been customers both in person and online. Now she couldn't even take an order over the telephone.

Not until the police finished their work.

Two uniformed officers had responded after Claudia's 9-1-1 call, and soon after, Hannigan showed up. He spoke with the officers, who both looked as if they'd just graduated from the academy and were stumped by the unusual crime scene.

Word had definitely spread, because Mallory's sister called, and Kip also got calls from his sister and then his father. Mallory had noticed no one called Claudia to check on her.

"Miss Monroe." Hannigan's deep voice had Mallory looking up from her tea. She'd barely taken a sip before finding the cryptic message left for her in the kitchen.

"When will we be able to open?"

"Soon." Hannigan pulled out a chair and settled across the table from Mallory. "When you and your staff arrived, you found the door unlocked. Correct?"

"I had gotten here earlier and chained my bike because I went to Heavenly Roast for drinks. You were there having coffee with someone." She waited for him to say something, like who he had been there with. When he didn't, she continued. "When I got back, Kip and Claudia had arrived and we then went to the back door together."

"Do you remember locking the door last night? We didn't find any signs of forced entry." Hannigan opened his notepad and was ready to jot down notes.

"I thought I had. It's my habit to do so, but I've been distracted lately." Talk about an understatement. She'd been juggling so many balls, it was no wonder she'd dropped one—securing her bakery from an intruder.

"Distracted by playing detective?"

"Distracted by being a person of interest in a murder investigation and watching my dream crumble down around me." She expelled a sharp breath. *Boy, that felt good.* Both the breath and the letting Hannigan know just how much his suspicion of her was costing her.

"I understand . . ."

She leaned forward. "Don't tell me you understand how I feel because you don't. Everything I've worked for could be gone, and for what? You really think I'd risk all of this over a cookie recipe? There are people who really had motives to kill Beatrice."

He dropped his pen and then rubbed his neck. "Miss Monroe . . ." He straightened and then stared into her eyes. In a blink, she was caught up in his gaze. "By insinuating yourself into a murder investigation you are risking your life."

Okay, reality check, and Mallory snapped out of her daze.

"How Mrs. Wright's body was found hasn't been released. So other than the police, only you and the murderer know about the flour outline, the rolling pin, and the letters."

Mallory's brow arched. Oops. She'd told Kip and Claudia. Also, Aspen knew from the interview at the police station.

"Is the rolling pin one of yours or your staff's?" Hannigan asked.

"No. Our rolling pins are accounted for. Whoever did this brought it with them." She should have installed surveillance cameras when she was remodeling the interior of the bakery.

Hannigan wrote on his notepad. "Have you had any other incidents?"

Mallory shook her head. "So you believe I'm not the killer?"

A rapid tapping drew Mallory's gaze to the window, and she found Aspen standing there with a concerned look on her face. She mouthed, "What happened?"

Not sure what to do, Mallory looked back at Hannigan.

"You can let your attorney in," he said.

"Great." She gestured to Aspen to go to the door. She promptly locked the door behind Aspen before returning to her seat.

"Is everyone okay?" Aspen asked. Dressed in capri leggings and a purple fitness tank, she looked as if she'd just come back from a workout. Her hair was swept up in a ponytail and sweat beaded at her temples. "Why are the police here?"

"There appears to have been a break-in, Miss Leigh," Hannigan said, cutting off Mallory's reply. Clearly, he wanted to limit the information released.

Aspen's hand flew up to her chest. "A break-in? How horrible. Was anything stolen?"

"I don't think so," Mallory said.

"Miss Leigh, did you hear anything during the night or early this morning?" Hannigan asked.

"No. I'm a sound sleeper, and I didn't wake up until twenty minutes before my four-mile run. I didn't see anyone lurking around when I left," Aspen added a little too quickly for Mallory's liking. Could she have been the one who'd broken in?

Hannigan closed his notepad and then stood. "We're about to wrap up, and you'll be able to open the bakery. Miss Monroe, please do yourself a favor and confine your activities to decorating cookies."

Confine her activities to decorating cookies? Mallory counted to ten before replying. "Thank you for the suggestion," she said flatly.

A small smile tugged at his lips before he walked away, exiting through the swinging kitchen door. Aspen quickly slid into the vacated chair and leaned her elbow on the table, resting her chin in her palm. "Now tell me everything. It wasn't just a break-in, was it?"

"You really don't know?" Mallory asked.

"Know what? About the break-in? Why would I know anything about it?" Aspen's fake lashes flew high as her eyes widened. She appeared to have come to a realization. "Do you think I had something to do with what happened here? I don't even know what happened."

"Someone left a flour outline of a body with a rolling pin. And the initials LL written in the flour. It was a reenactment of Beatrice's murder scene."

"Oh my gosh! It had to be the killer." Aspen pulled back, dropping her arm to the tabletop. "Wait. Do you think I'm the killer?"

Mallory remained silent.

"You do! Why would I have killed Beatrice? I didn't know her," Aspen said.

"And you don't know me, but here you are living upstairs, representing me, and now a part of my sleuth crew. I'd like to know why you really moved to Wingate."

"Wow. You think I'm stalking you? You think I'm a killer? Here I thought we could be friends."

"Why? Why do you think that? We don't know each other. We only met because I wanted to surprise Gil with dinner."

"I know how we met. It was the night my heart shattered into pieces. It was the night I realized I was alone. It was the night I knew I had to make a major change in my life. I thought you, of all people, would understand. But all along, you thought . . . it doesn't matter now." She wiped away a tear. "I'll leave you alone. You don't have to worry about me." She stood and took a few steps away from the table and then stopped, looking over her shoulder. "You also shouldn't flatter yourself that I would stalk you." Aspen picked her pace up and exited the bakery in a flash.

Mallory dropped her head in her hands. This wasn't how her day was supposed to start. She wished she could have a redo of the entire week, starting when she had the bright idea to surprise Gil with Chinese food.

Now she wasn't sure what to do with Aspen. She needed to think about how she'd handled her upstairs neighbor. What she was certain of was that she wasn't going to be intimidated or told what to do by Hannigan, no matter how handsome he was.

Or how right he was.

* * *

After the police cleared out, Mallory got to work. She had a pickup in less than an hour, and she had two orders to deliver by noon. One delivery was at Abernathy College, which meant she should stop to see Liz and fill her in on the break-in because she hadn't been able to talk long earlier. Though she wasn't up for a lecture, and she was certain Liz would give one. She *was* up for a strong cup of coffee, and she'd just heard the back door open. While Kip cleaned the kitchen floor, Claudia had gone to Heavenly Roast for another round of drinks.

Mallory dashed out to the hall and thanked Claudia for the coffee when she returned. With her coffee in hand, Mallory went into her office to finish some paperwork. A knock at the door drew her head up from the forms she had spread over her desk. She found Kip standing there.

"Mrs. Gable is here for the pickup," he said.

"So soon?" She glanced at her watch. Where had the hour gone? "Be right there." Before standing, she gulped the last of her coffee and dashed out to the front of the bakery. Kip had set the pastry box on the counter next to the register.

Mrs. Gable looked expectantly at the box. She was as excited as her eight-year-old son appeared to be.

Mallory lifted the lid of the pastry box to show Mrs. Gable and her son, Tyler, the special-order cookies for their puppy shower. Their family had adopted a nine-month-old Dalmatian puppy. Tyler's eyes nearly popped out of their sockets when he saw the two dozen cookies. Each in a proper sit position, the pups wore red scarves and had big floppy ears with black button noses and rosy cheeks. Mallory had taken creative license with the Dalmatian's eye-catching black spots and painted them on in heart shapes for more interest.

Mrs. Gable gushed over the cookies and gladly handed over her credit card so Mallory could charge the remaining balance. While she finished up with Mrs. Gable and Tyler, a few other customers came into the bakery, and Mallory's mood lifted. Her horrible start to the day had turned around.

Waving goodbye to mother and son, Mallory flashed the biggest smile she could muster at the other customers who'd entered the bakery. Two seniors muttered greetings as they walked to the pastry case. There they milled about discussing which cookies to buy. A third woman, who entered right behind them, flitted through the bakery. She ended up at the pedestal table where cookies and gourmet apples were displayed.

Mallory noticed the woman seemed to have an intense interest in the bakery's look rather than the abundance of tasty treats.

The stranger confidently carried herself in a well-tailored trench coat over navy ankle pants. Her black hair was cut in a pixie style, and her gold earrings were demure but impressive in their filigree pattern.

Mallory wasn't sure if it was the woman's presence or her interest in the bakery that made her feel something wasn't right. Then it hit her. The woman was probably looking for information about Beatrice's murder. Though she didn't look like the busybody type. Or like a reporter.

"Good morning," Mallory said as she approached the table. "All these apples are hand-dipped from caramel made right here in the bakery."

The woman lowered her phone and pasted on a smile. "How charming."

"We have premade cookie baskets and bouquets and offer custom-designed gifts."

Mallory usually didn't do a hard sell, but she was trying to get a read on the woman. "I'm Mallory, chief baker, decorator, and owner."

"Lovely shop." Her gaze traveled around the bakery as she stepped away from Mallory.

Okay, that was weird. Not wanting to alienate the potential customer, Mallory started to walk away. Then the woman's phone rang, and she answered the call. "Kyra Dunston." She listened for a moment and said, "Yes, I do interiors for cafés and restaurants . . . I think I can." Ms. Dunston walked to the door.

Mallory's heart sank. Kyra Dunston hadn't come in for cookies or hand-dipped apples. She had come in to scope out her next project. Mallory couldn't put it off any longer. She had to talk to Darlene.

"Excuse me," a cheery voice from behind Mallory said. "Could you help me?"

Mallory spun around, ready to make a sale, but nearly teetered over when she saw who was behind her. It was the woman she had seen earlier at the Heavenly Roast with Hannigan.

Chapter Sixteen

"Oh no," the brunette squealed as she lunged forward and reached out to help steady Mallory. Her kind hazel eyes met Mallory's gaze, and she offered an apologetic smile. "I didn't mean to startle you."

Mallory did her best to regain her balance and composure, but she felt a stinging heat on her cheeks. "You didn't. I'm just a little clumsy. Welcome to The Cookie Shop."

"Are those baskets for sale?" she pointed to the shelf behind the counter. Displayed was an assortment of premade cookie baskets. "I really like the small white wicker basket. I think my mom would love it."

"They are for sale. Let me get it for you." Mallory walked to the counter, the customer falling into step with her. They parted ways when Mallory stepped behind the counter and removed the Daisy Cookie Flowerpot from the shelf. It was a happy grouping of cookies. Nine daisy-shaped flowers, each decorated with bright pink dollops in the center, filled the container. Behind the cookies, green tissue paper added more volume and height.

"I don't know your mom, but I think she'll love it. Is it for a special occasion?"

"Not really. I'm hoping they'll lift her mood. It's been rough lately for her." The woman browsed the cookie case. "I'd love a few of those chocolate chip cookies too. Maybe four?"

"Four it is." Mallory set the Daisy Flowerpot on the counter, plucked out four chocolate chip cookies from the case, and added them to a brown paper bag. "These are my favorite cookie. Will you be sharing with your mom?"

"She's a chocolate fiend." She laughed. "This is the first time I've been in here. It's adorable. And these cookies are stunning. Are you the decorator?"

Mallory nodded and introduced herself. She folded the bag closed and carried it to the cash register.

"You know, I think I saw you earlier in Heavenly Roast." Mallory pressed the buttons on the register and totaled the order. "I love their chai tea."

"Oh my gosh. So do I." The customer tapped her credit card on the card reader when prompted. "Will suggested I stop in here."

"Will?"

"Will Hannigan. He told me about your amazing cookies. So I had to pop in." She returned her credit card to her wallet. "Geez. Where are my manners? I'm Caitlyn Baxter. Nice to meet you." She extended her hand to Mallory.

Mallory shook Caitlyn's hand and did her best not to jump into the myriad questions she had for the woman. Had Beatrice blackmailed her? Where had she been the night Beatrice was killed? How well did she know Detective Hannigan? Shoot. The last question was really none of her business. Well, maybe it was. Based on what Elana had said, Caitlyn was a suspect who was cozying up to the lead detective.

"I'm happy to hear Detective Hannigan suggested you stop in. You two good friends?" Mallory slid the cookie pot and pastry bag toward Caitlyn.

"Forever. We go way, way back. In fact, we have a standing coffee date every month. We missed it the other day because of his work." Caitlyn frowned.

"The murder. He must work twenty-four-seven when he's on a case like that," Mallory said.

"Pretty close. Sometimes he can lose himself in a case, so I told him I wouldn't take no for an answer and we'd meet this morning. Then he got called away for work." She sighed.

"The murder case must be his top priority. It's unsettling knowing her murderer is still on the loose."

"It was shocking. Unsettling? I don't think so. My guess is her murder wasn't random. Beatrice alienated a lot of people over the years."

"Is there anybody who comes to mind?" Mallory asked, leaning forward.

Caitlyn gathered her purchases. "It's a very long list." She fixed a puzzled look on Mallory. "Why are you so curious? Is it because you're on that list?"

Mallory's head jerked back at the question just as the kitchen door swung open and Claudia stepped out to the counter.

"I can take over so you can make those deliveries," Claudia said.

"Have a nice day." Caitlyn's words were as rushed as her footsteps to the exit.

"Thanks for the reminder." Though there was little gratitude in Mallory's voice. Her shoulders sagged as she tossed Claudia the side-eye. The baker's timing left a lot to be desired. Now Mallory would have to track Caitlyn down and figure out a way to pick up the conversation with her and tactfully let her know she was also on *the list*. The fact she was close to Hannigan would be a complication.

* * *

On her way to her first delivery at Abernathy College, Mallory made a detour, and it would set her back ten minutes in driving time. But it would be worth it. Evelyn Brinkley's house was on the way to the college. And it was where Mallory knew Darlene would be. She'd accessed her cousin's schedule through one of those files she'd still yet to review for the Garden Tour.

Knowing Darlene's obsession with schedules, time lines, and calendar blocking, Mallory knew somewhere among those files, there would be a document detailing every task, action, and step Darlene would take from the beginning to the end of the Garden Tour.

Mallory didn't know how long the conversation would take. But she figured it wouldn't be pleasant given the topic she would force her cousin to talk about.

Mallory hadn't counted on the uneasy feeling in the pit of her stomach when she arrived at the Brinkley house, which was next door to Beatrice's.

The murder scene.

Which had been reenacted at the bakery.

She parked her car on the road in front of Evelyn's meticulously maintained Dutch Colonial. She enjoyed the sight of the perennial beds that had come out of their winter slumber. Evelyn's gardens were breathtaking. And exactly what she needed to take her mind off the murder. Even if it was only for a moment.

Out of the car, Mallory walked up the driveway. There were three vehicles parked, one she recognized as Darlene's. Then she spotted her cousin. Dressed in wide-leg pants and a bright pink blazer over a white T-shirt, she juggled a clipboard, an electronic tablet, and a cell phone. Beside her was a petite blonde wearing gold-framed shades, nodding as Darlene spoke.

She caught her cousin's eye and waved, and Darlene looked down at her tablet. Mallory's fingers curled into tight balls as she huffed and then propelled forward, making a beeline for Darlene.

"The visitors will begin at the bottom of the driveway." The blonde made a sweeping motion with her hand. "All the parking will be on the street, none in the driveway, like Ms. Brinkley requested. Then they'll be directed up here." She angled her body and pointed to where the pergola stood off the two-car garage.

"We need to talk," Mallory demanded.

Darlene shook her head. "I don't have time. We're in the middle of something."

"Make the time." Mallory folded her arms and rooted herself. She wasn't budging.

The blonde, stuck between the cousins, looked nervously at them. "You know what, I'll go check on Ms. Brinkley." She offered a faint smile before fleeing.

Darlene let out a long, exasperated sigh. "Jake Lewis told me he ran into you and mentioned the offer I had on the building."

"So it's true? You're going to sell? What's going to happen to the bakery? What kind of lease will I have? Will there be a provision in the sale that my rent doesn't get jacked up?"

"We haven't gotten to those details yet."

"Then why was a commercial interior designer scoping out the bakery less than an hour ago?" Mallory unfolded her arms and propped her hands on her hips. Simultaneously, she lifted her chin, and her gaze locked on Darlene. This was a power stance from her days at the ad agency she had used when dealing with associates who had tried to undermine her.

Darlene blinked rapidly as she chewed on her lower lip.

It looked like Mallory hadn't lost her touch.

"I . . . I have no idea," Darlene said.

"Why are you selling the building? You know your mom wanted me to take over the bakery. Do you really hate me that much?" Mallory waited for an answer, but none was forthcoming.

"Silence? I guess I know the answer." She spun around and stormed off. She couldn't get away from her cousin fast enough.

Tears stung her eyes, and her chin quivered. This was why she'd avoided having the conversation with Darlene. She hadn't wanted to hear the truth that her cousin had found a way to truly hurt Mallory.

"Hello," Evelyn called out as she cut across her lawn, reaching the garden bed that stretched the length of the driveway. Her cotton skirt flitted in the soft breeze, and a sun hat shielded her porcelain skin from the sun. In the crook of her arm was a basket overflowing with fresh-cut flowers. As she got closer, tiny lines feathered out from her steel blue eyes, which appeared concerned. "Are you okay, dear?"

Mallory composed herself in record time, swallowing her hurt and anger.

Those emotions wouldn't serve her. Not now. She channeled corporate Mallory—the person who'd faced cutthroat competition every day at the ad agency. Also, the person who had ultimately lost out on a big promotion thanks to a ruthless coworker. Setting aside her career setback, she did what she'd always done: stayed alert and flexible. Now she had to remain open to whatever Darlene's decision brought her.

After all, what choice did she have?

"Hello, Mrs. Brinkley," Mallory said, grateful her voice didn't crack.

"It's Ms. Brinkley," she corrected. "I've been on my own for decades." She carefully stepped through the garden bed. Clusters of tulips stood tall and cheery while masses of hyacinths, snowdrops, and bluebells created a blanket of color that was a welcome sight after the harsh winter Wingate had endured. "But you can call me Evelyn. Are you helping with the tour?"

"I'm chairing the Pie Baking Contest. I stopped by to speak to my cousin." *To confirm she stabbed me in the back.* So it seemed Darlene and Mallory's former ruthless coworker had a lot in common. Though this betrayal had sliced straight through Mallory's heart like none other. Not even Gil's cheating.

"It's marvelous the contest is back. I so enjoy tasting all the entries. Darlene is doing a superb job, don't you think? She's so much more pleasant to deal with than Beatrice."

Well, it depends on who you are.

Mallory let go of the thought because at the moment it served no purpose. She was having a one-on-one with Evelyn, who might have had a motive for murder. She couldn't waste the opportunity, no matter how awful her cousin was.

"It must have been awkward having your garden on the tour while being in the middle of a property line dispute with Beatrice."

Evelyn tilted her head slightly, and her upper lip curled. "Our little disagreement didn't even escape the attention of the town's cookie baker."

"From what I heard it wasn't a little disagreement. Do you mind if I ask what caused the rift?"

"Never forget that people like to embellish things. It was just a misunderstanding. Beatrice had wanted to build a garden shed. You see, before this entire area was subdivided, it used to be farmland. The original owner wasn't careful when the land was broken up. As a result, the lots weren't cookie-cutter rectangular shaped. Instead, there are odd jags along the dividing lines. On the side of my property that borders Beatrice's land," Evelyn turned and pointed, "there's a huge oval cutout that's technically mine. I've always thought it would be perfect for another pond. Anyway, Beatrice had thought it belonged to her." Evelyn lowered her hand and slipped it into her skirt's pocket. "Thankfully, the matter is settled now."

"How so?" Mallory asked.

"Daniel isn't a gardener. The man has never once cut the lawn, so he won't be needing a garden shed."

Mallory shrugged. "Probably not. Now there's the whole matter of who killed her."

"Many people disliked Queen Bea. Including yourself." After adding those two last words, a small smile tugged at Evelyn's lips. "It was nice talking to you. Have a beautiful day." She turned and wandered away, crossing the lawn toward her home's front door.

Including yourself.

Those two words both stung and infuriated Mallory. They were also a reminder she had a lot of work to do to clear her name. If only the police would make an arrest. Then speculation about her involvement in the murder would subside, and life would return to normal. Okay, not exactly, since she had to deal with the possibility of relocating the bakery.

Where would she start that search? There weren't any available storefronts on Main Street. If there were, she doubted she'd be able to afford them. When she bought the bakery business, she'd negotiated a fair rent with her aunt. She worried a new landlord wouldn't be as accommodating.

Returning to her Jetta, the feeling of being overwhelmed consumed her. There were too many balls to juggle. And those balls were made of glass. One slip of the hand, and she was certain one, if not all, of the balls would fall and shatter into a million tiny pieces. She sucked in a ragged breath and tried to steady her racing mind. Then she tried sorting her thoughts into little compartments to keep her sanity.

There was the Darlene box stuffed to the top with hurt and betrayal.

There was the Aspen box packed tightly with ambiguity and suspicion.

There was the murder box overflowing with fear and curiosity. Whoa!

She stopped at box number three when it hit her. The technique had come from Claudia.

Okay, it was official. The only thing worse than Claudia being right was starting to agree with her life philosophy.

What was happening to her?

She'd arrived at the driver's side door, ready to get in, when she noticed a plump woman dragging a sign out of the back of a gray Lexus. She lugged the sign to a prominent space on the front lawn.

It was a For Sale sign.

It looked like Daniel wasn't wasting any time.

Mallory leaned her arm on the door's frame as she watched the real estate agent efficiently set up the sign. Even though Daniel's name wasn't on the deed, he was probably the beneficiary of his wife's will. Proceeds from the house sale could pay off some debts. How fortunate for him.

Chapter Seventeen

Mallory retrieved the Beary Good Luck to You Supreme from the back seat. Then, juggling the cookie tray, she closed the car door and proceeded to the administration building's entrance. When she reached the double doors, an exiting student held the door open for her. She nodded her thanks as she stepped into the hallowed halls of higher education. It was still unbelievable to her that her sister was a professor. When Mallory was in college, all her professors had seemed so much older than her. Looking back, several of them were probably close to Liz's age.

She strolled along the corridor, excited to be delivering the cookies. She couldn't wait to see the look on Martha Radcliff's face. After thirty years, Martha was finally retiring. Mallory remembered how helpful the secretary had been with Liz during her senior year in high school when she had applied to Abernathy. At the time, they hadn't known that Liz would flourish at the college and decide to build her career there. Because of the special connection, Mallory threw in extra cookies. She'd found out Martha loved teddy bears and had quite a collection, so she baked and decorated five teddy bear–shaped cookies.

Being a small part of Martha's celebration helped Mallory briefly shove aside all thoughts about Beatrice and Darlene. Now she was doing exactly what she'd dreamed of doing for years.

Up ahead, she saw the sign for the admissions department. Cheerful voices drifted from the office. It sounded like the celebrating had begun.

Her pace quickened, and she reached the partially opened door, prepared to make a grand entrance, leading with the massive tray of cookies.

"Happy retirement, Martha." Mallory stepped into the office, filled with a dozen people standing around the smiling retiree.

Gift bags and balloons covered her desk while a Happy Retirement banner was hung on the wall behind her. On the credenza was a half-sheet cake ready to be sliced.

Martha's pale blue eyes lit up as she clapped her hands together when she saw the cookie tray. Her coworkers parted, allowing Mallory to reach the desk. Standing off to Martha's side was Liz, who beamed with delight.

"Oh, look at those cookies!" Martha didn't waste any time inspecting her gift. "They're exquisite. Look at the teddy bears! They're adorable."

"Geez, they really look like the ones you collect," said the middle-aged man with a comb-over next to Mallory. His breath smelled of cigarette smoke, mouthwash, and coffee. Mallory eased away.

"This is from all of us," Liz said as she stepped away from Martha's desk and toward her sister. "It's gorgeous, Mal."

"Thank you." As much as Mallory wanted to stay a part of the celebration a little longer, she couldn't. She had another delivery to make. She also wanted to fill Liz in on the break-in at the bakery. "Do you have a minute?"

Liz nodded. "I'll be right back," she said, but everyone was so captivated by the cookies, they didn't acknowledge her.

Mallory turned and walked out of the office with her sister in tow. She recapped what had happened and shared the disappointing news that there were no leads yet. She also assured her sister everything would be okay.

"Everything is not going to be okay. Why would someone re-create the murder scene in the bakery's kitchen?" Liz asked. "I'll tell you why."

Mallory shook her head. "No need. It was a message, and I got it. Loud and clear."

"Good. Now I hope you've learned a lesson, and you'll let the police handle the matter with no further interference." Liz's attention drifted back to the office, where her colleagues munched on cookies.

Mallory hated bursting her sister's assumption bubble, but she had no choice. "I didn't say those words."

Liz's gaze shot back to Mallory. "You know, sometimes you can be infuriating. The killer left a warning for you. What more has to happen for you to back off?"

"An arrest to be made and my name cleared. Look, I'm not doing anything dangerous. I'm only coming up with theories and asking a few questions." So far.

"You're also exasperating," Liz said.

"And I'm running late. But I have a question before I go. What can you tell me about Chad Bellamy?"

Liz crossed her arms. "You think he killed Beatrice?"

Mallory shrugged. "I don't know."

"I think you're wrong in considering him. I don't believe he's smart enough to plan a murder. And he was Beatrice's nephew."

Mallory's mouth dropped open. Flabbergasted, her thoughts muddled together, and she couldn't say a word.

"Excuse me, ladies." Ernie Hollis appeared at the doorway with a briefcase in one hand and an oatmeal raisin cookie in the other.

Liz shuffled back, giving him space to exit. "You're not staying for the party? Martha still has to open her presents."

Ernie flashed an amiable smile. "I have to meet somebody. So you all have fun." He then slid his gaze to Mallory, and his smile faded.

Mallory hadn't moved when Ernie came out of the office. Instead, she was busy putting together the bits of information she'd collected.

Chad was a lackluster student and related to Beatrice.

Ernie was an unlucky gambler.

Beatrice had been accused of blackmailing people for favors.

Mallory came up with one possible favor that included all three of them—Beatrice had wanted her nephew to get into a good college. Hence, she dug up dirt on Ernie and leveraged it to get Chad admitted to Abernathy.

Liz cleared her throat, prompting Mallory to say something. "Too bad you have to leave. Enjoy the cookie."

Ernie simply nodded and then took off.

Mallory couldn't help but wonder where was he going in the middle of the workday? A quick trip to the casino? Or was he meeting with a bookie? Were there any in Wingate? There was only one way to find out what he was up to.

"I have to go. Talk soon. Love you." Mallory bolted, not giving her sister any time to object.

Outside, she spied Ernie getting into his dark sedan. She raced to her car and got in. When he pulled out of his space, she did too. Slowly, she followed him through the winding two-lane road that cut through the campus. Once they passed through the main gate, she kept a safe distance behind Ernie's car to avoid being noticed.

What on earth was she doing? Following a murder suspect? He could have been on his way to the Massachusetts or New York border for all she knew. Or to an underground gambling den. She shuddered at the thought of some dingy location with no cell service. Or he could be headed to Mohegan Sun for an afternoon of blackjack. At least there was cell service there, and food.

Or to a storage unit?

Up ahead, Ernie pulled into the Make Space Storage facility, which was a short drive from the college campus. In a split second, she decided to follow when she noticed the entry gate was open. It looked like the security keypad was for decoration only. She drove slowly, keeping ample space between their cars. Lucky for her, the grounds of the storage facility were spacious. It was amazing how much stuff Americans had to store.

Ernie's car turned left down a row of exterior units. She considered following, but she didn't want to be seen, so she parked along the end of the building. Mallory got out of her car and darted to the corner. Slowly, she extended her neck, and she had a view of the two rows of storage units. Ernie's vehicle wasn't the only one parked there. In front of another unit was a pickup truck.

Ernie got out of his car and walked toward the man standing between the black truck and an open unit. While she couldn't get a clear look at the stranger's face, she saw Ernie pull out a thick envelope from his jacket pocket and hand it to the man. They exchanged a few words, and then Ernie returned to his car. The stranger then tossed the envelope onto the front seat of his truck as Ernie drove away, following the exit signage.

Mallory pulled back and raced back to her Jetta. She'd wait a few minutes before driving through the row of units to leave the facility's property. While waiting, she realized Ernie would pass her on his way out, so she ducked down so she wouldn't be seen when he drove by. She was crouched down for a few minutes, and when she heard a vehicle pass, she slowly eased up and saw the taillights of Ernie's car reaching the open gate. She wasted no time in starting the ignition and getting out of there. Though she had to drive by the stranger Ernie had met with. The upside was that she could get a look inside his storage unit. The downside was she could be noticed. But there wasn't any choice. She had to leave. Mallory made her way around the loop, getting only a quick glimpse of the unit because the parked truck blocked most of the view. Lucky for her, the stranger was inside the unit, so he didn't see her pass by.

A few minutes later, she arrived at the exit. Ernie was long gone, and she was ready to pull out onto the main road. While she waited for a break in traffic, she thought about what she'd seen. The unit had been packed with construction supplies, and it looked like Ernie had been making a payment to the stranger. After all, what else could have been in that thick envelope?

After leaving the storage facility, Mallory drove to her next delivery stop. Before getting out of her car at Judith Madison's home, she mustered her best smile. She channeled the enthusiasm she had felt when she'd arrived at Abernathy to deliver Martha's cookie tray. The delight on Mrs. Madison's face was a mood booster, but unfortunately, the elation didn't last very long. By the time she was back in her car, her energy had depleted. Poof. Vanished. Gone. She should have been shifting the car into drive and going back to the bakery. Instead, she called Kip to tell him she would pick up lunch and be back later.

Mallory drove around for thirty minutes before deciding on dining by the water. Her nerves had been on edge all day, causing an antsy feeling she couldn't settle no matter how many deep breaths she took. Perhaps getting away from Wingate would help.

She eventually arrived in Middletown, a city located along the Connecticut River. Once a thriving port town, it was now home to Wesleyan University and to a thriving Main Street that maintained its historic character by careful preservation.

She parked her Jetta and then got a sandwich and soda from a deli. She found a bench with a view of the Connecticut River, the longest one in the New England region, and sat to enjoy her meal. She forced herself not to think about the murder or Darlene or following Ernie. The lull of the slow-moving water steadied her frayed nerves. And the birdcalls filling the air as she sipped her drink brought her a joy she'd been craving since the morning Beatrice had crashed her interview with Dugan. A few times, her gaze turned upward toward the lyrical notes and the sun's warmth.

When she was left with nothing more than a sandwich wrapper and an empty bottle, Mallory knew her respite from life had come to an end. It was time to go back to Wingate. Back to the bakery. Gathering her trash, she reluctantly stood and gave one last sweeping look out over the river.

* * *

She arrived back at the bakery in time to witness a mini-rush of customers. This boded well for her psyche, encouraging her to get into the kitchen and bake and decorate her heart out. All the while, careful not to step on the spot where the flour outline of a body had been. A few times when she sidestepped the area, she earned a disapproving look from Claudia. While the cookies baked, Kip handled the front of the bakery. He'd reported that word had spread about the break-in and the flour outline.

"It was all they were talking about." Those were his exact words when he came in looking for more of the Almond Melt-aways. They'd become the bakery's top seller. The reason was morbid, but Kip reminded her the money was much needed. So she baked more of the infamous cookies.

By the time Mallory turned over the closed sign on the front door, her whole body ached. From her toes to her scalp; she felt achy and fatigued. Claudia had also looked tired when she said goodnight. Meanwhile, Kip lingered and invited Mallory out to dinner. The offer was thoughtful, but all she wanted was to go home, feed Agatha, forage for whatever leftovers she had, and then go up to bed with a book. Waving goodbye to Kip, she tossed her backpack into the Jetta and then got in.

Her night's plan also included an attempt to channel her afternoon by the Connecticut River. She'd love a night free of racing thoughts and too many tosses and turns to count. Of course, an easy way to end those things would be to heed the warning left for her that morning. Too bad she never listened well.

* * *

Another fitful night of sleep resulted in Mallory giving up and reading into the wee hours of the morning. When her alarm went off, she hit the snooze button repeatedly. Finally, she decided to call Kip and tell him she'd be in later. Groggy from lack of sleep, she wasn't sure if she made sense, but by the end of the call, he'd told her to take the whole day off if she needed to. She thanked him for his support but planned to be in the bakery at some point. Not having to rush first thing in the morning would allow her to ease into her day, and maybe she'd be able to put everything into perspective.

As she dropped a pod into her fancy coffee machine—a treat she'd purchased after buying the bakery—she considered how she would start the new day. Since taking over the business, the only mornings she had to herself had been Mondays when the shop was closed. It hadn't meant she wasn't working because there were house chores to do, and she was always practicing her cookie art or recipe testing. While she waited for her dark rich roast to brew, she fed Agatha. With the cat taken care of and her coffee mug filled, she walked out of the house through the back door. Her destination was the pond.

The ground was soft from a passing shower overnight. She'd heard the rain tapping against the bedroom window while reading. Now droplets remained on the leaves of the tall, broad trees that lined the path to the pond. There the body of water was still, unlike the river yesterday. After wiping the Adirondack chair with a paper towel, she sank into it and sipped her coffee.

She'd been wanting to do this since moving into the cottage. It looked like she needed a serious problem to work through to spend time by the pond. Well, now she had one. After sipping her coffee, she dropped her head back, closed her eyes, and let her mind sort through what had turned into a devil of a week. From the scene at the bakery with Beatrice, which still had her cringing, to finding the dead body, to the threat, to Darlene's secret real estate deal, to following Ernie. Out of those things, what disturbed her the most was her impulsive decision to tail Ernie. Who knew what kind of trouble she could have driven into?

She stared at the calm water, wishing her life was as tranquil. Her life would have been if she'd stayed at the advertising agency. Working sixty-hour weeks, seeing when their schedules aligned, and spending nights curled up with Agatha reading a book.

But would she have been happy?

She took another sip of her coffee. Despite the crappy days life was hurling at her, she was happy with her new life in Wingate. She was doing what she loved, making new friends and becoming a part of a community. Though recent events were starting to outweigh those good things.

Her life had been threatened, her love life had blown up, and her business was at risk of failing. And she could be arrested for murder.

She shook her head. Sitting there feeling sorry for herself wasn't helping. She set her mug down on the arm of the chair and looked around. This was supposed to be her contemplating spot, not her pity-party spot.

Time to stop wallowing. Time to pull up her big girl panties and face every obstacle in front of her head on. Then knock them down.

Mallory pushed herself up from the chair and inhaled a deep breath before stepping forward. Her steps were small and light as she made her way to the pond. She didn't want to disturb the stillness that surrounded her. Instead, she tried to absorb it into every fiber of her body.

She was tempted to kick off her sneakers and let her toes wiggle in the water. A warm breeze trickled by, gently swaying the branches of the nearby trees and sweeping a fragrant scent around her from the wildflowers. Lulled into the tranquil state she'd been yearning for, she undid her ponytail and shook her hair free, running a hand through it.

This was her life. Nothing had been guaranteed, so she needed to make the best of it, whatever happened. If her fledgling business could survive this bump in the road, it could withstand anything.

A sound caught her attention. The crack of a tree branch? A squirrel rummaging? A deer grazing?

There it was again. The same sound she had heard the night she'd found Beatrice's body. Right before she approached the kitchen door.

She listened again.

Silence.

Just because it was quiet didn't mean she was alone. Someone was there. She was certain.

Goose bumps skittered over her already crawling skin.

She reached into her jogger's pocket for her phone. Shoot. She'd left it on the kitchen counter.

She began to turn around, but a blow to the back of her head stopped her.

A sharp pain ricocheted through her skull, rocking her body. She screamed as a kaleidoscope of colors burst in her eyes. Her cry faded as her body crumpled to the wet ground, landing face down in the dirt.

Chapter Eighteen

Mallory's body stirred as her eyes flickered open and closed while her brain tried to process why she was lying on the ground. And why she had the mother of all headaches.

"Mallory! Mallory! Are you okay?"

The alarmed voice wreaked havoc with the throbbing in Mallory's head. Too, too loud. She pushed herself up, giving space between her muddied thermal shirt and the cold, wet earth.

"What happened?" Dugan appeared, crouched beside her and reaching for her arm to help her up. "Did you faint or something?"

"No . . . I don't think so." Her rapid heart rate made it difficult for her to think clearly. Too much oxygen was being used up, her brain was foggy, and she hurt.

"What happened?"

"I came out here to think . . . then I got up and walked to the water . . . then . . . fainted? No, no. I didn't faint! I was hit on the head!" She recoiled from Dugan's hold, throwing her body off kilter. She wobbled to regain her balance and sat up.

"Whoa!" Dugan's palms raised. "You think I hit you?"

Mallory swallowed, and she remained silent for a moment as her body trembled. Honestly, she didn't know what she thought. She wasn't even sure of what had happened.

"I didn't see anyone. But you're the only one here." She wiped her hands together to remove the dirt and then wound her right hand around to the back of her head, where she remembered feeling the strike. She flinched when her fingers touched the spot.

"And you should feel lucky that I'm here. We have to call the police and report this." He pulled out his cell phone and punched in three numbers. "You have no idea who did this to you?"

"No." Mallory's lips pressed together. She'd sensed someone behind her. Why hadn't she reacted sooner? Faster? Defended herself? She could have drowned if her face had fallen into the water.

She stared at the pond. To think, not too long ago, she'd thought the still water tranquil.

"She's conscious now." Dugan finished with the emergency dispatcher and ended the call. "The police are on their way."

"Lot of good it'll do. I didn't see anything. I only heard . . ."

"Heard what?"

"I guess it was someone approaching. They must have stepped on a branch or something." Mallory moved to stand up, but Dugan intercepted, lunging toward her and grabbing her arm again. "I think I'm okay to stand."

"At least come and sit." He assisted her up and then guided her to the Adirondack chair.

As Mallory eased into the chair, she noticed she'd gotten dirt on Dugan's gray button-down shirt. And then she glanced at herself. Dirt smudged all over her top and joggers. Settled, she propped her elbow on the chair's arm and rested her forehead in her palm.

"I can't believe someone did this to me."

"Someone is sending you some very serious messages. Yesterday, there was the flour outline at the bakery, and now this."

"You heard about that?"

"Are you kidding me? The whole town has by now. It's one reason why I'm here. I called the bakery, and Kip said you were coming in later." Dugan pulled back from the chair and looked around. "Nice place you got here. Quiet, remote."

"Perfect place for a crazed killer to visit." Mallory cracked her first smile of the day.

Dugan chuckled. "I'm sure that wasn't on the real estate listing."

"Are you sure you didn't see anyone when you arrived?" It disappointed her when he shook his head. "Darn. I'm going to be of no help to the police. Why exactly are you here?"

"I have a few questions about yesterday," Dugan said.

"I'm afraid I can't tell you much. Someone gained access to the bakery and left an outline of a body in flour with a rolling pin next to it."

"Rolling pin?" Dugan tapped on his phone, and then his fingertips flew over the keyboard.

Oops. That probably was a detail Hannigan hadn't wanted to be released to the press.

"It's not much of a stretch to think that these two incidents are connected." He looked up from his phone. "What have you been up to?"

Before Mallory could tell him, sirens broke through the quiet morning air. She'd have to give another statement. Number three. Carefully, she twisted and then peered over the back of the chair in time to see Lauren exit her patrol car.

As Lauren got closer, a deep look of concern was etched on her face.

"Are you okay?" Lauren asked when she reached Mallory and Dugan. "Do you need an ambulance?"

Before Mallory could answer "no," Dugan stepped forward and said, "She'd been unconscious and was only starting to come to when I found her."

Lauren nodded and wrapped her hand around the radio mic on her vest. "The hospital it is."

"No. Wait. I'm fine," Mallory insisted.

"Not if you were struck on the head and unconscious," Lauren replied before requesting an ETA on the ambulance. "Mr. Porter, what are you doing here?"

"I wanted to ask Mallory about the incident at the bakery yesterday," Dugan said.

"Why aren't you at the bakery now?" Lauren asked her friend.

"I didn't sleep well, and I needed to think through some things, so I took the morning off." She'd think long and hard before taking another morning off again.

"Who else knew you were home?" Lauren asked.

"Kip and Claudia. But I don't know who else they told," Mallory said.

"Kip told me when I called the bakery earlier," Dugan added.

"What time did you call him?" Lauren had pulled out her notepad and jotted something down.

Dugan shrugged. "About fifteen minutes ago."

"Did you come straight here after the call?" Lauren looked up from her pad, her pen poised to write.

"You think I hurt her?" Dugan's voice was filled with indignation.

"I'm only asking questions to gather information." Lauren lowered her notepad and rested her hand on her utility belt. Her next question was to Mallory. "Did you see the person who hit you?"

Mallory shook her head. Big mistake. A sheath of white-hot pain shot through her head, down to her neck and shoulders.

When she stopped seeing stars, Mallory said, "I was facing the pond. Then I was struck from behind."

"Do you have any idea what was used to hit you?" Lauren asked.

"A rolling pin?" Dugan guessed. His comment got him a glare from Lauren. Mallory hoped he wouldn't reveal that detail in his article. More importantly, she hoped he wouldn't reveal who had told him.

"I'm not sure," Mallory said. "Maybe something like a thick tree limb. If it was a rock, I doubt I'd be conscious right now."

"Let me take a look." Lauren stepped forward and gestured for Mallory to lower her head for inspection. Mallory inhaled the clean scent of Lauren's body spray. When she was on duty, Lauren maintained a professional appearance with minimal makeup and jewelry. But she wouldn't forgo her favorite fragrance. "No bleeding. You're lucky. Maybe it was a tree limb or thick stick, and whoever did this didn't use too much force."

"It sure didn't feel like it," Mallory quipped.

Lauren stepped back from her friend and looked at Dugan. "Where did you find her?"

He pointed to the spot by the edge of the pond. "She was face down."

Lauren cautiously approached the area and looked in all directions—up, down, and sideways. "I'm not seeing anything that could have been used as a weapon. The attacker probably took off with whatever was used to hit you. There are some footprints. Looks like they came from over there." She pointed to a thicket of skinny trees in various stages of decay. It was an area in desperate need of clearing, but Mallory had noticed it provided shelter to some wildlife. And now, possibly, a killer.

"The attack was planned." Dugan lifted his phone and started typing again.

"I can't speculate." Lauren shifted and then noticed Dugan on his phone. "What are you doing? Are you here as a reporter?"

"Well . . . I came to ask her questions about the incident yesterday," Dugan said.

"Then you need to go back to your vehicle. I'll get your official statement in a few minutes," Lauren said.

"He's not here as a reporter. He did come to ask about yesterday but only because he was concerned, right, Dugan?" Mallory's eyes narrowed, and her lips pursed as she attempted to mentally will him to say the right thing. Like it or not, he was starting to grow on her. And she wasn't a hundred percent sure that he had hit her. Mostly because she couldn't figure out why he would have.

"Right. She's right," Dugan said, lowering his phone.

Lauren's expression made it clear she wasn't buying what Mallory and Dugan were trying to sell. But with a shake of the head, she'd moved on, past the blatant fib.

"So that we're all on the same page, everything is off the record." Not waiting for a response from the reporter, Lauren returned to her friend's side. "Let's get you in your house, and I'll write up the incident report."

Dugan slipped his phone back into his pocket and went to Mallory's other side to help steady her.

"I'm fine. I can manage on my own." Mallory swayed a bit as she found her footing and quickly flashed a reassuring smile. But the movement was too fast and left her light-headed.

"Ah-ha." Lauren sounded unconvinced as she walked alongside Mallory to the cottage's back door.

Dugan bypassed them and reached the door first. He pushed it open and stepped aside to let Mallory and Lauren enter ahead of him. Inside the utility room, Agatha greeted them. Meowing loudly, she slinked around Mallory's legs, causing her shaky balance to waver.

"I wish you'd reconsider going to the emergency department." Lauren pulled out a chair at the table for Mallory and then sat across from her. "If you don't go, I have to insist, as your friend, that someone stay with you."

Mallory looked at Dugan, who now stood at the island. No, he couldn't stay. Lauren couldn't stay either. She had to get back to work and find the person who hit Mallory.

"I'll call Kip." She hoped that would suffice for Lauren. "Maybe he can come over for a few hours. Claudia can handle the bakery for a little while."

"Go ahead, call him. I'm not leaving until someone is here with you. Head injuries are serious. Last year I responded to a wellness check and found the man dead on his sofa. After hitting his head while playing some hoops with his buddies, he'd fallen asleep. No one stayed with him."

"That poor guy." Mallory chewed on her lower lip, rethinking her decision not to be checked out by a doctor. "Maybe I should go to the emergency room. But I don't want to go in an ambulance."

"I'll drive you!" Dugan offered, perhaps a little too eagerly, Mallory thought.

"I'd prefer an ambulance transport. However, I'm happy you're going to the hospital. I'll cancel the ambulance." Lauren stood, seemingly satisfied she'd gotten her way. "Where are your purse and keys?"

Before she knew it, Mallory was seated in Dugan's pickup truck. A stale odor hung in the air, and she guessed it was from the trash that had littered the seat and floorboard. It'd taken him a few minutes to clear off the bucket seat, stashing loose papers, empty soda bottles, and potato chip bags on the jump seat.

It looked like he lived in his vehicle.

While she sent off text messages to Kip and Liz, her driver jogged around the truck's hood and then climbed behind the steering wheel. He wasted no time getting his truck on the road to the nearest emergency room.

And Kip and Liz wasted no time in replying to Mallory's update.

First, from Kip—**OMG. You know what this means. You're making the killer nervous.**

Next, from Liz—**You're on your own telling Mom about this. Let me know what you need me to do. Hugs.**

Mallory turned her phone over on her lap and stared out the windshield.

"I don't think what happened was random. Now tell me what you've been up to." Dugan slowed as they came to a yellow light at an intersection. "I know it's why you got knocked on the noggin."

Staring at his profile as he kept his eyes on the road, she couldn't argue with his assessment of her current predicament.

"Why are you staring at me?" He gave her a quick glance. "You still don't trust me, do you?"

"I sort of do," she said with a half shrug.

"Yeah, very reassuring. Here's the deal, Mal. May I call you Mal?"

"Sure."

"You want to clear your name, and I want a front-page byline in print and on the web. I figure we work together to get what we both want. Sound good?"

"I suppose."

"Again, very reassuring." The sarcasm in his voice was thick as he swerved to miss a pothole. "Now is when you tell me what you've been up to."

Mallory leaned her head gently against the headrest and then took him through her day yesterday, starting with entering the bakery and finding the flour outline of a body. She'd gotten to returning to Wingate after lunch as Dugan pulled his truck into a parking space at the hospital. He offered to walk her in, but she declined, insisting she could handle the short walk into the building. Dugan said he'd remain in place until she got inside safely. True to his word, he didn't pull out of the parking lot until she entered the automatic door. Through the floor-to-ceiling window, she saw his truck drive away.

* * *

Three hours later, Mallory had been examined, evaluated, and released. A competent nurse handed her the discharge papers. She reviewed with Mallory the signs and symptoms to look out for and instructed her to return to the hospital if she experienced them.

Mallory had no intention of returning to the hospital. She made her way along the corridor, heading for the exit to leave behind the bright white lights and antiseptic scent. Since Dugan had driven her to the hospital, she had to figure out a way to get home. Maybe Kip could get away from the bakery? If not, she'd have to do a rideshare.

"Miss Monroe, good to see they've released you." Hannigan pushed off the information counter and caught up with her. "Officer Winslow filled me in on the incident. I'm sorry you had to go through that."

"So am I." Mallory continued walking. She passed a waiting room full of patients in various stages of discomfort. Each had a story, just like hers. Attacked while pondering by the pond—so much for self-care.

"Have you remembered anything else about the attack?"

Mallory shook her head. Still a bad move. It still hurt. "No."

"Maybe you heard a vehicle? Or caught a glimpse of the person before you collapsed?"

"I've been replaying the incident, and there's nothing else. I told Lauren everything."

Mallory pulled out her phone, ready to text Kip, as she exited through the automatic door and stepped outside. A metal and glass canopy covered the department's entry. At the curb, other discharged patients waited for their rides while others were assisted into vehicles. Off to the side was a bench where she'd wait for her ride.

"Including your snooping?" Hannigan followed her to the bench and waited for an answer. "This isn't a game, Mallory."

The use of her first name had Mallory whipping her head up. Again, bad move.

"There is a *very* dead woman, and you have been on the receiving end of two *very* direct threats. Anything you can remember, no matter how small or seemingly insignificant, can be helpful." He sat next to her. His thigh grazed hers, setting off a fluttering of butterflies in her belly. Mallory swallowed. This wasn't good. She willed her leg to move slightly, but it felt as heavy as a rock and wouldn't budge. The butterflies fluttered faster. "You're lucky you're not dead."

And just like that, the butterflies petered out.

She recoiled at his harsh words. Tears stung her eyes, but she willed herself not to cry in front of the detective.

"I don't think this is a game. Never have." She blinked several times and was able to stave off a crying episode. "Did you really think I'd be able to sit quietly on the sideline while a murderer is on the loose and my future hangs in the balance?"

"You're not a suspect, Mallory."

There it was again. Her first name. The way he said it sounded so familiar and intimate that she could forget why they had come into each other's lives—a murder.

"Then tell everyone," she pleaded. "I'm losing business because people think otherwise."

"Is it worth losing your life?"

"Will." Yes, she was going out on a limb and using his first name. When there was no objection, she continued, "You know nothing about my life."

"I'd like to," he said, his voice warm and deep.

A breath hitched in Mallory's throat, and before she could speak, she heard her name. She looked in the direction of Kip's voice and saw him approach at full speed.

"Thank goodness you're okay. You had me scared to death." He swooped down and pulled her into a big hug. "You're okay, right?"

"They wouldn't have released me if I weren't. But you're squeezing too tight. Crushing me," she said.

"Oh, sorry." He released her and then straightened. "Lauren called after you left for the hospital. I can't imagine someone sneaking up behind you and then hitting you. Who would do such a thing?" He looked at Will. "Any leads?"

Will shook his head. "Not at this time." He stood. "Mallory, I'll follow up with you tomorrow. And I'll want a complete rundown of who you've talked to about Beatrice's murder."

Mallory knew better than to nod. "No problem."

"Let's get you home," Kip said as he reached out to help Mallory stand. "There's a glitch, Mal. I can't stay with you. I have a thing. Gram's eightieth is tonight."

"It's okay." Mallory eased her arm from Kip's hold. She didn't like to be fussed over.

"No. It's not." Will arrived at the passenger side of Kip's car. "You shouldn't be alone after a head injury."

Mallory wasn't about to invite him to stay over. That would be asking for a whole new kind of trouble, and her heart wasn't ready for it.

"I called Liz, but she has a faculty thing she can't miss but could come over later." Kip opened the passenger side door. "But don't worry. I got someone who can stay with you all night and until the morning."

Paused at the opened door, foreboding rippled through her body. "I'm almost afraid to ask who."

"Aspen." Kip lowered his head, breaking eye contact.

"What?" Mallory's voice was louder than she expected.

"It's the best I could do on short notice," Kip said.

"Next time, I'll schedule my assault," Mallory shot back.

Kip grinned. "Very funny."

"She's really staying with me?" They hadn't ended their last conversation on a friendly note. So why would Aspen agree to help her?

Will's cell phone chimed, and he pulled it out of its pouch on this belt. After glancing at the screen, he said, "I have to take this. Follow doctor's orders, and we'll talk tomorrow." He turned and walked away with the phone pressed to his ear.

"Aspen will meet us at your house." Kip closed the passenger door after Mallory slid onto the seat and buckled up. He then walked around the front of the car and got in. "Don't worry. It's going to be fine. You'll see."

Mallory relaxed back into the leather seat, and while Kip pulled out of his spot, her throbbing head pain returned at the thought of spending the entire night with Aspen.

Chapter Nineteen

On the drive home, the sky had filled with dark clouds, and the temperature dropped. The change in weather seemed fitting for the day Mallory was having. By the time Kip turned onto her street, she was deep in a text exchange with Liz. Despite her glib text earlier, Liz had been worried and, from her wording, felt guilty for not being able to stay with her sister. Mallory assured her she would be fine and that she understood the importance of the faculty event. Mallory had blown off a family get-together more than once because of work commitments. Not wanting to add any more stress to her sister, Mallory simply ended the conversation with a text saying she'd call later.

"Everything okay with Liz?" Kip shifted his car into park after pulling into Mallory's driveway.

"She's feeling guilty for not staying with me tonight." Mallory slipped her phone into her backpack.

"I'm feeling a little guilty myself." Kip turned off the ignition. "You need me, and I'm going off to a party."

Mallory smiled. She tenderly cupped his cheek with her hand and looked into his guilt-ridden eyes. "It's your gram's big birthday. You need to be there. Besides, you got me a babysitter." She took back her hand.

"I did, didn't I?" Then, looking proud of himself, he popped open the door and got out of the vehicle.

"It doesn't take much," Mallory muttered as she exited the car.

Kip trotted around to the passenger door. "I'll make you tea before I go back to the bakery."

Mallory walked along the side of the house, passing under the flowering arbor. Before she reached the back door, the sound of a car engine drew her thoughts from a nice cup of tea to how she'd survive the night. The closing of a car door gave her only moments to brace herself.

"Yoo-hoo!"

Mallory scowled at Kip. "My babysitter is here."

"Be nice," he warned.

"Mallory! You had us so worried." Aspen dropped her designer overnight bag and threw her arms around Mallory. "I know we left off in a not-so-good place earlier. I have to admit, your words were a little hurtful. But it's water under the bridge now."

"What is she talking about?" Kip mouthed.

Mallory shook her head. She didn't want to discuss it.

Aspen let go of Mallory and then turned to Kip. "You can go now. I'll take it from here."

He frowned. "Okay. I'll call later."

In what felt like a whirlwind, Aspen shuttled Mallory inside the house, deposited her on the sofa, set aside her bag, and then put the kettle on. As she served the tea with a plate of cookies, she cooed about how lovely Mallory's home was. She adored the charm and the vintage vibe of the furnishings. She also zeroed in on the new hardcover Mallory planned to crack open at bedtime.

"You enjoy mystery novels, don't you?" Aspen settled on the chair and angled toward the sofa for easy conversation. "Have you read all those?" She gestured to the stacks of books on the old chest.

"Not yet. I have to rearrange the bookshelves. The house came furnished, which meant it also came with stuffed bookcases." Mallory nibbled on a cookie. At some point, she needed to pack up those books and store them in the cubby beneath the staircase. Then she'd display her collection of crime fiction. Maybe even start another book club.

"Guess with running the bakery, you're not left with much time for household tasks." Aspen sipped her tea. Her bright pink lipstick left an imprint on the cup's rim. A gust of wind rattled the cottage's old windows. "Looks like the meteorologist got the forecast right. Though the coastline is supposed to take the brunt of the storm," Aspen said.

"Fingers crossed we don't lose power." Mallory sipped her tea.

"I'm thinking since we're hanging out tonight, we should do some work. How about I order dinner, and then we can bring that murder board in here and try to solve Beatrice's case?" Aspen looked hopeful.

Mallory set her cup on its saucer and leaned back. The softness of the plump cushion felt good to her tired bones.

"Sounds good. We can order from the diner. They deliver." Mallory reached for her phone. After they decided what they wanted to eat, Aspen set the table, and in record speed, their meals arrived.

They ate over small talk. Mallory learned Aspen grew up in Oregon and came east to attend Abernathy. Which answered the question about Aspen's connection to Wingate. After college, she was off to law school and a series of jobs. The last one was where she met Gil, though she became vaguer when Mallory asked about her work status now. Mallory had a feeling that Aspen had not only changed her residence but also quit her job. She couldn't blame her if she did. After all, she'd have to work alongside Gil, even if it were only a few meetings. If her hunch was correct, it had been a gutsy move on Aspen's part. At least when Mallory left the advertising agency, she had a business waiting for her.

"This was too much food." Aspen wiped her mouth with a napkin and then dropped it on the table.

Mallory stood, but instead of heading to the living room, she walked to the island. "Thank you for setting the table and dishing out our dinners. At least let me feed Agatha."

"Guess it can't hurt." Aspen cleared the table and disposed of the food containers while Mallory dished out the cat's evening meal. "Wow. Look at how windy it's gotten."

Mallory looked over her shoulder, out the window over the sink. "I love a good storm," she murmured as she bent over and presented Agatha with her heaping food bowl. She dizzied a little, so her movement back up was slow and controlled.

"I've never been fond. And definitely not when there's a murderer on the loose." Aspen added the utensils and glasses to the dishwasher. After closing the door, she turned to Mallory. "Ready to get to work?"

"Sure." Mallory left Agatha to enjoy her meal. She returned to her spot on the sofa in the living room, and Aspen carried in the bulletin board. She set the board up on the other armchair and then gathered the pushpins, index cards, and pens.

A boom of thunder startled them both. While Mallory smiled at the momentary scare, Aspen looked uneasy. Gosh. If she was that spooked by a rumble of thunder, how would she help track down a killer?

"I've been thinking. Out of all the people you've spoken to so far, I'm leaning toward Ernie as the one who attacked you." Aspen filled out another index card with the information about his trip to the storage unit. "Or the man he met with. Too bad you didn't recognize him."

"I wish I had." Mallory's head was down, and she was scrolling on her phone. As they were finishing dinner, they'd discussed Luke Collins. She remembered Lauren's comment about him—she recognized him from somewhere but couldn't pinpoint from where. Mallory had had the same reaction to him. Why? Where had she known him from?

"What are you doing?" Aspen asked.

"I'm looking at a food blogger's social media account. According to Luke's résumé, he worked with this blogger. Yet I'm scrolling through her photos, and none of them seem like Luke's style."

After nearly a decade of working in advertising, she'd honed her eye in identifying styles of copywriters, stylists, and photographers. Each one had their own unique stamp on their craft. Luke Collins had not snapped the photos she was looking at. They were moodier than the ones she'd viewed in his portfolio and the photos he had taken of her cookie bouquets.

"Maybe it's what the blogger wanted. After all, they were paying." Aspen said as she stared at the pinned index cards.

"True." However, Mallory thought back to how much Luke had been in command when he arrived for her photo shoot. He hadn't seemed very open to collaboration. Or to talking about Beatrice. "This will gnaw at me until I know for certain." She typed a direct message to the blogger asking about Luke Collins.

Aspen wrote out another index card—questionable credentials—and pinned it beneath Luke's name. She leaned back on her heels and studied the board.

"Who would have thought there could be so many murder suspects in a hamlet like Wingate?" She looked at Mallory. "It's so ugly, isn't it?"

Mallory swallowed. Before she could say anything, a loud snapping noise drew her attention toward the front window. Her heart thumped. Then she realized it sounded like a tree limb breaking as sheets of rain battered the house and windows.

"Ugly like this storm. It's getting worse." Mallory's phone buzzed, and there was a reply from the blogger. "Oh, boy."

"What is it?" Aspen joined Mallory on the sofa.

"The blogger replied. She's never heard of Luke Collins." It appeared Lauren had been onto something. "He lied on his résumé. Why?"

"The same reason everybody else does," Aspen said. "To get the job."

The cracking noise Mallory had heard before finding Beatrice's body and right before being struck on the back of her head replayed in her mind, in sync with the wind's taunting whistling. Goose bumps pricked her skin.

"Mal, are you okay?" Aspen asked, placing her hand on Mallory's knee.

"Huh? Yes. I'm okay. We were talking about Luke. He was arguing with Beatrice," Mallory said.

"Let me add it to the board." Aspen rose but froze when a boom of thunder roared over them, and the lights flickered. "I don't like this."

"Neither do I." Mallory stood. She'd never been one to cower during storms, but she was a little scared given recent events. The lights flickered again. "I have candles and flashlights in the utility room. We should get them. We could lose power."

"Because of the storm or because the killer on the loose cut the power?" Aspen asked, wide-eyed and visibly freaked out.

Then the living room plunged into darkness. Aspen screamed and grabbed Mallory's arm, squeezing tightly and digging her nails into Mallory's skin.

"Oh my God, what was that? Didn't you feel it?" Aspen's grip tightened.

The lights came back on, revealing Agatha seated by their feet. The cat's eyes narrowed, and she flicked her tail.

"It's only Agatha. I wonder where she's been all night?"

"Who cares?" Aspen drew closer to Mallory, leaving no space between them. Her strong floral perfume was overwhelming, and her grip unrelenting. "This wasn't a good idea. We're isolated during a storm with a killer on the loose."

"You know you don't have to keep saying there's a killer on the loose."

"There's a murderer who hasn't been apprehended moving freely about in town. Better?"

No. It wasn't better. Mallory gritted her teeth. Unfortunately, she couldn't argue Aspen's point. So she needed to find a counter-argument. "We still have contact with the outside world."

"How long do you think it would take the police to get here? Maybe we should leave? Go to my apartment?" It'd seemed impossible, but Aspen's eyes had grown wider and more panicked.

Another crack followed by a crashing bam sent Mallory jumping. She ran across the living room to the front window with Aspen on her heels. She swept aside the sheer curtain panel with Aspen behind her and stared out into the pitch black of the storming night. Hundreds, if not thousands, of raindrops dotted the glass.

It took a nanosecond for her eyes to focus.

Then she and Aspen screamed when they saw a man staring back at them.

Their screams faded when they realized the peeping Tom wasn't a killer but a cheater. Gil. They shared an annoyed glance before Mallory broke away to open the door. A moment later, a waterlogged Gil entered. He was a soggy mess, from his dark hair plastered to his scalp to water dripping from his thick eyelashes to his soaked trench coat.

"What are you doing here?" Mallory moved only enough to let him in so she could close the door. She had no intention of allowing him any farther into the house. "I thought I made it clear I never wanted to see you again."

"I wanted to check on you. Make sure you're okay. I heard about what happened. I can't believe someone hurt you." He sounded genuinely sincere. Like he had when he had told Mallory he was going on a business trip.

"No need to worry. I'm here." Aspen's voice startled Gil.

He spun around, and when he saw her he paled. "What . . . are you doing here?"

"It's none of your business," Mallory said. "Neither one of us needs you to check on us. We're strong, independent women capable of taking care of ourselves." Providing the power stayed on. She wasn't sure how capable she'd be in the dark, knowing the person who attacked her was lurking around.

"You nearly scared us to death." Aspen propped her hands on her hips. "You shouldn't be looking into people's windows. Especially an ex-girlfriend's window. That's how you get in trouble for stalking. You know, it's a crime."

"A crime? I'm . . . I'm not stalking. My God. I can't understand why you two are together," he said.

"Afraid we're comparing notes about you?" Aspen asked.

"No!" His gaze bounced between Mallory and Aspen and back to Mallory. "I need to talk to you." He cupped her elbow and shuffled away from Aspen. Then he said, in a low voice, "I don't think you should be friends with her."

"Oh, we're not friends."

"Good."

"She's my lawyer." Okay, technically not anymore, but he didn't need to know that detail.

"What?!" Gil checked himself and lowered his voice. "It's not a good idea. She's infatuated with me, and I'm worried she blames you for our breakup."

"Oh, get over yourself, Gillie." Aspen's whisper into his ear sent Gil jumping. "The only person I blame for the breakup is you. So if you're so worried"—she used air quotes around the word worried—"then you should leave and never come back."

"Fine. Suit yourselves. Don't say I didn't warn you. Women are crazy," Gil muttered as he stomped to the door.

"And don't you forget it!" Mallory followed him to the door.

He stepped out onto the porch.

"One more thing, Gil."

He turned and faced her.

She smirked, and then she slammed the door in his face.

Aspen scooted to her side and gave her a high-five. "Well done."

"The nerve of him." Mallory closed and locked the door.

"I think we should wrap up the murder part of our evening." Aspen drifted back to the bulletin board. "What do you think?"

"Sounds good. I'm probably going to have a hard enough time getting to sleep without working on the murder board until bedtime." Mallory gathered the unused index cards and pushpins. She knew Agatha would have loved to take a swipe with her paw and knock the small bin off the chest, scattering the pins all over the floor.

"This record player is so cool. It looks like an original. Like one my grandma had." Aspen had moved over to the turntable stand and browsed albums stacked beside the player.

The mid-century-inspired cabinet had two drawers and four open cubbies for album storage. It was one of the few pieces of furniture Mallory had moved to Wingate with. To keep expenses low, she had only brought what was absolutely loved.

"Her favorites were Conway Twitty and Loretta Lynn. She played their records all the time. And she wondered why I never had friends over," Aspen said.

"You lived with her?" Mallory approached the stand. She loved streaming her music, but there was something special about a record. She believed it was the same reason she had a vast collection of print books. While she enjoyed the convenience of e-books, it wasn't the same feeling as holding a book in her hands when she was reading.

"My parents divorced when I was a baby. My dad took off. I think to California. And my mom died in a car accident when I was five. So it was just Grandma and me." Aspen attempted a smile, but it didn't reach her eyes.

"I'm sorry," Mallory said. She couldn't fathom losing her parents at such a young age. "You've never seen your dad again?"

"No. After a while, I stopped asking Santa to bring my daddy home." Aspen's shoulders drooped, and Mallory's heart ached for her. "Being raised by a grandparent wasn't easy. None of my friends lived with their grannies. She had a hard time doing the things the other moms did. But now, looking back, it was a blessing." Aspen gave a reassuring nod and then pulled out an album from a cubby.

"I'm sure it was." Mallory patted Aspen on the shoulder. "There's something I need to ask you. Why did you really move to Wingate? I know what you told me, but I think there's more to the story."

Aspen's eyelashes fluttered and she exhaled a deep breath. "My lease was up and I had decided not to renew it because I thought I'd be moving in with Gil."

Mallory sighed.

"I really thought that night you showed up with Chinese food was going to be the night he asked me to move in. Guess I read those signals wrong." Aspen blinked back tears and then pulled out an album from a cubby. "Dusty Springfield? I've never heard of her."

"Maybe not her name, but I'm sure you've heard her biggest hit." Mallory slipped the album out of the jacket and placed it on the player. "I got this at Rock, Pop, and Jazz. It's a cool shop on Main Street." It was time for them to stop thinking about Gil. She lifted the needle, set it on the vinyl disc, and then switched the machine on. A moment later, the song played.

Aspen nodded. "I do recognize it! 'I Only Want to Be with You.' I love this song. It's from the . . . what . . . the seventies?"

"Sixties," Mallory corrected. Smiling, she increased the volume and let the song ease all her worries, fears, and annoyance at Gil. The uplifting beat instantly perked Mallory up. The trumpets added a texture to the melody that gave it a special oomph.

Within seconds, she and Aspen were bopping to the music and singing along with Dusty. Mallory didn't give a darn how silly she felt. Or looked to Gil if he peeped into the window again.

When the song ended, they dropped onto the sofa, still giggling like teenage girls.

"Wow. How fun was that?" Aspen tossed her head back.

"A lot. But I think it's time to call it a night. I'm exhausted." Mallory slapped her hands on her thighs before standing. She might have overdone it with the dancing, but it'd been so long since she had let loose. Who knew spending time with Aspen could be so enjoyable? "Thank you for staying with me tonight."

"Thank you for slamming the door in Gil's face." Aspen's nose wriggled, and she winked.

A twinge of guilt pinged in Mallory at how she had tossed him out of her house. It wasn't very hospitable of her, especially on a night like tonight. But when she remembered how little respect he had shown for her and Aspen by two-timing them, she stopped her thoughts in their tracks. Gil deserved whatever they dished out. And getting a door slammed in his face during a storm wasn't all that bad. In fact, she considered he'd gotten off easy.

She retreated to her bedroom after setting out linens for the sofa. She'd hoped the guest bedroom furniture would have arrived, but deliveries were fickle. Aspen seemed to be a good sport about spending the night on the sofa. By the time Mallory had changed into her pajamas, Agatha had jumped up onto the bed and curled up into a tight ball, ready for a night of sound sleeping. Mallory slipped under the bedcovers and checked her phone's alarm for tomorrow morning. She couldn't help but wonder how Aspen would fare with Mallory's early rising time. With the clock all set, she placed her phone on the nightstand and adjusted her pillows.

She nestled her head into the pillow and closed her eyes. Her shoulders molded into the cloud-like mattress, and bit by bit, her whole body relaxed after a day of being on high alert. She inhaled and exhaled slowly in the darkness, allowing herself to float into a deep slumber. Then, right on the edge of the rest she craved and desperately needed, her mind grabbed hold of another question.

What had Will meant when he said he'd like to know more about her life? And why was she referring to him as Will rather than Hannigan?

Her eyes popped open, and she groaned. She needed no more complications in her life. Yet she was staring up at the ceiling thinking about a man. There was no way she could have romantic feelings toward Will Hannigan. She wasn't looking for a new relationship. But the tingling in her belly told her something different. And so did the urge to run her fingers through his loose curls. Her lips turned up at the corners at a memory she'd forgotten about. The boy she'd kissed during the Mums, Merlot, and Mozart had a mop of curly hair. Now she was thinking of kissing another boy with curly hair.

She pulled the pillow next to her, covered her face with it, and groaned again. She couldn't be falling for Detective Hannigan. Could she?

Chapter Twenty

Mallory eased the back door of her utility room closed, leaving her babysitter snoring on the sofa. It was far too early to wake Aspen. So she wrote a note, took out a coffee mug, and left them both on the counter. After popping two aspirins and feeding Agatha, Mallory grabbed her backpack and headed to the garage for her Jetta. There wasn't any way she'd miss another day of work. The thought of sitting around the house all day worrying and waiting for something to happen wasn't her style. However, she wasn't completely reckless with her health. She'd do her best to take it easy, and if she experienced any of the symptoms the nurse had warned her of, she'd stop working and go straight to the hospital.

Traveling along Main Street, the bakery came into view, and she smiled as she drove into the driveway. It felt good going back to work. After parking and exiting her car, she walked to the back door and unlocked it with trepidation.

Inside, she scoped out the bakery with her cell phone in hand, ready to dial 9-1-1. She found no messages or intruders. Now she could put into motion the plan she'd concocted while showering and finalized as she'd filled Agatha's bowl.

She texted Luke, telling him she wasn't happy with the photos and wanted a reshoot. While waiting for his reply, she turned on the ovens and gathered the ingredients for making a batch of royal icing. Kip would be coming in later, and Claudia had the day off. She was about to turn on the mixer when her phone pinged.

A text from Luke.

His response wasn't pleasant. But he said he would swing by in an hour and discuss what she didn't like and how they could fix it.

Mallory set her phone down. She had sixty minutes to fret over whether her plan was a good idea. By the time she glanced at her watch again, an hour later, she'd made a batch of royal icing, chocolate chip cookie dough, and organized her work tray for the day. She removed her apron and dashed out to the front of the bakery. She unlocked the door and returned to her spot behind the counter. She busied herself filling the cash register and wiping down the countertop.

She looked at her watch again and then stared out the bay window. The sun had come out, brightening and uplifting the morning after a night of battering rain and wind. There were no pedestrians at that hour, but there was traffic. Cars zipped by on their way to work. Everyone was in a hurry to get where they needed to go while she waited. Alone.

The front door opened, and Luke entered, his stride defiant and his posture stiff. The door closed behind him, and he stood with his hands jammed into his jeans pockets, his expression irritated.

She cleared her throat and prayed she wasn't going to regret this. "Thanks for coming."

"I have a shoot I need to get to. I reviewed the photos, and I can't see what you disapprove of."

Mallory was at a loss because he was right. He was also in a rush, and if she prolonged their discussion, he'd leave in a heart-beat. It was best to get straight to the reason why she wanted him there.

"You're right. The photos are good. Actually, they're amazing." She stepped out from behind the counter and approached him. "There's something I wanted to talk to you about, but I didn't think you'd come if I told you what it was."

"Mallory, you're a nice lady, but I don't have time for games."

"Murder isn't a game."

"Murder? What are you talking about?"

"Why did you lie on your résumé? I'm paying for your experience. Which seems to be a big fat lie. Did Beatrice find out you lied? Did she find out the reason why you lied? Is that why the two of you argued? My friend Officer Lauren Winslow agrees with me that you look familiar. Why?"

Luke pulled his hand from his pocket and raked his fingers through his hair. "Geez. What is it with you people? First Beatrice and now you. And police? I did nothing wrong. Ever!"

"Except lie about your work history," Mallory countered.

Luke took a big step forward, entering Mallory's personal space and staring her down. She gulped. But did her best not to show any of the fear coursing through her body. "Does the name Lucas Carnes mean anything to you?"

Mallory's heart pounded, and then it went into overdrive, beating so fast she was short of breath. The name certainly meant something to her and everyone else in New England.

Lucas Carnes had been the lead story for the regional news programs five years ago. And now Mallory was face to face with him.

"He killed his girlfriend."

"No! Lucas Carnes did not kill his girlfriend." Luke's jaw tensed, and his dark, brooding eyes that Mallory had believed came from his creative spirit darkened, but less with creativity and more with anger. "Juliette disappeared after leaving my apartment. We had a fight. She stormed off, and then she was gone. I have no idea what happened to her, but she was alive when she left."

"You didn't go after her?"

"I finished the wine we had with dinner and then opened another bottle. Before she left, she said we were done. Man . . . if I could take back everything I said and what I didn't do. I should have gone after her." Grief shadowed his face, and he looked away to regain his composure. "When the news got hold of the story, I went from dumped boyfriend to number one murder suspect."

"You really didn't kill her?"

He looked at her. His eyes softened, and his demeanor changed. Now he looked anguished, broken. Those emotions sparked empathy in Mallory, and she instantly regretted asking the question.

"I loved her. And I'll never forgive myself for not chasing after her. Instead, I drank too much and fell asleep."

"You changed your name for a fresh start?" she asked, feeling more comfortable with Luke, but she kept her guard up.

"Up in Maine, I couldn't get work, a place to live. I couldn't move on with my life. No woman would date me. No one would hire me. Let me tell you, being accused of a crime is worse than being guilty of one. At least guilty people eventually get paroled. And they're given a second chance."

Those words hit home for Mallory. After finding Beatrice's body, she'd been thrust into the public light with a cloud of suspicion over her. Five years from now would people look at her like she was looking at Luke? Would there always be a question of her innocence? She believed the answer was yes if she didn't find the murderer.

"I realized that I had to start over if I wanted a life," Luke said.

"With a new name?"

"New name, new state, new job. Photography has always been my passion. But over the past two years, I've gotten really good at it. Good enough to support myself."

"Somehow Beatrice found out who you really are, didn't she?"

He rubbed the back of his neck, and his gaze drifted off. "That woman was a piece of work. Like you, she discovered my résumé wasn't kosher. Don't you see, I didn't have a choice. I needed to get jobs, and for that to happen, I needed a work history. As I got jobs to build my portfolio, I've been deleting the ones I lied about. I'm not trying to scam anyone. I swear. Just trying to earn a living."

"You thought living under the radar behind a camera lens was a perfect way not to be recognized. But Beatrice figured it out. When she found out about your secret, what did she do?"

His eyes shot back to Mallory. "She threatened . . ." He paused a moment to control his voice. "Look, I don't want any trouble. But that's what Beatrice was. Trouble. She said if I didn't shoot her photos for free, she'd reveal who I really am."

"That's a lot of work for no payment."

"Tell me about it. In addition to her blog, she demanded I shoot her cookbook. She wanted to self-publish one. Her plan was to get it into every bookstore so she could do a book signing tour along with television interviews. She had grand plans," he snickered.

"I'm not surprised."

"She had the money to bankroll the project, yet she wanted me to shoot all the photos for the book for free. No way was I going to do it. I've worked too hard for my freedom. I had no intention of living under her constant threat. If she wanted to out me for being Lucas Carnes, then so be it. That's what we were arguing about. I told her I was done being blackmailed."

"Why didn't she reveal your secret?"

He shrugged. "Don't know."

But maybe Mallory did, and it had her taking a step back. The argument had happened a week before Beatrice was killed. It was possible that she hadn't gotten the chance to follow through on her threat because Luke had permanently silenced her.

"Now, with her gone, it seemed okay to stay and continue working, plant some roots here in Wingate. Too bad I have to leave." He stepped forward, putting just inches between them. "You had something in common with Beatrice. You both couldn't mind your own business. Do whatever you want with the photos. I won't be working for you again." He turned and stalked out of the bakery.

Mallory let out a breath that she hadn't realized she'd been holding. Luke Collins was a complicated man, and it made it difficult to know for sure if he was the killer she was looking for.

Had he been telling the truth about his girlfriend? Had he really drunk enough to knock himself out while she disappeared into the night? Had he really been willing to let his fate be decided by Beatrice?

Or had he taken fate into his own hands and gotten rid of the blackmailer once and for all?

What she needed to do next was call Will and tell him about Luke Collins and his motive for murder. But first, she closed her eyes and gave her brain a moment of silence. All she heard was her breathing—deeply in and out. Then, a loud knock broke her pseudo-meditation. She raced to the door and just as she grabbed hold of the knob, the door pushed opened and Ernie Hollis rushed in, practically shoving her out of the way.

His congenial disposition had morphed into a wild frenzy. He blinked rapidly, sweat beaded on his temples, and his white-collared shirt was rumpled.

You've got to be kidding me. First Luke, and now this?

"What's going on with you?" Mallory did her best to quell the rising alarm in her body.

"You have no idea who you're dealing with. You need to back off. Now. Before it's too late."

Mallory slipped her fingers into her back pocket for her phone with ease and as little movement as possible. Once she grasped it, she whipped it out and held it up in the air. Ernie let out a dark laugh.

"You think you're so smart? What? Are you going to call the police? Video me?" He advanced forward. "You shouldn't have followed me the other day."

"How . . . you saw me?" Mallory asked.

"No. But the man I met with did, and he told me. It's not a good idea to spy on him."

"Why? Who is he?"

"The man I owe a lot of money to. The man who controls my life."

"What are you talking about? Oh . . . he's a bookie? Loan shark?"

"I had to borrow money from him to pay my bookie. I was so stupid. I never realized I'd be paying him forever when I took his money. He's ruined my life." Ernie scrubbed his face and then dragged his hand through his hair. "Just like Beatrice."

"Why don't we sit and talk? Come on." Mallory reached for Ernie's arm and walked with him to a café table. There they'd be in view of passersby.

Ernie dropped onto a chair and slumped. He clasped his hands on his lap. He looked defeated, not menacing as he had when he first burst into the bakery.

Mallory sat across from him, poised to leap up and run out of the bakery if he showed any signs of aggression.

"Why are you here?" she asked.

"To warn you."

"About your loan shark?"

"He called me and wanted to know who you were. I had no choice. I had to tell him. Then I heard about your attack yesterday."

"You think he hit me?" Great. While tracking down a killer, she'd managed to get herself caught up in the crosshairs of a loan shark. Is that what was meant by unintentional consequences?

"Who else?" Ernie straightened up and leaned forward, dropping his hands on the table. "Why did you follow me? Are you trying to blackmail me too?"

"Was someone blackmailing you? Was it Beatrice?"

"I'm sick and tired of being blackmailed. Do you hear me? It's about time I come clean and face the consequences of my actions."

Mallory leaned forward. "What did you do?" She couldn't help herself. She had to know.

"I've always liked to bet. Nothing big. Football games, the ponies. But after Patty died, I found myself doing it more and more. It got to the point where I couldn't afford to lose. I did something foolish. I stole money from the college. Let's just say I did a little creative bookkeeping." Ernie dropped his head.

"Beatrice found out?"

He looked back up at Mallory. "Yeah, how did you know?"

"You're not the only person."

"Not surprised. I don't know how she found out, but I had to do her a favor to keep my secret and not go to prison."

"Which was what?"

"Get her nephew into Abernathy. Chad didn't have good grades. Actually, they were abysmal. And he had been part of a hazing at his high school that went bad. Very bad. It was no easy feat getting him into Abernathy."

"You abused your position as the admissions director?"

He sighed. "I had no choice. She pressured me. Believe it or not, I had integrity once. Everything is gone. I'm just glad my wife isn't here to see what a mess I've become." Ernie dropped his head into his hands, and he sobbed silently.

The front door swung open, and Aspen rushed in with a puzzled look on her face. While Mallory had only enough energy when she woke that morning to dress in a pair of black jeans and a white T-shirt, Aspen had gone full-on glam, with a slim lavender pantsuit and nude stiletto pumps.

"You nearly gave me a heart attack," Aspen said. "When I peeked into your room and you weren't there, the most disturbing thoughts raced through my mind."

Given the morning she was having, Mallory wasn't surprised by Aspen's drama. Had she really thought Mallory had been kidnapped from her bed in the middle of the night?

"I'm sorry. I didn't want to wake you so early."

"Apology accepted." Aspen then pointed at Ernie. "What's his deal?"

Mallory rose from her chair and quickly grabbed Aspen's arm. "Come, sit with him. Don't let him leave." She shuffled Aspen to the table.

"Why? What's going on? Did you solve the murder?" Aspen set her beige satchel on the table and eyed Ernie with distaste. "Why is he crying?"

"His life is a mess. And I don't think he's the killer." Mallory scooted over to the counter to call Will. After she found his number in her phone's contacts, she waited for him to pick up.

"Whoa! Looks like I'm late for the party." Kip walked through the kitchen's swinging door. "What's going on, Mal? Who's the guy crying with Aspen? Don't tell me another ex?"

Mallory waved her hand to shush him as she finished leaving a message for Will. After she lowered the phone from her ear, she gave Kip a quick recap of her morning. And what a morning it had been.

When Mallory finished talking, Kip stood staring at her with his mouth open.

"Say something," Mallory urged.

"I'm kind of at a loss for words. You met with someone who could have been the killer. No backup? Nothing. And then Ernie Hollis comes waltzing in, another suspect . . ."

"He didn't exactly waltz in," Mallory interrupted.

"Noted. Back to what I was saying. It turns out Ernie led you to a loan shark who knows who you are. Oh, and he confessed to embezzling from the college and to admissions fraud." Kip reached for Mallory's hand and dragged her out of earshot of Aspen and Ernie. "I thought we were a team?"

"We are."

"Really? Oh, let me check my phone for your call or message about your plans for the day." He pulled his phone from his pocket.

"Don't be so dramatic."

Kip cocked his head sideways.

"I'm sorry, you're right," Mallory said. "I should have kept you in the loop."

"What about me?" Aspen demanded from behind Mallory.

Mallory jumped and then swung around. Now she knew how Gil felt. "I thought I told you to stay with Ernie."

Aspen dismissed Mallory's concern with a wave. "He's not going anywhere. The man is a blubbering mess."

Mallory's phone buzzed, and it was Will returning her call. She moved away from Kip and Aspen so she could talk in private. Less than a minute later, he said he'd heard enough and he was on his way over.

"The bakery needs to open." Mallory turned to Kip. "Which means I can't have Will arresting Ernie out here."

"It's Will now?" Kip asked.

Mallory ignored the question. "I'm going to take Ernie back to my office. Kip, can you stay out here for now? Aspen, I think we have everything under control for now. Thanks for keeping an eye on Ernie."

"Sure. No problem. I'm going to unpack my bag. Call me later, okay?" Aspen turned on her heels and left the bakery.

"While you were on the phone, Aspen told me Gil showed up last night. What nerve." Kip returned to the counter.

"Tell me about it." Mallory walked over to Ernie and guided him up from the chair. "We're going into my office."

Ernie nodded as he allowed Mallory to lead him through the bakery. In her office, she settled him on the chair at her desk. It didn't take Will long to show up. Within minutes of talking to Ernie, he called for a uniformed officer to take the disgraced college admissions director into custody.

Standing in her office doorway with Will, watching Ernie being taken away, Mallory didn't feel triumphant at Ernie's arrest. Instead, she felt terrible for him. It appeared he'd turned to gambling to help sort through the grief of his wife's death. What he did was wrong, but she had no intention of casting judgment on him.

"Tell me, Mallory, what will it take to get you to back off my investigation?" Will leaned against the doorjamb with his arms crossed. His deep, authoritative voice had more than a hint of annoyance.

Indeed, that was a rhetorical question, so Mallory opted not to answer it. Instead, she walked into her office and sat at her desk. She sensed a lecture coming, and she wanted to be comfortable.

"It's not my fault Ernie came in here and confessed his crime to me."

That broke the severe line of Will's lips. "Of course it isn't." He walked into the room and cleared off the stack of file folders from the red plastic chair, and then sat. "You are a very stubborn woman."

She shrugged. "I've been called worse."

"I can't imagine that." He leaned forward, his forearms resting on his thighs and clasped his hands. "You were assaulted yesterday after a threat was left for you. And now you've gotten yourself caught up with a loan shark."

"Are you going to question him about my attack?" Despite what Ernie had said, she wasn't inclined to believe his loan shark was the one who'd attacked her. What would have been his motive? He was worried she followed Ernie to find out his identity? Possibly.

"I intend to. Though I don't think he was the one."

"Why not?" Mallory asked, wanting to compare notes.

"All you did was follow Mr. Hollis. I don't think his loan shark would risk going after you for something like that."

"I agree." She drummed her fingers on the chair's arm. "There's someone you should speak to about Beatrice's murder." She filled him in on her conversation with Luke.

Will jotted notes and thanked her for the information. He also advised her to stay away from Luke until he'd been interviewed. After he left, she hoped she'd done the right thing.

Chapter
Twenty-One

Mallory retreated into the kitchen after the bakery emptied of police and confessed embezzlers. Okay, it was only one, but it was more than enough. When she'd first texted Luke, she had no idea her morning would be so eventful. Standing at her workstation, she had her earbuds in and was decorating a dozen deer-shaped cookies. The concentration required to create the whimsical forest animal forced her to push away the morning's events. How had two men she hardly knew bared their deepest, darkest secrets to her? She didn't know, and now wasn't the time to think about the reasons. The little deer lying on the parchment paper needed a tail.

She leaned forward and guided her piping bag fitted with a number two tip to outline the animal's face, ear, and part of its tail with tan-colored royal icing. Without missing a beat, she filled in those parts with a flooding consistency of the same icing. To finish, she used her scribe tool to get the flooded icing to the edges of the outline and pop any air bubbles. The little guy was coming together. She reached for the chocolate brown icing bag, which she used to outline the entire cookie. For the next thirty minutes, Mallory reveled in the enjoyment of creating her edible works of art. And her tummy rumbled. Inhaling the sweet scent of the sugar cookie had kick-started her appetite. She hadn't eaten since dinner last night.

"Hey, Mal." Kip popped his head into the kitchen. "Mrs. Tomasini just called. She needs a get well bouquet ASAP. Her neighbor fell."

Mallory set her piping bag down. "Oh dear, I hope he's okay."

"Mr. Sullivan twisted his ankle and his pride. I've heard through the grapevine that the widow is sweet on him," Kip said.

"The grapevine?" Mallory walked to the sink and washed her hands. "My guess is it's either Mac or Ginger." *Wait until they get hold of Luke's secret.* The grapevine would be working overtime.

Kip laughed. "Both. Anyway, Mrs. Tomasini ordered the medium Bee Well bouquet. She asked for delivery to her house."

Mallory frowned. It was only her and Kip in the bakery that day. Then again, business wasn't exactly booming.

"I can make the delivery," Kip said. "She'd like for it to arrive in the afternoon. She has a doctor's appointment this morning."

"Okay. We'll figure it out. I want to finish these cookies and then bake a batch of snickerdoodles. There are also two bouquets to pack for shipping." Mallory returned to her workstation and scanned her handwritten to-do list. Always on the list was administrative work. She had a good hour of work at her desk to look forward to.

"Sounds good. How about I call the diner for delivery of some breakfast? I'm starving." Kip patted his stomach.

"Yes, please. I'd love an egg sandwich on multigrain." Mallory returned to her cookies while Kip returned to the counter and called the diner. Perhaps the day was turning around. They had a new order, breakfast was on its way, and the deer cookies were absolutely adorable. She couldn't help herself. She reached for a cookie and took a bite. Adorable and delicious. So good.

By midday, Mallory had eaten her breakfast, finished decorating the woodland creature cookies, and tackled the stack of papers on her desk. Then, with the Bee Well cookie bouquet in her hands and on her way out the door, she promised Kip she'd be fine. And that she wouldn't go looking for trouble. Sort of.

While making the delivery, she knew it was the perfect opportunity to visit Daniel Wright again. However, the chance that she'd have a door slammed in her face was very high. If it happened, she'd knock again. And again, if necessary. One way or another, she would find out where he was the night of his wife's murder and the morning of Mallory's attack.

As she drove down Main Street, she slowed her car as she passed the building where Daniel's office was located. She recognized his Mercedes parked at the curb in front of the white clapboard building. A discreet plaque identified Daniel's business, and the lights were on inside. Good. Because she'd be back.

After delivering the cookies to Mrs. Tomasini, who gushed over the bouquet, Mallory headed back to town, intending to stop at Daniel's office.

She parked a few spaces behind Daniel's expensive car and then got out. Main Street was humming with shoppers and retail employees. Above, a slit of sunshine was widening as the clouds rolled out. All in all, it looked as if the day was shaping up to be a good one. Her phone buzzed with a text from Lauren. As she approached Daniel's office building, she checked the message.

What the heck happened this morning? Ernie Hollis has been charged and is waiting for arraignment. Call me.

Before Mallory put her phone back in her backpack, another text came in, and it was from Liz.

You got Ernie Hollis arrested? Why? Call me. ASAP.

Dropping her phone back into her bag, Mallory realized that the clearing sky and warming temperature were the calm before the storm. She was about to feel the full-on wrath of her sister because of Ernie's arrest. But she was confident once she explained everything, Liz would calm down. At least she hoped so.

When Mallory reached the front door of Daniel's office, she peered into the window. The interior office appeared empty, but the lights were still on. She shifted back to the door and twisted the knob to enter.

The entry hall was long and narrow, just like the building itself. Off to her right were two closed doors. The office she'd peered into was to her left, and its door was also closed. Up ahead, the next office door was ajar. She walked across the gleaming hardwood floor, and when she reached the door, she pushed it open, prepared to recite the words she'd memorized.

Hi, Mr. Wright. I apologize for dropping in without an appointment.

Though she never got those words out.

Instead, she let out a blood-curdling scream at the sight of Daniel Wright's bloodied body on the floor.

When the scream faded, she realized someone else was in the room.

A man stood over Daniel's body, and he looked as horrified as she felt. He held a crystal paperweight, and instantly she knew it had been used to knock Daniel unconscious because of the blood smeared on its edges.

Her legs went weak as the only sound she heard was her heart-beat thrashing in her ears as she tried to make sense of what she was seeing.

Once she stopped screaming, she was able to speak. "Is he dead? What happened? Who are you?" Why was she asking questions? She needed to get out of there. Now!

"He's dead," the man said with certainty as he shoved his fingers through his hair and looked pale. Very pale. "I don't know what happened. I found him like this."

"Really? You found him?" Mallory's mind raced with warnings to flee. She spun around so fast that she got dizzy. Not good, considering her whack on the head yesterday.

But there was no time to worry about her head injury. Getting out of there was a straight run down the hall. Her legs propelled her down the corridor as the man chased her.

"I swear! I didn't kill him!"

Closing in on the front door, she was inches from the exit. Until she was tugged back by the arm.

He'd caught her.

He whirled her around, but she wasn't about to be his next victim. She swung her backpack and whacked him in the face with it.

"Ouch!" Stunned, he let go of Mallory, allowing her to make her escape. She yanked open the door and nearly jumped out of her skin at the sight of someone standing there.

Elana Peterson.

"Mallory. Are you okay?" Elana asked. The stranger's moaning drew Elana's gaze from Mallory to the entry hall. "Jared? Oh my goodness." She pushed Mallory out of the way and raced toward the man. "What happened to my husband?"

"She hit me with her bag!" He got to his feet. "She's crazy."

"He attacked Daniel with a paperweight," Mallory countered as she peeled her body from the door.

"Did not!" Jared countered.

"The bloodied paperweight was in your hand." Mallory retrieved her phone. "I'm calling the police."

"Daniel's hurt? Have you called an ambulance?" Elana shoved her husband out of the way and ran toward the office.

"Wait, Elana!" Mallory followed her. So much for promising Kip she wouldn't get into trouble. She'd gone and found another dead body. This time with the possible murderer on the scene.

When Mallory reached the doorway with Jared catching up to her, they found Elana kneeling beside Daniel's body. Her fingers were pressed against his neck, and her face crumpled as she dissolved into tears. "He's de . . . dead."

240

"We shouldn't be in here," Mallory said. She tilted her head at Jared and signaled he should go to his wife.

"She's right. We should wait for the police outside." He went to his wife and reached for her shoulders.

Elana softened with his touch and allowed her husband to guide her up. She leaned into him as he escorted her to the doorway. "This is all my fault. All my fault."

Mallory watched as the couple headed toward the front door and wondered if she'd actually heard a confession. She gave a final look at Daniel. He'd been killed the same way his wife had been—struck on the head. And it was the same way she'd been attacked. Only she'd gotten lucky.

She shuddered. She needed to get out of that room. When she reached the exit, a police car had pulled up with lights flashing, and Lauren was at the steering wheel. Didn't she ever take a day off?

Lauren exited her vehicle and paused a moment, giving Mallory a *you-gotta-be-kidding-me* look. Then, shaking her head, she pasted on a no-nonsense expression. She stepped up onto the sidewalk with both hands pressed on her utility belt.

Another police car pulled up and double-parked as pedestrians gathered, gawking and buzzing with questions about what was going on.

Lauren instructed Mallory to stay put while the other officer kept watch over Jared and Elana before she disappeared inside the building.

Mallory studied the couple, separated, silent, and not making eye contact with each other. She had so many questions. What had Elana meant that Daniel's death had been her fault? Had she been the one who whacked him on the head with the paperweight? Then why come back? Had she known Jared was there?

Elana's arms wrapped tightly around her body, and her gaze was focused on the sidewalk. She looked lost, scared, and devastated. Six feet from her, Jared still looked as confused as he had earlier when Mallory discovered him standing over Daniel's body. Mallory's eyes narrowed, and she reconsidered her assessment of Jared. It wasn't confusion. Instead, it was fear. What was he afraid of?

Lauren emerged from the building, talking on the walkie-talkie secured to her vest. The police shorthand and codes were a foreign language to Mallory. But she understood that Lauren had requested another unit to respond to the scene.

"Everyone is going to the police station," Lauren proclaimed. "Mal, can you get over there on your own?"

Mallory nodded. Given the chagrined look on her friend's face, she decided to be as agreeable as possible.

"What about the Elana and Jared?" Mallory asked.

"Don't worry about them. You can go to the station now. Officer Fitz will be waiting for you." Lauren gestured for the other officer to remove Jared from the scene. Mallory guessed the additional officer Lauren requested would escort Elana to the station. Before she pivoted to return to the building, she asked Mallory, "Why aren't you moving?"

"Do you think Jared Peterson killed Daniel?" Mallory asked.

"No comment."

"Could he have killed Beatrice?"

"Still no comment. I need to get back to work. And, as I said, Officer Fitz is waiting for you." Lauren disappeared inside the building.

Mallory looked over her shoulder and scowled. Her plan to drive to the Wingate Police Department was thwarted thanks to a line of emergency vehicles that had blocked her car. Considering the circumstances, there was no way to ask them to move.

The walk to the police station wasn't far, but she worried about being stopped by curious onlookers. But, she reasoned, the farther she got from Daniel's office, the less likely it was that people would know she had been at the crime scene. As she passed people coming and going from shops, she heard snippets of buzz about the police activity just up the street. She kept her head low and stayed the course. Just a few more feet.

Mallory finally arrived at the police station. She entered the lobby and asked for Officer Fitz. Instructed by the officer behind the partition to have a seat, she drifted to the row of plastic chairs and sat. She hadn't waited long before Fitz appeared.

"Miss Monroe, come on back with me." Overweight, balding, and with jowls that reminded Mallory of her great-aunt's old hound dog, Fitz waved to her. "We're going to take your statement, and then you can be on your way. Sound good?"

"Are you taking my statement?" Mallory walked along the corridor, racking her brain for the name of the hound dog.

"Yes, ma'am. Detective Hannigan has been dispatched to the crime scene, and Officer Winslow can't get back here." Fitz stopped when he reached a closed door. "Can I get you something to drink? Coffee? Water?"

"Spencer!" She knew she'd remember the dog's name.

"Pardon me?" The officer gave her a curious look.

"Sorry. It's nothing. And no, thank you. I don't want anything to drink. I'd like to get this over with." Mallory entered the familiar interview room after the officer opened the door. Based on experience, she went straight to the rectangle-shaped table and sat.

Fitz asked questions for the next forty minutes and Mallory answered. However, one question nagged at her—what had Elana meant that Daniel's death had been her fault? When she asked Officer Fitz his opinion, he had no comment and then wrapped up the interview.

"I expect Detective Hannigan to do a follow-up, so let us know if you need to leave town. Also, if you think of anything, don't hesitate to call us." Fitz rapped his knuckles on the table and then stood.

Stepping out of the room, she turned left, traveling along the corridor as she headed for the exit.

She reached the reception area and stopped to check her messages before exiting. There were several waiting for her response. She scrolled. Dugan had questions about the latest murder. Kip and Aspen wanted to know what was going on. Liz was waiting for a reply about Ernie.

They could all wait. She lowered her phone and passed through the vestibule, exiting the building. After being in a stuffy room for close to an hour, she welcomed the fresh air.

Her intention to walk to her car was deterred because she spotted Elana seated on the stone bench beneath a tree, the canopy of full green leaves shielding her. She couldn't walk away without checking on her.

Mallory had expected Elana would still be inside, detained for extensive questioning. After all, it had been her husband found over the body.

"How are you doing?" The closer Mallory got, the answer to her question became evident. Elana's posture was rigid, her gaze down and her face puffy and red from crying. "Where's your husband?"

"Inside. They're going to charge him with Daniel's murder," she said, dabbing her eyes with a tissue. "I don't know what to do."

Mallory rushed to her side and sat next to her. When she first met Elana, it was apparent the woman was troubled, and she had wanted to help. Like then, now all she could do was lend an ear since she had no experience with how to handle life when your husband is charged with murder.

"I'm so sorry. I understand this is difficult and scary." She craned her neck, looking around the perimeter for any sign of the press. "I don't think you should be out here. It's only a matter of time before reporters show up." She was surprised news vans hadn't lined up outside the police station already. She knew one reporter who was for sure champing at the bit for an inside scoop.

Elana leaned back and crossed her legs. "My sister, Rochelle, is coming for me, and I'm going to stay with her." She reached into her purse for another tissue.

"Good. Good." Mallory rested her hand on Elana's shoulder for reassurance. "Does Jared have an attorney?"

Elana nodded.

"Do you? Did you answer their questions without an attorney?"

"Of course I did. Why would I need one?"

"When you saw Daniel's body, you said it was your fault. What did you mean?"

Elana stiffened, and Mallory removed her hand from her shoulder. "I didn't kill him. Not directly."

"I don't understand." Elana was talking in riddles, and Mallory wasn't in the mood for a cryptic conversation. Technically, Mallory had no right to be asking questions. So she didn't want to push too hard, fearing Elana would stop talking.

"In hindsight, it was foolish. I found out about Daniel's affair with Natalie." She sighed. "He'd caused so much pain for Jared and me, and I wanted him to feel some of that. We're nearly broke because of him!"

"What did you do?"

Elana broke eye contact. "I took a photo of him and Natalie together. Then I sent it to Beatrice the day before she was murdered."

"That's how you were going to hurt Daniel? By telling his wife about his relationship with Natalie?" From what Mallory had learned about the Wrights, she doubted Daniel would have cared if his wife had found out.

"I figured Beatrice knew about them, but I wanted her to know someone else did too. It would put a crack in her perfect façade of a life, which would make her angry, and she'd tighten the screws on Daniel. After all, he wanted out of the marriage with his finances intact."

Now, that theory made more sense to Mallory.

"Do you know why your husband was at Daniel's office?"

"He called on his way there and said he would give Daniel one more chance to make things right. If not, we'd have no choice but to get a lawyer and sue. I really don't understand all the legal stuff. But I know we can't afford a drawn-out legal battle."

"It's possible things got out of hand between them," Mallory said.

"And what? My Jared killed him? He's not a killer."

"From everything you've said, he's been under a lot of stress."

"I know my husband." Elana wiped her eyes dry for the last time. "If anything, he could have been defending himself. What if Beatrice confronted Daniel and showed him the photo? Maybe Daniel lashed out at Jared for what I did."

"Elana! What are you doing out here?" A slim woman with narrow features and a deep-set frown rushed toward the bench from the parking lot. "There's a news van up the street. I have to get you out of here."

"I needed some air, Ro." Elana's voice was shaky. "I can't leave Jared."

"You can't stay here. We don't have much time before the reporter shows up," Rochelle said, looking over her shoulder.

"She's right. You need to go with her. Since they're charging Jared, it's unlikely you'll be able to see him until arraignment," Mallory said.

"Who are you? Why are you talking to my sister? Elana, you didn't say anything that could hurt Jared's defense, did you?" Rochelle asked.

"I'm not stupid." Elana shot up from the bench and marched off. Exasperated, Rochelle threw her hands up in the air.

"She didn't. I'm Mallory Monroe, and I found Jared standing over Daniel's body." She stood and braced herself. She expected Rochelle wouldn't be pleased with Mallory's role in the matter.

And she was right.

Rochelle pointed a finger at Mallory. "You better not twist anything my sister said in her moment of vulnerability."

"I would never do that. I'm not her enemy," Mallory said.

"Be sure of it." Rochelle turned and chased after Elana. Both women eventually disappeared, and Mallory knew it was time for her to leave. She'd get her car—hopefully, it was no longer blocked in by emergency vehicles—and drive back to the bakery. She had a lot to tell Kip.

And she had to sort out the murders. On the surface, it was clear that Jared had a reason to kill Daniel. But what would have been his reason to kill Beatrice?

And Elena? She'd admitted she wanted to humiliate Beatrice. Maybe sending the photo wasn't enough. Maybe Elana confronted Beatrice, things got out of hand, and she killed her.

Mallory spun around so fast that she didn't see the person behind her until she crashed into his chest. Again.

"Whoa! What's the hurry?" Will asked as he steadied Mallory.

"You're letting a murderer get away! I know who killed Beatrice and why!"

Chapter Twenty-Two

Okay, so maybe Mallory didn't know who killed Beatrice. How could she? She didn't get a confession from Elana or have any proof. All she had was a theory, which she had laid out for Will to consider. And he said he would. With his word, she left the police station and returned to the bakery and filled Kip in on everything that had happened—from every detail of the most recent murder scene to her conversation with Elana. The day had definitely been one for the books and one she hoped never to have a repeat of. When her alarm went off the next morning, she checked her phone for a message from Will. She was hoping for an update, possibly something about whether her theory panned out. There was nothing from him. But there was one from Lauren.

The one and only text told her that Jared had been charged with both murders and his arraignment was scheduled for that afternoon. She dropped her head back onto her pillow. It looked like her theory was just that—a theory. As far as Will was concerned, his two cases were wrapped up.

Her second alarm, a hungry cat, nudged at her. Mallory swept Agatha up and snuggled, dotting a kiss on the feline's head. Maybe it was time to put the murders behind her. It was definitely time to get out of bed and get ready for her workday. She had cookies to bake.

*　*　*

Mallory's start to the day was more energized than she'd expected. In fact, she only needed one cup of coffee before she got her hands into some cookie dough. On a whim, she decided to make a batch of Mexican Wedding cookies. Rolling each ball of dough between her palms was time consuming, but it allowed her thoughts to slow down. Until each cookie was placed on a baking sheet, ready for the oven, her mind let go of thinking about the murders, the arrest, and losing her first corporate order. One by one, each ball of cookie dough reclaimed her joy of baking. And after the last few days, she desperately needed that feeling again.

Once the cookies were in the oven and the timer set, Mallory cleaned up her workstation and retrieved the money bag from her office safe. Claudia arrived at her scheduled time and offered to take over the kitchen while Mallory went out to the front of the bakery to get it ready for the day.

Mallory opened the cash register, turned over the closed sign on the door, and wiped the café tables. She'd just gotten back to the counter when the kitchen door swung open.

"The Mexican Wedding cookies are cooling." Claudia emerged from the kitchen carrying a clipboard. Once a week she did an inventory of all the supplies and ingredients.

The front door opened and in walked Kip looking chipper and accomplished. "The new sidewalk sign is all set up."

While Mallory had retreated to her cottage last night, Kip had worked on his new marketing idea. He purchased a large chalkboard, some chalk, and got creative, drawing a cookie basket and offering a buy two cookies and get one free promotion. Mallory loved his enthusiasm and gave her blessing. And she was willing to try anything to bring in more business.

"It's still hard to believe that you found another dead body yesterday," Claudia said flatly.

"I didn't go looking for one." Mallory heard the defensiveness in her voice and instantly regretted it. She strived for her interactions with Claudia to be conflict-free and professional. She regrouped and tried again. "I'm glad I was there, because Elana Peterson was very distraught."

Claudia scoffed. "I'm certain she was. Her husband had just murdered a man."

Don't engage. Don't engage.

"Anyway, I hope this means things will go back to normal." Claudia looked up from the clipboard. "I saw you signed the bakery up for some bridal shows in the fall."

"I did." Mallory filled the napkin dispenser. "Though I'm not sure the murders of the Wrights are completely settled."

"What are you talking about?" Claudia asked.

"Mal, let it go," Kip said. He approached the counter. "Don't go looking for trouble. We have the media connecting Jared to the murders and The Cookie Shop to the Garden Tour. Which you need to start spending some time on."

"Everybody is buzzing about the Garden Tour." Claudia set her clipboard and pencil down. Her expression became thoughtful. "Though I wonder if it's more about Beatrice's passing and Darlene taking over. All eyes will be on your cousin."

"I'm certain Darlene will rise to the occasion. The Garden Tour will give the bakery a lot of free publicity." Kip dashed around the counter and headed for the swinging door.

"That PR isn't really free because we have a lot of work to do." Mallory rubbed her forehead. It was time to sit down and do a brain dump of everything they needed to get done before the weekend. She moved over to the desk, pulled out the chair and sat. "Give me a few minutes and I'll have a new schedule for us."

*   *   *

It took longer than a few minutes to write up a schedule for the three of them. There were so many things they needed to accomplish between now and the cookie decorating workshop at the Garden Tour. Then there was Mallory's own personal to-do list for the Pie Baking Contest. Despite all the tasks listed, she was confident that they'd get everything done.

The front door opened, and the real estate agent she had seen putting up a sign at the Wrights' house entered. She waved to Mallory as she made a beeline to the gourmet apples display on the coral pedestal table. She scooped up five in her hands and carried them to the counter.

"My assistant brought these into the office the other day. I had one, and it was divine. These are going to make perfect gifts." She unzipped her quilted leather purse and reached in for her wallet. "I also need your most fabulous cookie bouquet."

"Absolutely." Mallory's smile stretched from ear to ear. A most fabulous bouquet came with a most fabulous price. "Would you like one of our premade gifts, or would you like it custom-made?"

"Oh, custom-made, of course. I sold a house, and the cookies are for the buyer. She loves gardening. Could you do something flowery?" the agent asked.

"Yes, I can." Mallory snatched an order form from the desk and began filling it out. "When would you like to pick it up, or if it's local, we can deliver?"

"Delivery would be great. It's for Evelyn Brinkley. You know where she lives. I saw you at her house the other day."

"I was there on Garden Tour business. She bought another house?" Mallory filled out the delivery address information.

"The house next door."

"The Wrights' house?" Mallory stopped writing. "She bought it?"

The real estate agent nodded. "When I heard about Daniel's death last night, I was devastated. Then first thing this morning, Ms. Brinkley called and made a full cash offer. Between us, I was so relieved. Having Mrs. Wright murdered in the house would have made the sale challenging. You know how people can be . . ."

"About murder," Mallory said.

"Exactly. But Ms. Brinkley doesn't care." The agent beamed. "Easiest sale I've made all year."

"How exactly does the sale happen since Beatrice and Daniel are dead?"

"Their deaths complicate the process, but I'm confident the sale will go through. Ms. Brinkley is very eager to purchase the property." The agent tapped her oval-shaped fingernails on the counter. "What other information do you need for the cookie bouquet? Remember, it needs to be fabulous."

"We just need to ring up the sale, and you're all set." Mallory moved through the motions as questions bounced around her head. Why would Evelyn buy the house next door? And pay cash for it? Did it have something to do with the property line dispute?

* * *

The remainder of the day passed without any further excitement. Which Mallory was grateful for, considering it seemed she'd been either finding a dead body or on the receiving end of a threat for too long. Mac came in with the day's mail and looking for some juicy tidbit about Daniel's murder she could share at her next stop. Unfortunately for her, Mallory was too tired to chitchat. By the time the bakery closed, a handful of customers had come in. She

252

suspected they had the same ulterior motive as Mac had. Mallory kept her lips zipped about the murder and thanked the customers for their business.

"You sure you don't want to get dinner? We can go somewhere *not* in Wingate," Kip offered.

"I'm sure. All I want to do is heat up leftovers, pour a glass of wine, take my book upstairs, and soak in a hot tub." So much had happened over the past few days that Mallory had had little time to process it. That would change once she arrived home. And after she fed Agatha. Her feline didn't really care about Mallory's mental health.

Kip shrugged. "Okay." He grabbed his bag off the peg and slipped on his baseball cap. He reached the back door and then stopped. "I completely forgot. Lauren texted me this morning about Luke Collins. So the guy is really Lucas Carnes? Talk about deception. I hope you got your money back."

Mallory chewed on her lower lip. She hadn't. And she wasn't sure she'd call what Luke had done deception. Yes, he'd lied about his work history. As for his name, he'd legally changed it three years ago. The bottom line was that she liked the photographs he had taken of her cookies and intended to use them in her upcoming sales campaigns.

"He has enough problems without me demanding my payment back," she said.

"You got that right. His girlfriend disappeared, and he was the last person to see her." Kip thought for a moment. "Maybe we should try and solve that case next."

"Oh no, no. I'm happy to leave crime-solving to the fictional sleuths I spend my evenings with, thank you very much." She laughed. But she was dead serious.

"Got it. Call me if you need anything." He pulled open the door and left for the day.

Mallory went into her office and spent a few minutes cleaning off her desk. After turning off the computer, she looked around the small room and decided it needed a makeover. A little spruce-up. When she had worked at the ad agency, she had a spacious cubicle with a window that had given her a view of midtown Manhattan. Now her view was a wall of open shelving stocked with supplies on one side and fading twenty-year-old wallpaper on the other wall. Behind her desk hung an oversized bulletin board that had seen better days.

She tucked the chair beneath the desk and walked to the doorway. She gave the office one last look before leaving for the day. She added one more task to her nightly routine—scour Pinterest for design inspiration.

Outside, she walked toward her Jetta after she double-checked that the back door was locked. Her workday had worn her out and her body was relieved when she tossed her backpack on the passenger seat. Then, just as she was about to slide into the driver's seat, she saw her cousin.

"What are you doing here?" Mallory's grip on the car door tightened. Her last conversation with Darlene hadn't been great, and she wasn't in the mood for a repeat.

"I heard what happened at Daniel Wright's office. It's terrible." Darlene's typically energetic disposition seemed muted, and her brown eyes looked remorseful.

"Yes, it is." Mallory moved to get into the car, but Darlene darted forward.

"I'm here to apologize. What I did was wrong." Darlene wrung her hands. "I shouldn't have gone behind your back and tried to sell the building. It put the future of your bakery in danger."

Your bakery?

Had Mallory heard right?

"I'm here to let you know I won't be selling the building. It's not what my mom would have wanted. And it's not what I want. I'm sorry. Do you think you can forgive me?" Darlene looked at her cousin hopefully.

How could Mallory not forgive her? Darlene had apologized, canceled the sale, and said without a hint of sarcasm or distaste, *your bakery.*

"Of course I can." Mallory let go of the car door and pulled her cousin into a hug. She understood Darlene had been trying to cope with her mother's death. For the first time in months, she had hope for their relationship. Their friendship.

"Thank you," Darlene said, and then she pulled back. "I'm also sorry that I rented the apartment to Aspen. Can you forgive me for that, too?"

Mallory let out a laugh. "Please tell me it's only a one-year lease."

Darlene nodded. "It is."

"Okay. Then we're good." Mallory was set to leave, but she hesitated. "I have a question about Evelyn Brinkley. The real estate agent handling the Wrights' house came into the bakery earlier today. She said Evelyn bought the house. And that she's paying cash."

"I didn't think she had that much money. Good for her," Darlene said.

Mallory dreamed of being financially independent. But a quick glance at the bakery's building reminded her she had a long way to go before she'd be declaring that independence. "Why would she want to buy the house?"

"No idea. Evelyn isn't much for sharing. All I know is what everyone else does. Her husband, Mason, left one night thirty years ago. My mom had been friends with Evelyn and always said that losing her husband was the best thing that ever happened to her."

"Why?"

Darlene shrugged. "I got the feeling he hit Evelyn. But I don't know for sure. She's very private about her personal life and her money situation. Maybe she's going to rent the house?"

"Guess she could do that. Did Mason have any family in town?"

"I remember Mom saying that his sister died just before he left town," Darlene said.

"I have one more question. You and Beatrice had an argument before her death. What was it about?" Mallory prayed she wasn't about to hear a deep, dark secret from her cousin.

Darlene's eyelids lowered and she sighed. "It was one of many stupid arguments about the Garden Tour. I wanted the Pie Baking Contest back on the schedule."

Mallory let out a relieved breath. "That's all?"

"Yeah. What did you think I was going to say?"

"It's a long story. I'll fill you in another time."

"How about tonight? Want to come over for dinner? Hazel would love it."

Mallory groaned inwardly. She hated disappointing her favorite little cousin. "Can I get a raincheck? It's been a busy day, and I need some downtime."

"Sure. No problem." Darlene gave Mallory a quick hug before breezing away to her minivan. Her energetic bounce was back.

Mallory got into her car and followed her cousin out of the driveway. At the light, they parted, heading in different directions.

Mallory couldn't resist the lure of the new window display and found herself parking outside Just One More Chapter. Inside, she was drawn to a table of new releases and picked up three of them. Winding her way through the shop, passing several cozy reading nooks and more displays of enticing reads, she reached the mystery section. She added two more books to her haul and then dragged herself to the counter before she spent her entire budget in one visit.

She backtracked to the front of the shop and made her way to the cashier, who seemed to be missing. As at her bakery, there was a bell on the counter. She tapped it once and the tinny noise had someone hustling from the backroom. Mallory was surprised to see Caitlyn Baxter approaching her wearing a Just One More Chapter nametag.

"I hope you found what you were looking for," Caitlyn Baxter said as she pulled the books closer to her.

"Hi, Caitlyn. Remember me? Mallory from The Cookie Shop?" Mallory placed her books on the counter. "I didn't know you worked here."

"I remember you." Caitlyn scanned each book. "I've been working here for a while. Part-time. Do you need a bag?"

"No." Mallory pulled out a canvas bag from her backpack and unfolded it. "You can use this."

Caitlyn took the bag and added the books to it. "Anything else?"

"That's it." Mallory unzipped her wallet. She took out her credit card and tapped the card terminal. "Now that the murder cases have been wrapped up, you and Will can get back to your regular coffee dates."

"We have one scheduled next week. And he'll have no reason to cancel. Would you like your receipt?" Caitlyn asked after the charge went through.

"No, thank you." Mallory reached for her bag. "Do you mind if I ask you a personal question?"

Caitlyn tilted her head, and she smiled. "Will and I are only friends. My brother went to college with Will. It's nice having a connection to my brother." Her smile dimmed. "He died three years ago in a car accident."

"I'm sorry for your loss." And Mallory was sorry for the awkwardness now between them. She wasn't sure how to bounce back from that conversation downer.

"I appreciate it." Caitlyn's gaze darted from corner to corner, then she leaned forward. "I know Elana told you about my indiscretion."

Mallory hadn't thought their conversation could have become any more awkward. She'd been wrong.

"In my defense, I was trying to find a murderer." *And clear my name.*

"Don't worry, I'm not upset. Anymore. You have to understand, I'm sorry that Beatrice is dead, but she wasn't a nice person. She leveraged the worst mistake of my life to get something she wanted."

"A position on the Mums, Merlot, and Mozart board? Do you know why?"

Caitlyn gave an exaggerated nod. "To get close to Emerson Lewis. She's in charge of the festival. Her nephew is the co-host of *Connecticut Daily.*"

"Now it makes sense," Mallory said. "Beatrice was lining up her television appearances to promote the cookbook she planned on writing." The cookbook she had blackmailed Luke into photographing for free. The woman had been a piece of work.

"She'd mentioned the book a few times. So she was going through with it? Huh. Maybe you can figure out why she hired a private investigator," Caitlyn said.

"She did? When?"

"A few months ago. I only know because I overheard her on a call." Caitlyn's body shifted so she could look behind Mallory.

"Sorry, I have to help Mrs. Morris. She always wants the books on the very top shelf."

"No problem. Thank you for the information." Mallory left with her new books and some answers she'd been searching for. The question she was most happy that had been answered was the one about Will. He and Caitlyn weren't a couple. She wasn't sure how she felt about it, but let's just say she wasn't unhappy about it.

Chapter
Twenty-Three

A couple of days later, Wingate was still buzzing about Jared's arrest for both murders. Media coverage had been swift and overwhelming after Daniel's body was found. News vans from all the local media outlets had converged on the town. Reporters camped outside the Petersons' home, waited at the police station, and swooped down on residents as they walked along Main Street. Claudia complained that she'd had a microphone shoved in her face when leaving work. To keep the press out of the bakery, Mallory hung a sign on the door announcing that the press was not welcome. It killed her to turn away media attention, but the coverage she would receive wasn't what her business needed.

While trying to stay out of the spotlight, she did give in and grant one interview request from Dugan. He simply wore her down, and she felt that she owed him since he had helped her. When the interview wrapped up, she shut down all other requests. He got an exclusive and a byline, and she got him to stop blowing up her phone.

Mallory also tried to get some much-needed rest, but running a bakery didn't allow for such indulgences. The day after she walked into Daniel's office and found Jared standing over the dead body, she was up early and baking cookies. Like nothing had happened. She'd reasoned that getting back to normal would be good for her. And it had been. Until she started thinking about how quickly everyone had accepted Jared's guilt.

But they hadn't seen the look on his face when Mallory caught him standing over the body. He'd looked just as surprised as she was, and afterward, his behavior hadn't jibed with that of a murderer, even though he had chased and then grabbed her. Yet something didn't fit. And it gnawed at her.

She shook her head, hoping to shake out the thought. The police knew how to do their jobs. While she'd had difficulty finding a motive for Beatrice's murder, it was easy to imagine that Jared had gone to the Wrights' house, believing that since she had been married to Daniel, she had some financial interest in the company. Or maybe he hoped she would convince Daniel to do the right thing. Unfortunately, things hadn't gone as he had planned. They argued and then, in a rage, he'd lashed out and killed her. He'd simply lost control.

She'd read an article about Jared's dire financial situation. So it was easy to see why Jared might have snapped.

But had he?

Mallory carried the tray of black-and-white cookies to the pastry case, slid open the door, set the tray inside, then closed the door. Her intention was to also close the door on the murders of Beatrice and Daniel Wright. According to the police, the case had been solved, and now it was in the hands of the courts.

Her cell phone rang, and she pulled it from her back pocket. After she accepted the call, she said, "Hey, Darlene. What's up?" They'd made plans for a family dinner with Liz and her husband after the Garden Tour. Darlene would make her mom's famous pot roast, Liz would bring the wine, and Mallory would bring raspberry thumbprints cookies, one of her aunt's favorites.

"Everything is falling apart!" Darlene cried. "I scheduled five volunteers to set up, and only three are here. The handouts have more than a dozen typos. Apparently, Mrs. McDougal doesn't proofread. So I need to get hundreds of new ones printed today. There's a construction crew here! Of all days! Something to do with a busted pipe in the basement, and something needs to be dug out. Oh, and my babysitter called out sick. So I'm trying to keep an eye on Hazel while managing this zoo."

"I don't know what to say." Mallory truly didn't. She'd never heard her cousin have a meltdown. Darlene always maintained a cool, calm exterior. Not once had Mallory seen a crack in that façade. Until now.

"Say you'll come and help. Please. I need someone I can count on," Darlene said. "Please."

Mallory looked over her shoulder at the swinging kitchen door. Kip and Claudia were both working, so they could cover while she went to help her cousin. She'd been asking a lot of them lately and didn't want to burden them anymore. Yet Darlene needed help. Besides, hearing that Darlene counted on her gave her all the warm fuzzies and more hope that they'd become friends again.

"Okay. I'll come over. But I can't stay long because I have to be at the community center to set up the Pie Baking Contest later."

"No problem. Thank you!"

"Where are you? Whose house do I need to show up at?"

"No! That's not how we agreed to set it up. Wait. I'll do it." Darlene's voice had drifted, and she was talking to someone else. "Sorry, Mal," she said, returning to her conversation with Mallory. "I'm at Evelyn Brinkley's house. See you soon." The call ended.

Evelyn's house? Mallory lowered her phone. She had a few questions, and if Evelyn could answer them, she believed she'd be able to ditch the nagging doubts about Jared's guilt.

Mallory had to finish decorating a batch of bunny cookies for a children's birthday party, and Kip had to finish dipping and decorating two dozen apples for a family reunion before she could leave the bakery. While she'd love to work at warp speed like she had when she was an account manager with a deadline looming, she couldn't hurry with her cookies. They were little works of art she took pride in. And earned her income from. So she couldn't rush decorating.

With the cookies all finished, Mallory took off her apron and grabbed her backpack, leaving the bakery in the hands of Kip and Claudia. They seemed to have come to a truce. It looked like Mallory's frequent absences had helped forge a bond between them.

Things were turning around.

Orders were flowing in, she was no longer a murder suspect, her relationship with Darlene was getting a fresh start, and it had been over forty-eight hours since she had cried over Gil. Those tears had been coming in the late hours of the night, but not anymore. She was keeping that little change to herself. If she shared with Lauren or Liz, they'd take it as a sign she was ready to move on.

She wasn't so sure her heart was ready to be vulnerable again.

Then, out of nowhere, Will's face popped into her head. His way-too-sexy grin and his deep, thoughtful eyes. A gal could get lost in them. And that would be risky for someone like her, just coming out of a relationship.

Mallory arrived at Evelyn's house and her cousin was nowhere to be found. She caught the attention of a flustered volunteer who had her hands full with a heavy potted plant and found out that Darlene was somewhere, maybe around the back of the house. Mallory thanked the woman and continued to look for her cousin. On the patio, she found Natalie Kellogg busy watering plants.

"Hey there." Mallory kept her voice light and breezy, just like the afternoon, as she approached. Through a set of French doors, she caught a glimpse of Evelyn's kitchen. Not updated as Beatrice's had been. Then again, Evelyn preferred to spend her time out in the garden, not cooking. "I didn't know you'd be here."

"I love being outside in the gardens. Being cooped up in the senior center all day isn't for me. Glad you're here to help. We're shorthanded, and there's so much to get done." Natalie carried a lavender-filled pot to a petite wrought-iron accent table. Her shoulders drooped, and her steps in her floral-patterned crocs were heavy. It looked as if she was carrying the weight of the world on her. Or was it grief? "I could use a hand with watering. There are dozens and dozens of containers. Here, out front, scattered among the garden beds."

"Sure. No problem." Mallory went for a watering can, filled it, and then approached a collection of pots. She angled the nozzle over the petunias, geraniums, and lavender and let the water spray down on them. The varying shades of purple grouped together were striking. "I've been thinking a lot about the murders."

"It's all anybody is talking about." Natalie had returned to watering and didn't look up at Mallory. "It feels like the whole town is grieving. This Garden Tour will be good for us."

Mallory understood what Natalie was talking about. After Aunt Glenna passed, she had kept herself busy baking dozens of cookies and then delivering them herself, no matter the distance. Focusing on work had helped her work through her grief. And a knot in her stomach formed. Should she be intruding into Natalie's mourning? She had no idea if the woman loved Daniel or if she killed him and Beatrice. But what if she was guilty of the murders? She had to take the risk and ask.

"What I've been thinking about is the possibility that Jared isn't guilty." Mallory moved her watering to the next section of pots, which were arranged on a tiered plant stand. "That someone else had motives to kill Beatrice and Daniel."

"It's probably best to leave this to the police. After all, it's their job." Natalie peered at Mallory and then started to turn away. "I'm going to water the containers by the front door."

"I know you were having an affair with Daniel," Mallory blurted out.

Natalie came to a hard stop. Her shoulders squared as her body elongated. When she turned to face Mallory, there was a look of contempt on her face. "You have no idea what you're talking about."

"I saw you two together, and so did Elana."

Natalie gasped.

"I think you wanted more of a commitment from him, but Beatrice was dragging out the divorce." Mallory searched Natalie's guarded eyes for an indication that she was right. But there was none. She wasn't sure how far she should push. Either Natalie was innocent and mourning her deceased lover or she was a cold-blooded killer. She had to say something. "Though, with Beatrice gone, Daniel was free to marry you."

"How dare you! I know what you're insinuating, and I'll have none of it." Natalie set the watering can down with a thump and crossed the patio toward Mallory, getting into her face. "You have no idea what you're talking about. Let me set you straight, missy. Daniel wasn't important enough for me to kill for. He was nothing more than a fling. I've been a widow for ten years and I don't plan on marrying again. Though I still enjoy a man's companionship. Before you go and judge me, know that Daniel's marriage to that horrible woman had been over for years before I started dating him."

"You didn't want to marry him?" Mallory hadn't expected to hear that from Natalie. With marriage off the table, she had no motive for murder.

"Absolutely not. You ought to be careful with the accusations you sling around town. Everybody loved your aunt, but remember, you're not her." Natalie returned to the watering can and picked it up. "I'm not sure why you're snooping, but you should look at Evelyn since you are. Now there's a woman who is holding a tremendous amount of anger beneath the surface. She probably has bodies buried all over her property." Natalie turned and walked away, heading for the front of the house.

It hadn't taken much for Natalie to throw Evelyn under the bus. Mallory wondered if Natalie had been projecting when she said that Evelyn held onto a lot of anger. It seemed the merry widow had her own issues. Mallory realized there wasn't much more she'd get out of Natalie, so she decided to finish watering the plants on the patio. After all, she was supposed to be there to help Darlene. The thirsty plants soaked up all the water, and when she finished the task, she gave all the plants a once-over, looking for any brown leaves or bare stems. She'd hoped keeping busy would keep her mind off Natalie's comment about buried bodies on the property, but it didn't. In between plants, she glanced out at the yard. How many acres were there? Three? Four? More than enough to dig a six-foot-deep hole that would be unnoticed. Being worried about having a body or bodies dug up would explain Evelyn's reaction to Beatrice wanting a property survey.

She homed in on the section Evelyn had pointed to the other day—the overgrown, messy area way in the back— and then looked around for volunteers. Spread throughout the gardens on display, they were busy prepping for the visitors. She could sneak off for a moment without anyone noticing, like Darlene.

She crossed the lawn on a diagonal and continued toward the rear of the property, in search of what Evelyn didn't want revealed.

There had to be something. As she traipsed along the freshly cut grass, she passed a garden statue, one of many scattered throughout the gardens. With a border of bright pink flowers surrounded the crouching stone angel, she looked so tranquil. Farther ahead, a garden shed, adorned with flowering window boxes and a weathervane, stood solid, ready for seed starting or container planting. Perpendicular to the shed was a towering tree with a massive trunk. A row of hedges jutted out from the other side of the tree, creating a makeshift border that shielded the area where Mallory wanted to go.

Not deterred, she continued along the path, which became rugged terrain with a gully and random rock boulders. It was quite a stark contrast to the lush lawn and landscaped area she'd just left. As she moved forward, Natalie's morbid words echoed in her head.

She probably has bodies buried all over her property.

Mallory reached a swath of prickly overgrowth. The bushes intertwined, creating a barrier like barbed wire protecting a secret. She stopped, propping her hands on her hips. She surveyed the area and noted that it would have been a perfect place to bury a body.

Now there's a woman who is holding a tremendous amount of anger beneath the surface.

Mallory's gaze skimmed across the neglected landscaping as past conversations replayed in her head.

Her husband, Mason, left one night thirty years ago, Darlene had said.

She stared ahead, piecing together fragments of information she'd collected about Evelyn since finding Beatrice's body.

Evelyn was a private person.

Evelyn made a cash offer to buy Beatrice's house.

There had been a property dispute between the women.

This *section* of the property had been in question.

Guess he never filled out a forwarding address card, Mac had said.

Mallory's eyes widened. Could it be? She shook her head at the thought of Mason being buried there. Then again, it would have explained his vanishing in the middle of the night, never to be heard from again. With no family, who would miss him? She had to tell Will about her suspicions.

A chill shimmied along her body even though there was no breeze, and a snapping noise set her body on alert.

She wasn't alone.

"I think you're somewhere you shouldn't be." Evelyn's tight, menacing voice had Mallory jumping and spinning around. "What are you doing back here?"

With her hand over her heart, Mallory caught her breath, and her eyes bulged at the sight of the shovel in Evelyn's hand. Uh-oh.

"Your shed is adorable, so I had to check it out. I'm sorry if I ventured where I'm not supposed to be. I'll get back to the other volunteers."

"The shed is back there." Evelyn pointed. "And you're here. Where there's obviously no garden."

Think quick, Mal.

"I thought there might be a secret garden." What was she saying? Secret garden. More like secret burial grounds. "I apologize. I should get back and join the other volunteers."

Evelyn blocked Mallory's attempt to walk away.

"What are you really doing back here?"

"I told you." Mallory tugged at her lower lip. She had to convince Evelyn she wasn't suspicious. "Let's get back to everybody, okay? We have a tour to get ready for."

"You've been snooping around Beatrice's murder, asking questions you shouldn't be asking. What did you think you'd find?"

"The truth. The killer." Though standing there, Mallory discovered how unprepared she was for a face-to-face with a killer. "The police suspected me. What choice did I have?"

Evelyn took a step forward. "It's the same question I asked myself thirty years ago. What choice did I have? And I'm asking myself the same question right now."

Mallory's mouth went dry, and her chin trembled. The person standing in front of her wasn't the Evelyn she'd sold Almond Meltaways to a few days ago. No, this person was dangerous, unpredictable, and a murderer.

"This time, I'll make sure to bury the body on *my* property."

Mallory blinked as her mind processed the confession she'd just heard. "Your husband didn't disappear. You murdered him!"

"If I hadn't, he would have killed me. He liked to slap me around for sport. I had no choice. So one night, with a concussion and bruises all along my stomach, while he slept, I smothered him. He'd drunk too much, so I finally had an advantage. The only one I ever got."

"Why didn't you call the police? Have him arrested?"

"His brother was a captain. Nothing would be done to him. Nothing," she spat out. Her eyes grew cold and hard.

"So you buried him here?

"Not me." Beatrice shook her head. "I was a wreck after I killed him, I had to call my brother. But the idiot buried Mason on Beatrice's property."

Mason? *Right*. That explained the letters scrawled in flour next to Beatrice's body. She knew about him.

"He's barely on Beatrice's property, but just enough. My brother thought he was digging on my side. He blamed the darkness." Evelyn huffed. "I couldn't exactly dig Mason back up. Could I?"

"There wasn't a reason to until Beatrice decided to build a garden shed, which meant she'd be digging up her property."

"For decades, I was able to claim that section as mine. Beatrice never cared. But once she found out it was hers, she'd start digging for a foundation. It was going to be quite a garden shed."

"You tried to talk her out of the survey, of building the structure." Mallory's gaze darted side to side; she was searching for anything that could help her out of her precarious situation.

"She could never leave things alone," Evelyn said.

"My guess is that she got curious about why you were fighting so hard over the property line. That's when she hired the private investigator, isn't it? She'd known about Mason's mysterious disappearance years ago and she wanted to find out where he was. My bet is that the PI couldn't find Mason. He'd truly disappeared without a trace. And that's when Beatrice became more suspicious, didn't she?"

"Seems you know a lot for a cookie baker." Evelyn stepped forward. The edge of her lips twitched. "You're right. She hired the PI. She stood right there in her kitchen, all smug and conniving, telling me that she wasn't going to wait any longer to dig up the property since I wouldn't give her money."

"She told you she'd keep your secret if you paid her?"

"Daniel had gone through her inheritance, and she was almost broke. I told her I didn't have that much money. And she said, too bad. She'd scheduled her contractor to start the next week. I didn't want to kill her, but she left me no choice." Evelyn's gaze flitted upward for a moment, and when it returned to Mallory, a flicker of regret flashed. "The rolling pin was on the island. I reached for it and when she turned to face me . . . I . . . hit her with it. And down she fell."

Mallory's stomach soured at the image of Beatrice's final moments. The queasiness spread through her body, and she thought she'd be sick.

"I checked her pulse. She was dead. There was nothing I could do for her. If only she had left it alone and not demanded money."

"You were a battered wife. They'll understand." Mallory believed that but recognized the fact that Mason's murder hadn't exactly been self-defense.

"And what about Beatrice's murder? And Daniel's? If only he had agreed to sell the house to me." Evelyn dragged in a breath. "The police won't understand. And I have no intention of spending the rest of my life in a jail cell." She tightened her grip on the shovel. "You had a lot in common with Beatrice. You both stuck your noses in where they didn't belong. I thought you would have backed off after seeing Beatrice's crime scene reenacted at the bakery or when I struck you on the head by your pond."

Hearing the confession turned Mallory's stomach. She couldn't fathom how someone could have so little regard for life.

She instinctively backed up, but the prickly branches stopped her. Getting away from Evelyn in that direction was out of the question. She'd never make it through the bramble.

That left only one other way out, and Evelyn was blocking it.

Mallory had only one option because she couldn't talk her way out of the situation—move Evelyn.

She braced herself to rush Evelyn, but the murderer lunged forward, shovel raised, ready to strike.

Mallory's heartbeat kicked up to double-time, adrenaline pumped through her, and she ducked. She got low enough to miss the swinging shovel. And to grab Evelyn's legs. Then, in one swift motion, she yanked hard, throwing Evelyn off balance. She fell backward, and Mallory's body slammed on top of her.

Evelyn still held the shovel in one hand, and Mallory wrestled for it. Finally, she was able to pull her torso up, giving her more leverage to break the hold Evelyn had on the weapon. Evelyn resisted as much as she could, grunting as she tried to hit Mallory with her other hand. But Mallory evaded the strikes as she pried the woman's fingers from the shovel's handle and finally took possession of it. She pressed it against her chest, pinning Evelyn to the ground.

"What on earth is going on?" Darlene's demanding voice broke the silence. "Mallory, why are you *wrestling* with our tour host?"

"Get your cousin off me. She's crazy!" Evelyn shouted.

Mallory looked at her cousin and let out a cry, tears stinging her eyes. "Call the police! She killed the Wrights and tried to kill me!" She was light-headed but wouldn't release Evelyn. "Her husband didn't disappear. He's buried over there." She nodded in the direction of the bushes.

Darlene paled, and she fumbled to pull out her phone from her pocket. "Are you sure?"

Mallory rolled her eyes. "Look at us. What do you think?"

"Um . . . right." Darlene punched in the numbers and, in a moment, was on the line with an emergency dispatcher.

* * *

"Good grief. The Garden Tour starts tomorrow, and one of our most stunning gardens is now a crime scene." Darlene paced the patio with her arms folded and her lips set in a grim line. "You just had to go and confront a murderer today . . . of all days!" Her pacing halted, and she glared at her cousin.

"It's not like I planned to find an old grave or nearly get killed." Mallory sat on a chair at the table with her legs crossed and her arms wrapped around herself. Even though it was a warm, sunny day, she felt chilled to the bone.

"Sorry to keep you waiting," Will said as he approached the table. "This won't take long, and then I'll have someone drive you home."

"Detective, this garden is supposed to be open for tours tomorrow," Darlene said.

"Darlene!" Mallory unfolded her arms, uncrossed her legs, and leaned forward. "There's a murdered man buried on this stunning piece of property."

"Well . . . according to what Evelyn said, he's been there for a long time. What's two more days?" Darlene asked.

"Do you hear yourself?" Mallory stared at her cousin with utter shock.

"I do," Darlene exhaled. Her shoulders slumped, her eyes watered, and her words choked. "This whole event has been a nightmare, and now this . . . I'm sorry. This location is off the weekend schedule. I need to make some calls." She pulled out her cell phone and stalked off.

Mallory shifted to Will. "When will you start digging up Mason's body?"

"Once we obtain a search warrant." Will pulled out his notepad and opened to the page where he'd left off jotting notes when he first arrived on the scene.

"But Evelyn told me that her brother buried Mason back there." Mallory pointed and her insides quivered. She'd been standing just feet from where a man's body had been dumped and left to rot for decades. Even if he'd been as horrible as Evelyn had said, he hadn't deserved to die that way.

"Unfortunately, the information is based on a third-party statement, so in order to dig up that area we need a search warrant. Your concise statement and the fact that Mason Brinkley hasn't been seen or heard from in years helps make the case for the search warrant stronger."

"And that she tried to kill me with the shovel. If she wasn't hiding a body, I don't think she would have come at me like she did." Mallory tried to squash down that memory, but she feared it would be forever etched in her brain. "The way she lunged at me . . . she wasn't playing. She wanted me dead."

Will scooched his chair closer to Mallory and leaned forward, resting his hand on her knee. "Are you okay?"

The innocent touch sent a spark through Mallory, and she didn't know how to react to it. One part of her wanted to throw herself into his arms because she thought his firm embrace would make her feel safe. Another part of her wanted to push his hand away because she didn't need to be coddled. She wasn't fragile and at risk of falling apart. Then there was another part of her that wanted a happy medium. Though she wasn't sure what that looked like. Maybe just stay there and talk with him until the fear that was still coursing through her body dissipated.

Mallory nodded. "I'm not hurt. Though I'll probably be sore tomorrow."

"Good to hear you don't have any injuries. But I'm talking emotionally. You've been through a lot." His voice softened. "There are counselors for victims of crimes available for you to talk to."

He did think she was fragile. And she hated it. For some reason, she wanted Will Hannigan to see her as strong and resilient. But in his eyes, she was anything but.

"I've given you my statement." She shifted in her seat, letting his hand fall to the wayside. "I'd like to go home now."

Will pulled back and straightened. He snapped his notepad shut. "I'll get an officer to drive you home."

"No need," Darlene said as she returned to the patio. "I'll drive her home. All the volunteers have left, so there's nothing for me to do here. Can we pick up her car tomorrow?"

"Sure." Will's phone buzzed and he retrieved it from its pouch on his belt. "Hannigan," he said, standing and walking out of Mallory's earshot.

"Thanks," Mallory said as she stood. "I appreciate the ride."

"This is all so unreal. How did this happen?" Darlene took a final look around the perfectly manicured and maintained property. "She murdered three people."

Mallory stepped toward her cousin and wrapped an arm around Darlene's shoulder. She resisted the urge to look back to where she'd come face to face with evil.

"And to think people were afraid of Queen Bea."

Chapter
Twenty-Four

Mallory and all of Wingate had less than twenty-four hours to process what had gone down at Evelyn's home. The gossip mill was both shocked and devastated by the breaking news. Kip had called Mallory first thing in the morning and said Heavenly Roast was buzzing with the topic when he stopped in on his way to the bakery. Bless him, he bought three large coffees because they had a long day ahead of them.

The Garden Tour's general committee had held an emergency meeting last night, which Mallory missed because she had been too wiped out physically and mentally. They decided to carry on with the event. Gretchen Ford had been adamant that it would have been impossible to reschedule the tours, though a somberness overshadowed what was usually a fun weekend for Wingaters and visitors to the town. Hearty New Englanders, as Mallory's aunt used to call her neighbors, would weather the storm of Evelyn's heinous deeds with grace and a stiff upper lip.

Mallory wasn't sure if she had enough grace to extend kindness to Evelyn, but she hoped she would find it because at one point in her life Evelyn had been a victim. As for a stiff upper lip, hers felt like it trembled at every flashback of her rolling around on the ground fighting for her life. The one thing she was certain of was that the large coffee Kip had picked up for her wasn't large enough. She'd need at least a gallon to get through the day.

While she loaded her Jetta with all the equipment she needed for the cookie decorating workshop, Claudia opened the bakery. She'd staff the counter, leaving Kip to divide his hours to help in the kitchen and at the senior center.

For the first part of the day, Mallory taught a workshop to a packed room of kids. The senior center's meeting room had been converted into a cookie decorating factory. She'd recruited another volunteer to work as her helper. Having an extra set of hands came in handy when Hazel's bestie, Mariel, had a meltdown because she squeezed all the icing out of her decorator's bag. And when little Boyd dropped his cookie and he let out a string of expletives that had Mallory and her volunteer helper blushing. Luckily, Boyd's mom was nearby and took her son for a time-out. Once the workshop was over, Mallory darted down the hall to the community room to check on the Pie Baking Contest. The contestants had delivered their pies and the volunteers had arranged the tables and put out the plates and forks and then set up the refreshment station.

Somewhere between waking and arriving at the senior center, she had reviewed the list of entrants and their pies. Many of the names were familiar to her, but there was one name deleted—Ernie Hollis. She swallowed the lump in her throat. To think, she believed he'd been the one who had killed Beatrice. And that his bookie had attacked her at her pond. Boy, had she been on the wrong track with those theories.

Ernie needed help, not to be accused of murder. She promised herself that when he was released from rehab she'd apologize. Hopefully, she'd get the chance before he faced the criminal charges that were looming over his future because of embezzling funds and manipulating Chad's admission into Abernathy.

While Ernie's name was missing from the list, there was one addition that surprised her. Mallory had no idea Wingate's resident romance author could bake. And she was dying to see the pie.

"Mallory, dear! There you are." Ginger swept into the room wearing a tangerine-colored puffed shoulder, ruched midi-dress and a chunky white necklace. In her right hand she carried a nude clutch. Who carried one of those during the day? Mallory needed to be hands-free all the time.

"You've entered the contest?" Mallory moved away from the tables and approached Ginger. "I had no idea you could bake."

Ginger tilted her head slightly. "Dear, there are many things you don't know about me. In due course, you'll learn a few of them."

"Only a few?" Mallory teased.

"A lady needs to keep a few secrets." Ginger laughed and then reached out to Mallory and pulled her into a hug. She smelled like gardenias. "You must have been terrified yesterday."

"I've never been so scared in my life." When Mallory pulled back, she fixed a smile on her face. She knew she'd be haunted by her encounter with Evelyn for a long time to come. She also knew she couldn't let it absorb her completely. "It's over. I'm safe. And you've entered a pie contest."

"I did a live video with my readers' group while I was baking it. I can't tell you how many likes and comments I got!" Ginger looked like she was about to burst.

Kip poked his head into the room. "Hey, I'm going to start packing everything up to take back to the bakery."

"Okay, thanks. Sorry, Ginger, I have to go. Good luck in the contest," she said, breaking away from the author. If she helped Kip collect all the supplies, he'd get back to the bakery faster. From his constant updates so far, business had picked up, and that was music to her ears.

"How's everything going?" Darlene rushed in with her electronic tablet and phone in hand and a harried look on her face. Her outfit of white ankle jeans and striped pullover was a smart choice since she'd spend the day going from garden to garden and checking in at the senior center too many times to count. "Please tell me everything is going okay."

"Don't worry, Mal. I got this." Kip disappeared from the doorway.

"Darlene, everything is fine," Mallory assured her cousin. "The workshop went well, and the pie contest is ready to start. All the judges are here and so are all the entries." Her gaze swept over the long line of tables topped with delicious-looking pies. Her tummy grumbled. She hadn't eaten since breakfast, and that was only a slice of toast.

"Excellent." Darlene consulted her tablet, nodding as she read the screen. "The ribbons are set out?"

Mallory hesitated. She never got any ribbons. "Maybe?"

Darlene sighed. "You're in charge of the contest and ribbons are a big part of it."

"Well, I've been busy." *Like almost getting killed.*

"Then why on earth did you volunteer to chair the contest?" Darlene shook her head. "Never mind. I'll check. Maybe Freida brought them with her. She's been a judge for years and is very conscientious."

"I'm sure she is." Mallory resisted rolling her eyes. And a good thing she did, because an older woman came into the room with a big smile on her round face. "Can we help you?"

"Mrs. Cranston. So good to see you," Darlene said, lowering her tablet. "Mal, Mrs. Cranston lives in the blue Cape Cod down the street from where my mom lived."

"I've been there since I was a newlywed. Raised my three children there." Mrs. Cranston's blue eyes twinkled. "Now my eight grandchildren visit." She moved farther into the room. "I wanted to talk to you girls. If you have a moment?"

"Of course. What can we do for you?" Mallory asked, curious what the older woman had to say.

"There's something I think you both should see." Mrs. Cranston reached into her large purse and pulled out a worn book and handed it to Mallory. "That's a Wingate Women's Club cookbook. It was published over fifty years ago."

Mallory and Darlene exchanged glances. Both were unsure why Mrs. Cranston was showing them the old cookbook.

"In that cookbook, I shared a recipe that was given to me by my mother. It was for her Almond Meltaway cookies. If you check Glenna and Beatrice's recipes, you'll see that they're the same as my mother's. It seems they forgot about the cookbook, which I'm sure they purchased a copy of, because that's what we did back then to raise money for our charities."

Mallory opened the book and scanned the list of contents and then went to the recipe page. After a quick read of the Almond Meltaway recipe, she concluded it was the same one she'd found in her aunt's recipe book.

"This is where the recipe came from. Finally, we know." Mallory closed the book. She looked at her cousin and they both smiled.

"My mom didn't steal the recipe from Beatrice," Darlene said taking the book from Mallory and then flipped through the pages.

Mrs. Cranston reached out for Darlene's arm. "Your mother didn't steal the recipe. She shared it. And I hope you both continue to do so. I better get going. I don't want to be late for the tour of Nancy Johnston's garden."

"Thank you for letting us know about the recipe." Darlene went to hand the cookbook back to Mrs. Cranston.

"You keep it." Mrs. Cranston turned and shuffled out of the room.

"All that drama over a recipe neither my mother nor Beatrice created." Darlene laughed. "How about we schedule a night to go through these recipes? Kind of like a girls' night with wine, some pasta, and old recipes?"

"I'd like that." Mallory's heart swelled. It seemed like her relationship with her cousin was on the right track.

* * *

Once Mallory finished with her responsibilities at the Pie Baking Contest, she returned to the bakery to work the counter until closing time. It'd been a long day, and just as she'd expected, there hadn't been enough caffeine. So she was reaching for another source of energy—sugar—by way of cookies. She reached for a peanut butter cookie and took a bite. The soft, sugar-dusted cookie melted in her mouth. It was the perfect way to end the day.

"I think I'm going to stay right here," Mallory said after she swallowed the bite. She was seated at a café table with her legs propped up on another chair. After closing the bakery, she'd filled a plate with an assortment of her favorite cookies and settled at one of the tables by the bay window. Once the cash register was closed out and the baking equipment turned off, Kip joined her. Claudia had declined the offer to hang out, stating that she had plans with a friend. "I don't want to move."

"Suit yourself. But you'd probably get a better night's sleep in your own bed." Claudia stood beside the table holding her purse. "After all the hoopla, you should get some rest."

"It was a lot of hoopla," Kip said with a grin before biting into an oatmeal raisin cookie.

Mallory shot him a warning look.

"Most of it could have been avoided, if you ask me," Claudia said.

"Nobody—" Kip started to say.

"I don't think now's the time to do a postmortem on the events of the past few days," Mallory interrupted. "Actually, maybe never." She took another bite of her cookie. The mild peanut butter flavor mingled with the sugary coating made for a little bite of pure joy.

"You're lucky you didn't get yourself killed." Claudia reached out and rested her hand on Mallory's shoulder and then squeezed. "Thank goodness for that."

Mallory choked on her cookie while Kip went bug-eyed at the comment. She reached for her bottle of water and took a drink. She wanted to say something, but she was speechless.

"After all, you've made so many changes to the bakery, who could run it now?" Claudia took back her hand, turned, and then walked across the bakery, disappearing into the kitchen.

Mallory's gaze shifted to Kip, and they both stared at each other. It looked like there was hope for a friendship with Claudia after all.

"Are these macadamia nuts?" Aspen asked, clearly oblivious of the *moment*, as she lifted a chocolate cookie from the plate and then settled on a chair at the table. She'd stopped in when she returned from the tour and declared it wonderful and that she was looking forward to it next year. "I'm going to have to run an extra two miles tomorrow to burn off all these calories."

"You said you had news when you arrived." Mallory hadn't expected to be hanging out with Aspen, considering how they'd first met, but the redhead had grown on her and she actually liked her company. Who knew?

"I have an interview on Monday at Abernathy College. If all goes well, I'll be teaching at my alma mater." Aspen's flawless face lit up and she clapped her hands together.

"You're going to teach law, aren't you?" Kip asked.

Aspen nodded. "I thought I'd explore a new career change. I figured, why not? It seems to be working for Mallory."

A tap on the bay window drew all their attention to the three people standing on the sidewalk. Ginger, standing in the middle of Paddy Hannigan and his nephew, Will, pointed to the door. In her other hand was her first place ribbon.

Mallory was surprised when Ginger's name had been announced, but she'd wowed the judges with her blueberry pie. Kip popped up and hustled to the door and let them in.

"What a day!" Ginger radiated happiness as she glided to the tables. Behind her was Paddy, and he pulled out a chair for her. "I'm still on cloud nine about winning first place."

"You deserve it." Mallory reached for the plate and then stood. It looked like more cookies were needed. "Your pie was delicious."

"It most certainly was." Paddy sat next to Ginger and stared adoringly at her, making Mallory wonder if there was a romance brewing between them. "See, I told you you'd win."

"You did, dear." Ginger caressed Paddy's face and then kissed his cheek.

"My, my," Mallory murmured as she walked to the pastry case, leaving her friends gabbing. All except Will. He'd pivoted and followed her to the pastry case. "I thought you'd be working today."

"I was but I'm off duty now. Unfortunately, I missed getting a slice of Ginger's pie." He frowned. "So I'm hoping I can get a cookie."

"Take your pick. It's on the house." Mallory's irritation with Will—well, it really was with herself—had faded thanks to some self-reflection. She realized she hadn't looked weak or fragile yesterday. She had survived a murder attempt. It took strength and a strong will to do that. "I heard Jared was released yesterday."

"He was." Will studied the pastry case. "Can I get one of those chocolate walnut cookies?"

"Absolutely." Mallory opened the case and took one out with a piece of tissue paper and then handed it to Will. "I wonder what will happen with him and Elana. They've been through a lot. Will their marriage survive?"

"Guess only time will tell." He bit into the cookie and his face lit up. "You're an amazing cookie baker. This is so good."

"Thank you. Maybe it'll be the next cookie of the month," she said.

"You're going to continue with that? Didn't it get you into a sticky situation this month?" Will asked.

She shrugged. "It hasn't been all bad."

"You're right." Will finished the cookie and then plucked a napkin out of the dispenser. "We finally got to meet again."

"Again?" Mallory repeated, confused. Her mind raced to remember meeting Will Hannigan before. She couldn't.

"At the Mums, Merlot, and Mozart Festival. I was fifteen, and I met a pretty girl with long hair and wide eyes who was drinking a Mountain Dew."

A Mountain Dew? Mallory's mouth gaped open. When she was fourteen, she had gone through a hard-core Dew phase, and she'd been drinking one when she met the boy with brown hair who was her first kiss.

"You're him? The boy with the curly brown hair?" she asked, her heart thumping against her chest. She came out from behind the counter. "I always wondered what happened to him."

"Same here." He stepped forward, closing the space between them.

"You were my first kiss. Ever." Thoughts of a second kiss with Will flitted in her mind, and he was so close to her. What could it hurt? Her eyes started to close as she leaned forward when Kip up and ruined the moment.

"Hey, what do two cookies say when they're getting ready to fight?" Kip waited a beat. "Let's get ready to crumble!"

Laughter spread out among the group and even Mallory found herself joining in. It felt good to laugh. And it felt even better to finally be in a place where she felt at home. Mallory flashed a smile at Will as she reached for the plate on the counter and headed back to her friends. "I've got more cookies!"

Recipes

The Cookie Shop, located in Wingate, CT, sells so many different cookies. And now the bakery offers cookie bouquets for all occasions. This new feature took some time for people to get used to, but Mallory Monroe knew in her heart it was the right decision for the bakery her Aunt Glenna opened decades ago. Even with the changes, Mallory made sure to keep the beloved cookies customers have been enjoying for years. And here are three of those cookie recipes. Enjoy!

Almond Meltaway Cookies

This cookie sure did cause quite a stir in Wingate. And it's not surprising. They are soft, tender, and will melt in your mouth!

Ingredients:

For the cookies:

2 cups all-purpose flour
½ teaspoon baking powder
¼ teaspoon salt
1 cup unsalted butter, room temperature

¾ cup granulated sugar
1 large egg
2 teaspoon almond extract

For the almond icing:

1 cup powdered sugar
1 tablespoon milk
1½ teaspoon almond extract

Instructions:

Preheat the oven to 375°F. Line baking sheets with silicone pads or parchment paper. Set aside.

In a medium bowl, combine flour, baking powder, and salt. Set aside.

In a stand mixer, beat butter and sugar until light and fluffy. Add egg and mix together. Add almond extract and mix together. Add in the flour by spoonfuls, mixing until completely combined.

Roll 1 tablespoon of dough and then press with your hand or the bottom of a measuring cup to form a disk shape. Place each cookie on the baking sheets.

Bake for 8 minutes. The cookies will not look cooked, but they will finish setting up as they rest on the baking sheet for 5 minutes. Then transfer cookies to a cooling rack.

For icing: Whisk together powdered sugar, milk, and almond extract in a small bowl until smooth.

Using a spoon, smooth the icing on top of each cookie and let set until icing is hardened.

Store in the refrigerator until ready to serve. Let come to room temperature before serving.

Yields about 28 cookies, depending on size.

Peanut Butter Cookies

These cookies are soft, chewy, and coated in a light layer of sugar—and addictive.

Ingredients:

1⅓ cup all-purpose flour
¾ teaspoon baking soda
½ teaspoon baking powder
¼ teaspoon salt
½ cup unsalted butter, softened
½ cup granulated sugar
½ cup packed light brown sugar
¾ cup creamy peanut butter
1½ teaspoon vanilla extract
½ cup sugar for dredging, set aside
1 large egg

Instructions:

Preheat oven to 350°F. Line baking sheets with silicone mats or parchment paper.

In a medium bowl, whisk together flour, baking soda, baking powder, and salt. Set aside.

How the Murder Crumbles

In the bowl of a stand mixer, cream together butter, granulated sugar, and brown sugar until combined.

Mix in peanut butter, then add in the egg and vanilla, and blend together. Lower the speed on the mixer and add in the flour mixture. Do not overbeat.

Scoop dough (about 2 tablespoons) out and shape into balls, then roll in bowl of sugar that was set aside. Place balls onto baking sheet, press cookie to flatten.

Bake for about 9 minutes (cookies will appear pale and slightly under-baked when taken out of oven but will continue to cook as they cool).

Let cookies stay on baking sheets for 5 minutes. Then transfer cookies to a cooling rack.

Store in airtight containers.

Oatmeal Raisin Cookies

This classic cookie is soft and chewy and filled with just the right amount of raisins.

Ingredients:

1¼ cups all-purpose flour
1 teaspoon baking soda
½ teaspoon kosher salt
3 cups old-fashioned rolled oats
1 teaspoon cinnamon
½ cup granulated sugar
1 cup light brown sugar
2 eggs
1 teaspoon vanilla extract
1⅓ cups raisins
¾ cup butter, softened

Instructions:

Preheat oven to 350°F. In a stand mixer, beat the butter on medium high speed until smooth and fluffy, about 2 minutes.

Add the sugars and continue beating until the mixture is light and fluffy, about 4–5 minutes.

Add the eggs and vanilla and continue beating until smooth.

In a large bowl, whisk together all the flour, oats, baking soda, salt, and cinnamon. Gradually add this mixture to the wet ingredients in thirds. Mix until completely combined. Add the raisins and stir well.

Using a medium-size scoop, drop the dough onto baking sheets lined with silicone mat or parchment paper.

Bake 8–9 minutes. Remove from the oven before the cookies are browned and still look soft in the center.

Let the cookies cool on the tray for 5–10 minutes; they will continue to finish baking. Transfer to cooling rack.

Acknowledgments

When I sat down to write this novel, all I had was a vague idea of a main character owning a bakery, a sidekick who told corny baking jokes, and the support of my agent, Jill Marsal. Five months later, I had fleshed-out characters and a story to tell.

During the process of writing what is now my twelfth book, I had friends, family, and readers cheering me. I'd like to take this opportunity to acknowledge those closest to me who have cheered me on, used a red pen when necessary, helped brainstorm, and ultimately made this book possible.

My husband, George. Without your support and encouragement, none of my books would have been possible. Debbie Mulach, your daily messages helped keep me focused and allowed me to do what I truly love—write. Ellie Ashe, Jenny Kales, and Denise Pysarchuck, you gals brainstormed, edited, and in the end made this book so much better than I could have imagined. Sgt. Michael Confield, my go-to consultant when I have police procedural questions. Thank you for your time and for helping me keep it real in my story. Finally, to my editor Faith Black Ross and the whole team at Crooked Lane. Thank you for believing in Mallory and her story.

And thank you for choosing to read this book. It means the world to me.